$\mathcal{F}$IRST
$\mathcal{B}$ITE

DANI HARPER

FIRST BITE

THE **DARK WOLF SERIES** BOOK ONE

Montlake
Romance

The characters and events portrayed in this book are fictitious. Any similarity to real persons, living or dead, is coincidental and not intended by the author.

Published by Montlake Romance

PO Box 400818
Las Vegas, NV 89140

ISBN-13: 1477807594
ISBN-10: 9781477807590
Library of Congress Control Number: 2013904921

I've had a lifelong fascination with books
that started long before I could read.
I credit my parents, Bill and June, for
taking me to the library at an early age
and making sure there were *always*
books in the house for me.
As for my obsession with the paranormal,
it was probably a rogue gene.

"Everyone is a moon, and has a dark side

which he never shows to anybody."

—*Mark Twain*

ONE

At least she'd picked a scenic place for her last night.

Geneva Rayne Ross—*Neva*—hugged herself tightly against the night wind as the waxing moon rose like a frosted pearl overhead. It silvered the wide river far below, lighting its serpentine path along the feet of the Blue Mountains. Frozen sparks of light glittered in the blue-black sky. Was it Van Gogh who said the sight of stars made him dream?

She used to have dreams, too, for herself, for her life…But as Neva gazed at the sky, she felt a tug within her, a deep longing and an excited recognition by something inside her, something that was wild and alien and *other*. It scared the hell out of her. That's what had brought her to this beautiful place, driven her to her lonely purpose.

*Only a few more nights till the moon is full…*And she wouldn't see it. Not here, not anywhere. The enormity of that fact chilled her much more than the wind, and she shivered. How was she supposed to do this?

I don't want to die.

Well, duh, that was a given. But she couldn't live with what she'd become, either. She had to protect her family, her friends, all the people whom she loved. All the people who wouldn't understand what was happening to her.

And why she was killing them.

She sat on a large square boulder, one of many that jutted from the grassy hillside. These mountains were filled with memories for her—clambering on the rocks as a child, sunning on them with a book as a teenager. She'd grieved her first broken heart right here, where the breeze in the tall pines breathed peace. The hilltop was considered sacred by the local natives, and she could see why. But Neva had always thought of it as her own special place. And it was the first place she thought of when she made the most difficult decision of her life.

She stared determinedly at the edge of the cliff, at the path she intended to take. *They'll just think I slipped.* That wouldn't be hard for anyone to imagine. Neva had always been, well, a little on the awkward side. Earlier this year she'd managed to trip on a sidewalk crack and ended up with a cast on her wrist. Of course, that was *before*. Lately she couldn't help but notice a new agility, an almost feline grace to her step. She hadn't needed so much as a Band-Aid for weeks. There could be real advantages to—

No. She wouldn't be swayed. Neva didn't think of herself as a particularly brave person, but she had to find some shred of courage in her, something that would allow her to do what she had come here to do. And she should do it now, she really should. She'd never be able to make herself climb the steep, rocky trail to this isolated spot again, knowing what she was coming here for.

Neva stood on shaky legs, her focus on the cliff's edge. It was maybe a couple dozen steps if she ran, and she was going to *have* to run if she wanted to clear the chalky sandstone side of the hill. She blanked out that dreadful image and took a step forward.

Two steps. Three.

Her heart was pounding so hard that she could hear it throbbing in her ears, feel it in her throat. There were tears streaming down her face now, but she took another step. And another. Her knees were jelly, and if she didn't hurry, her legs might give way—

Suddenly, that *something* deep within her stirred again. She heard it call out to her as she took another wobbly step, but she dared not listen, she dared not heed.

Six steps. Seven.

(((((

He didn't know why his lupine persona had brought him here. Travis Williamson had wanted, no, *needed* to go for a run, and he'd simply given his inner wolf its head.

You damn well better know the way back. His alter ego ignored him, too busy enjoying its freedom to respond. Boxy boulders erupted through the steep, grassy hillsides like a giant's molars, and pine trees punctuated the slopes, their roots clinging to the sharp incline. As he trotted along the ridgeline, he felt himself relax. The air was clear and cool, the pale moon's light throwing every plant, every rock, and every tree into sharp relief. It was a perfect night to be a wolf, and Travis couldn't help but enjoy the view—until he saw a human figure emerge from the trees on a narrow plateau far ahead of him.

Even with the moon's help and the night vision common to his kind, the distance made it difficult to see much detail. He could tell that the person was pacing as if agitated. But there was something more, something about the *way* they moved—

A woman? *What the hell's a* woman *doing all the way out here, alone?* And in the dark, no less. Curious, he headed in her direction.

As he got closer, she stopped pacing and faced the valley, hugging herself with her arms as if she was cold. Or maybe comforting herself, although Travis wasn't sure why he thought that. Was she nervous because of the height? The plateau topped a section of hill that was steeper than the rest and jutted like a stone chin over the forested valley. The vantage point would be a photographer's dream, but as the stranger suddenly took a shaky step in the direction of the edge, his gut said she wasn't there for the view. Her body language spoke of fear and terrible resolve as she took a second step. A third.

And he wasn't nearly close enough to stop her.

He wasn't waiting around for his human brain to come up with an idea, however. He was already running flat out with all the speed his kind was capable of. If only he could distract the woman, Travis thought, make her stop, give him *time*, goddammit. In this form he couldn't yell at her, but he let loose with a flurry of yips and barks as if he was an excited yearling on a pack hunt.

The woman froze, and her shoulder-length hair whipped around as she scanned the hillside for the source of the lupine sound. It was unlikely she'd see him at this distance—his tawny-gold coat blended with the dry grass, day or night. *Yet she did.* She stared directly at him, and he was close enough to see her dark eyes widen with terror. Then she ran—

"*No,*" he yelled as she vaulted from the edge. But all that came from his throat was an agonized howl as he skidded to a stop a scant few feet from where she had disappeared. Unbidden, the wolf howled, too, long and loud until it echoed over the valley and drew answering cries from the natural wolves that roamed there.

Shit. Shit. *Shit.* He'd known he couldn't save her. He'd known he was too far away. Knowing didn't prevent the bare-knuckled punch to his heart, though. A drop like that was guaranteed fatal to a fragile human. All that was left was to walk away…But at that, a snarl broke from his lips, a clear message from his ever-rebellious animal side. *Forget it*, Travis argued with his lupine self. *There's nothing more I can do here.*

But his damn wolf wasn't taking *no* for an answer. Trotting to the west side of the promontory, it was already picking its way down the sheer hillside. There were narrow goat trails hidden in the grassy rocks, most just a few inches wide. One misstep and Travis would reach the valley floor in a helluva hurry. Worse, he'd probably live through it—and wouldn't that be fun? His species could survive a lot of damage, thanks to regenerative healing powers, but that didn't mean it was a painless process.

No broken body lay among the rocks at the base of the cliff. Travis breathed a sigh of relief—he hadn't been looking forward to finding what was left of the woman. But where the hell had she gone? Baffled, he looked around and tried to catch a scent. Suddenly the wolf took him toward a thick stand of pines, a family group with the tallest tree in the center, the ancient giant surrounded by dozens upon dozens of younger trees that had sprung from its cones over the decades. *Not possible*, thought Travis. She couldn't be there; it was too damn far from the cliff.

Yet as he approached, he caught a whiff of newly released sap. Cautious, he pushed his way through into the heart of the forest, where a falling twig suddenly made him look up. Overhead, a few of the trees had freshly broken branches from crown to floor, their jagged edges exposing moist wood that gleamed white in the moonlight. It marked the path of descent as surely as if a small comet had crashed to earth here—only it wasn't a comet. Swallowing hard, Travis lowered his gaze and cast his nose over the needled floor. The tang of blood was in the air now, mixed with the heady pine.

He found her beside a rotted-out stump that was feeding a tall stand of maidenhair ferns. Her dark clothing and dark hair made her a crumpled shadow in the tangle of broken branches and crushed fronds. Only her pale, drawn face caught what little

5

light filtered down to the forest floor. She was young, maybe just twenty-five or so...

What a goddamn waste. Travis gently nosed the pine needles and leaves from her fine features as he wondered what to do. He could bury the poor girl, he supposed, but someone out there was probably missing her. He didn't relish the thought of having to call the cops. They'd want to know who he was, and try to pinpoint the call, and—

She opened her eyes, and Travis nearly yelped in surprise. And then he *did* yelp as the knife struck his chest.

TWO

The tawny wolf leaped backward and landed several feet away, growling and baring its teeth. A sudden flurry of pine needles and dead leaves flew up from the forest floor, forming a whirling vortex around the snarling creature. Seconds later, the plant debris fell back to the ground, accompanied by a scattering of tiny blue sparks that winked out as they struck the earth. The wolf was gone. Travis stood in his human form, a small knife protruding from his sternum.

"What the fucking hell was that for?" he shouted as he grabbed the hilt and yanked. Then yanked harder since the damn blade was wedged in the bone. "Ow, dammit!" He pressed the pad of his thumb hard against the hole in the front of his favorite T-shirt to stop the bleeding as he regarded her with narrowed eyes. She could have stabbed him in worse places, he supposed glumly. He threw the knife into the forest and most of his anger with it, then approached her cautiously and knelt beside her. "Got any more surprises on you?"

She was terrified but defiant, and Travis was reminded of an animal gone to ground, backed into a corner with no chance of escape, yet determined to battle on. "I wish I did," she spat out, her voice raspy. "I'd kill you. I'd kill *me*. You're not taking me back."

Right. In that case, Travis was almost glad that she *had* stabbed him—at least he'd gotten the weapon away from her.

What if she'd chosen to do herself in first? He couldn't have reacted fast enough to stop her. But why the hell was she so damn determined to die? And what was so terrible that she felt she had to jump off a damn cliff to escape it? Of course, she couldn't be in her right mind at the moment, not after that landing. He'd just shape-shifted right in front of her, and she hadn't turned a hair.

"You're in shock," he said. "And you're hurt." Nothing like stating the obvious, but maybe she didn't realize how bad off she was. He could see from here that her left leg was broken. Her left arm was broken, too. And she was bleeding from scrapes and gashes in a dozen places that he could see and goddess knew how many places he couldn't. "You're not going anywhere but a hospital."

He ignored her protests as he pulled his cell phone from his pocket, thankful anew for that little Changeling quirk that allowed him to retain his clothes and everything that was within his aura each time he shifted. Christ, if life was like the movies, he'd end up naked and penniless every damn time he ran as a wolf. No wonder Hollywood werewolves were insane with rage. Probably pissed off at the sheer inconvenience of their lives.

Travis dialed 911 on just two bars—it was amazing he had any at all—and thanked all the stars when someone answered. He spelled out the location, described the woman's injuries.

"What happened to her?" asked the dispatcher.

He considered revealing exactly how she'd gotten her injuries; he really did. Then after Search and Rescue delivered her to a hospital and she was treated, she'd be held for seventy-two hours in a psych ward to protect her from herself. But it didn't feel right. Maybe his inner wolf was repelled by the thought of the woman being locked up, or maybe his human side was just getting soft in the head, but Travis heard himself say, "She fell out of a tree."

When he was asked for his name, he gave the one that the phone was registered to. No one would know until much, much later that it didn't belong to him.

"Please stay on the line until the crew arrives," said the dispatcher.

"No problem," he said. He didn't plan to hang around, though. Instead, he positioned the phone on top of the stump, where it glowed like a beacon—the rescuers would be able to zero in on the cell's location. "There," he said to the injured woman. "Help is on its way."

"I don't *want* help," she hissed.

"You're welcome." The flippant remark fell flat as he looked at her drawn face. A strange greenish light shone momentarily in the depths of her big dark eyes. *What the hell?* He inhaled sharply, but her scent hadn't changed. *Human.*

In his whole long life, he'd only seen that flash of green in the eyes of one other creature—a Changeling like himself. The glow vanished as fast as it had appeared, however, leaving her eyes as human as before. Apparently he was imagining things, likely because he was spooked by the whole situation. He was no medic. He knew enough not to move the injured woman and that was about it. He had no supplies, no equipment. And if he did, where the hell would he start? Best to leave it to the pros. In fact, he'd done his good deed for the year, so he should probably just leave, right?

Wrong. She was pale and her teeth had started to chatter. He understood that shock was dangerous, but how did he treat it? Warmth? That sounded right, she needed to be kept *warm*. She needed blankets, lots of them. The only things at hand were pine boughs, however—and how helpful would that be? His inner wolf whined softly, urging a different course of action. *No.* He'd already done plenty, and nothing good ever came of getting too cozy with humans. *No way.*

Unable to come up with another solution, Travis sighed and resumed his wolfen form. This time, though, he was careful to approach her from the left. Her good hand, the one she'd stabbed him with, was her right. Even if she came up with another weapon, it was unlikely she'd be able to reach across her battered body.

"Get away from me." Her voice was a faint whisper now, her head was lolling, and she had to fight to keep her eyes open. Carefully, he used his front claws to scrape away the branches and debris from her left side and made a place where he could lie down with the full length of his large body pressed against her shivering one. A Changeling's core temperature ran much higher than a human's, giving him far more body heat to share. Despite his efforts, however, his heightened senses told him that it wasn't going to be enough.

She wasn't going to live long enough for her rescuers to find her.

It was a damn shame. She was pretty and young, and her whole life had been ahead of her…Just like him. His whole life had been ahead of him once, too—and like her, he had contemplated ending it all. Only he hadn't been trying to escape anything. He'd been trying to atone for what he'd done.

Shit. Travis shook his great wolfen head, making his long ruff stand out almost like a mane. He didn't like unscheduled trips down memory lane, and it pissed him off when he was blindsided with one.

Atone. He needed to make amends where none were possible. Restore harmony where none could exist.

He sighed, feeling every ounce of the crushing weight he carried on his shoulders. What had driven this young woman to such extremes? Maybe he wasn't doing her any favors by interfering, but he was going to anyway. It was time to pull his last card out of his pocket.

It took a helluva lot of energy for the human body to transform into a wolf. Changelings learned to draw it from their surroundings, particularly from the earth. It led to an enormous buildup of static electricity, which was why shifts often ended in a flurry of blue sparks. But in times of extremity, Changelings could sometimes collect that energy for another purpose. When he was lying this close to the injured woman, his aura and hers intersected. It would allow him to give her an infusion, not just of energy, but also—if his wolfen side permitted it—of a portion of his life essence.

The inner wolf was devoted to his survival. It would rise to the surface without being called if Travis's life was threatened, force a shift, and deal with the problem with tooth and claw—a fact that Travis knew all too well. It was against its very nature to allow what he wanted to do for this woman, and without its cooperation it wasn't possible. So he couldn't let the wolf say no.

Listen, you, he addressed his lupine self. *I don't care what your mission statement is; I need to give this woman a second chance. Understand?* He waited, prepared to fight his alter ego if necessary. (And wouldn't Freud have a field day with that?)

Help. Give.

If Travis had been in human form, his eyebrows would have disappeared into his hairline. The wolf had actually communicated with words, a rare event—the animal persona knew language but seldom used it. Even more rare was that the wolf had actually agreed with Travis. *All right then. Let's do it.*

((((● ●

Geneva finally gave in and agreed to meet up with her coworkers, Candace and Amber, at a popular rave club. "Neva, come have a couple drinks with us and dance." "Neva, you'll never meet anyone if you stay home all the time." "You need to loosen up, Neva. Have some fun."

Fun? Her life hadn't contained much of that, and really, she felt a little old for the whole rave scene. But to her surprise, she enjoyed herself. Three Jell-O shots and she was ready for a lot more fun, too. Amber loaned her a pair of LED gloves. Circles and spirals and even squiggles of brightly colored UV light appeared to dive through the air overhead as the techno music moved her.

Neva was having so much fun on the dance floor that she lost track of her friends. A dedicated raver, Candace wore waist-length faux dreads in Day-Glo pink. Even in the midst of the crowd of dancers, she should have been visible. And Amber's vivid blue tutu should have stood out as well. But Neva didn't see them among the bodies thrashing in unison to the music's primal beat.

She made her way off the dance floor, but the table they'd been sitting at had been taken over by another group. Restrooms? She checked all four of them. They were large enough to do an airport proud, but her friends weren't in them. Neva cruised the balcony that overlooked the enormous dance floor, to no avail. The massive dance room branched off into a warren of smaller rooms: a few specialty bars but mostly offices and storerooms. No Amber, no Candace. Had they left without her?

The last door opened into a cozy pub. Although most of the chairs were upside-down on the tables, the lights were on and Anderson Cooper was on the big-screen TV. No one was there, and it was tempting to sit down for a moment. The pounding techno tunes she'd enjoyed so much were starting to give her a headache. Not that it was quiet here—just a few decibels lower than the main dance hall. Tired of the hide-and-seek, Neva decided to go home.

That's when she discovered two things. One, the door was locked. Two, she wasn't alone after all...A silver wolf of nightmarish size emerged from behind the bar, its broad back level with the *bar stools. Slowly, silently, the creature turned its massive head toward her and regarded her with glowing eyes—*

Neva regained consciousness with a loud gasp. The distant clatter of trays, voices, carts intruded on her senses, and her eyes flew open, then squinted under the bright fluorescent lights. *Hospital*, said her brain, which was the first and last thought she managed before raw pain slammed into her from every quarter. The sheer surprise of it caused her to yell out. And that brought a nurse on the run.

"Relax, honey. It's going to be all right. You're pretty sore right now, but we can fix that, no problem." The woman had dyed-red hair tied back in a ponytail and a scrub top with colorful parrots and palm trees on it. A clip-on ID showed a picture of her in the same bright shirt, and Neva could just make out the name *Fern*. Her hands were deft and competent as she administered a syringe to the IV line taped to the back of Neva's right hand. "Just breathe steady, hon. You're going to feel a lot better in just a couple minutes."

"You're not going to knock me out, are you?" Neva's voice came out like sandpaper on stone as she discovered just how dry the human mouth could get.

"Not at all. My goodness, you just woke up—you've been out for two days straight. Let me get your vitals, and I'll get you some ice water."

As the nurse checked pulse, blood pressure, etc., Neva closed her eyes. The pain was sliding into the background, but horror was taking its place. Two days? *Two whole days*. The full moon was close, much too close.

She had to get out of here—

Omigod, I don't even know if I can move. What if I'm paralyzed? Damn that big werewolf! She'd managed to carry out her desperate plan—and thanks to his interference, all she'd accomplished was to injure herself severely, maybe permanently. All she could hope for was that perhaps she wouldn't be of any use to—

Fern brought her a cup and held a straw to her lips. The water was cold and sweet, and Neva imagined the parched cells in her mouth and throat expanding and uttering a collective sigh of relief. "Thanks," she said, and her voice sounded better.

"I'll leave it right here where you can grab it." The nurse pushed a table close to the right side of the bed and set the cup on it. Neva lifted that hand experimentally, opening and closing her fingers. She wasn't prone to tears, but the discovery that at least some part of her still worked was overwhelmingly wonderful.

"I've got some things to do, but I'll be back at the end of my shift. We'll get that catheter and IV out and see about helping you to the bathroom."

"I can walk?"

"Well, it's going to be quite a challenge with a broken arm and a broken leg on the same side, but the X-rays and the CT scan say you're okay otherwise. Crutches won't work for you, but I'll see if I can find a cane. We'll try to get you mobile enough to shuffle to the bathroom when you want to."

The nurse smiled and left, and Neva exhaled a breath she didn't know she'd been holding. She pulled aside the blanket and did a quick survey—not hard when the silly hospital gown was so small. Her leg was in a cast from her ankle to the top of her thigh. Her arm was in an L-shaped cast. Quickly, she tried each one of her fingers and toes. Everything obeyed. The ones on the left were damned stiff and sore, but that was to be expected. All the skin she could see was garishly multicolored with the fading remains of spectacular cuts and bruises. *Two days?* There was far more than two days' worth of healing there—more like two *weeks*—and Neva realized the creature within her was to blame.

The creature she had to destroy before it was too late.

THREE

As motorcycles went, the Triumph Thunderbird was one of Travis's favorites. This particular bike had been out of the showroom for over nine years, so it had enough wear to make it look ordinary—an important feature, since *fitting in* was the unwritten code of all Changelings who wanted to survive. But the Thunderbird also had just enough retro styling to give it some class. Travis didn't want to be *too* ordinary.

Best of all, it was a great cruising machine. He'd checked out of the motel at six a.m. and been on the road for the entire day. Straddling an 885-cc engine at high speed was the closest thing his two-legged form could get to the thrill and the freedom of running as a wolf.

But today his *Canis lupus* had grumbled nonstop. His *Homo sapiens* wasn't overly happy either. He tried to ignore both and just ride and ride and ride...until his stomach got louder than both the engine and the voices in his head, and Travis was forced to stop at a Denny's in Idaho Falls. Shapeshifting burned a virtual *ton* of calories, and he'd been foolish to go without breakfast, crazy to go without lunch. He was ravenous. There were better restaurants, certainly, but Denny's was his go-to place when he needed a lot of calories *fast*. Maybe he'd be lucky and they'd have that bacon-on-everything special. Thank the goddess, Changelings didn't have cholesterol issues.

A wild-haired man in ragged clothes stood quietly in the parking lot, a tin can at his feet labeled *Thank U*. He was holding an enormous cardboard sign: *You can't go back and fix the past.*

Travis threw a dollar into the can as he passed. The slogan had proved disturbingly true in his life, although he could have done without the damn reminder tonight.

He'd finished his double cheeseburger and was halfway through his country-fried steak when both sides of his personality ganged up on him. It started with his wolf, of course. That was normal—his alter ego was always nagging him about one thing or another, and he was used to it. The lupine persona had a moral compass that exceeded that of many humans, probably because life was simple to a wolf. Black and white, no gray at all. Still, Travis didn't understand why on earth it wanted him to *go back* to the woman he'd barely managed to rescue.

By then his human brain had started laying out clues like breadcrumbs, all the bizarre things he'd been doing his damnedest to ignore. Like how the woman had failed to react to his Change. Sure, she'd been injured and in shock, but even the most stoic person would at least raise an eyebrow when someone shape-shifted right in front of them. And then there was how she'd somehow managed to leap far enough out from the ledge to land in the trees. Without a hang glider or one hell of an updraft from the valley, it should have been impossible. And of course it should also have been impossible that she survived it. Even with the tree branches slowing her descent, they could only break her fall to a degree. She shouldn't have been alive, never mind *conscious*, when he found her. Humans could be tough spirited, but their bodies were all too fragile.

The real clincher, however, was that momentary flash in the depths of the woman's dark brown eyes, like the elusive glimmer of green in a tropical sunset at the precise moment the sun disappeared into the ocean. Travis had tried to talk himself out of it—just imagination, a trick of the light, all those lame-ass explanations—but the truth was, he knew what he'd seen.

And he knew what it meant.

She was a Changeling, just like him. Her scent had said *human*, however, and there was only one possible reason for that: she hadn't made her first shift yet. His inner wolf radiated approval—no doubt relieved at having finally gotten through to the thickheaded human it shared its existence with. And the thickheaded human's mind seemed satisfied, too. Both fell silent as Travis finished his meal. He even got to eat his bacon-maple sundae in peace. He paid his bill and walked out into the parking lot, and knew without looking that the moon was only a day or so from being full. He could feel the lunar tug, but he wasn't subject to it—he took on his wolfen form as he pleased. Or not. But then he'd been born a Changeling, not *made*. A human who had been bitten would turn at the very next full moon. And it wasn't pretty.

The woman he'd rescued was in the worst of all possible places for such an event: a hospital filled with witnesses. As a loner, Travis didn't give a damn about pack protocol, but it was in his own best interests to make sure that the world at large didn't suddenly find out about Changelings. But what made up his mind was the knowledge of what a first Change entailed. It was difficult enough for those born to it, but for a human? It was the sire's responsibility to both guard them and coach them through the ordeal. Why the hell was this woman alone at such a critical time? Where was her sire, her pack? *If* she lived through the Change—not a given, especially in her condition—a freshly made wolf left to its own devices could do a lot of damage in its terror and pain. It was something that Travis knew all too well. And while he definitely did *not* want to babysit this already troubled young woman, he couldn't stand by and allow her to hurt somebody.

As he headed to his motorcycle, he pressed a bag of hot food into the hands of the homeless man and nodded at the sign.

"S'true, man," the man said as he clutched the bag to his chest.

"More than you know," muttered Travis. He straddled the Triumph and cruised out of the parking lot, heading in the direction he had come from. He could swear his damn wolf was smug as he opened up the throttle.

((◖ ◗ ●

Fern was as good as her word, and a few hours later, Neva was sitting on the edge of the bed, free of all tubes, needles, or other accoutrements. Her toes touched the cold floor, and her right hand gripped the mattress cover beside her. She wished she had the full use of her left one to clutch something, anything else. "No crutches, huh?"

"Not with that arm. I brought you a cane instead." Neva's expression must have been totally transparent because Fern waved a calming hand at her. "I know, I know, it looks like a little old lady's cane, but maybe you can steady yourself with it once you're up."

I ought to be able to steady a Buick with it. The jack for her car wasn't as solid as the thick cane that Fern parked beside the bed. As utilitarian as an army jeep, it was made of plain gray metal, but any hope it had for a neutral appearance had been utterly compromised by its four heavy-duty rubber feet.

Neva slid some of her weight off the bed. The broken leg throbbed, and she leaned on her right foot. Now what? She was unsure of herself, but Fern had obviously been around this block before.

"Put your hand here. Hang on to me like this. Let me take some of your weight."

"You sound like my dance instructor," said Neva.

"A little two-step music and we'd be all set. Ready?"

One moment Fern was bracing her, and the next, she was standing. As her weight settled onto her feet, she straightened and couldn't help stretching just a little bit. Instantly, pain threatened to break through the buffer of the medication, but Neva could sense that she had improved just since she'd awakened. In any other situation, it would have been great news. But she knew the rapid healing was caused by the animal entity that was threatening to take her over, so her emotions were a toss-up between depression and stark fear.

Fern chattered as they "waltzed" a few steps, and then Neva used her good right hand to lean on the cane instead of clinging to the nurse. Thankfully, it was every bit as solid as it was ugly. And there were other things to be grateful for. Her leg cast was long, from thigh to ankle, but it didn't encompass her foot. She might be stiff-legged, but at least she was level. She could walk—okay, it was more like a bad zombie shuffle. But a visit to the bathroom on her very own (Fern being right outside the door notwithstanding) proved that she was ambulatory, she could get around. And if she could do that, she could escape. But first she was going to sit down—no, better make that *lie* down, for just a little while.

((((●

The hospital *stank.*

Barely inside the front doors, Travis shook his head, trying unsuccessfully to clear it. A human would only smell disinfectant, which was bad enough. A Changeling smelled *everything* the disinfectant was supposed to hide. Topping the list of aromas were blood and urine, but emotions had a scent, too, and the acrid tang of fear was the strongest. It set his teeth on edge. Under normal circumstances, both his human and wolfen selves would have voted to leave this place as fast as possible.

He sighed and tried to focus on the job at hand, which was figuring out just where the woman was in the enormous building. Travis had no name, just a vague description based on what his natural night vision could tell him about her. Still, as a Changeling he had everything he needed in order to find someone: a scent. As with all things olfactory, his inner wolf had automatically filed it away. Memories could fade; the way someone looked or sounded could become fuzzy over time. But scents? They were never forgotten.

Travis followed the signs to the emergency ward, where he knew the woman would have been brought first. It was a tough place to pluck a specific scent out of the air, especially one that was already two days old. His wolf chuffed in disgust as it fought to sort out the tangle of smells. It came out like a human cough, and a nurse commented cheerfully on the dryness of the air as she hurried by.

Finally the wolf found what it was looking for. *Here.*

Travis inhaled, and the wolf helped his human nose to perceive the woman's scent. Light and airy yet spicy and warm, like wild roses after a rain…Travis started walking quickly. Trailing a scent always seemed to him as if he were trying to follow a single thread out of a vast conduit of fibers—like maybe a transatlantic cable. It would have been a helluva lot easier in lupine form, of course, but that option wasn't open. All he could do was give his inner wolf its head and let it guide him.

Which worked until the elevator doors shut in front of his face.

Now what? What floor would she be on? Luckily, visiting hours were in full swing, and Travis was quickly joined by several humans. Several averted their eyes, however, and a few shrank away. Between his motorcycle leathers and his size, he probably looked like a badass to them. Normally that would be fine with him, but it wasn't going to help him today. He whipped his sunglasses off in hopes of appearing less intimidating, barely remembering in time to wipe the frown off his brow, too. "Excuse me," he said politely to an administrative-looking guy in a suit. "Where's the orthopedic ward?" It was a flat-out guess, but it was a place to start. "Mom said my cousin's in here with a broken leg, but she couldn't remember the room number."

"Adult? Probably on the fourth floor, south wing. Hope your cousin gets better soon."

"Me too. Thanks."

Several people got off at four, and he followed them. The wolf picked up the scent immediately, but beelining was out of the question. Both visitors and patients thronged the hallway. Travis shortened his steps so he wouldn't run over a convoy of wheelchairs. Several flower arrangements sat on a cart just outside a room, and he scooped up one as he went by and tucked it in front of him without missing a beat. No one noticed. The hallway branched into two at the nurses' station, and he smiled at the clerk behind the circular desk as his inner wolf steered him to the left.

This hall was crowded, too, and he hugged the east wall as he made his way through the people. Tripped on an IV pole and apologized to an older man in a plaid bathrobe. Still, the woman's scent was getting stronger, and Travis knew he was close. Then he spotted his quarry through the open door on the opposite side of the hall. He expected his wolf to be pleased with itself (it was always terribly self-satisfied after a successful hunt), but this time it was full-out triumphant. For a strange moment his human brain reeled, too, and Travis had to shake his head to clear it. *Weird.* Clearly his senses were just overloaded after tracking her through this olfactory nightmare.

Hidden by the tide of visitors and patients between him and the door, he watched her for a few moments. She was in an armchair, beside the bed rather than in it, which meant she was healing up fast, even for a Changeling. The long, faded blue bathrobe was hospital issue, but he liked the look of her dark-brown hair tumbling over it. Her face was pale in comparison with vivid freckles that marched up and over her nose and across her cheekbones. Her eyes were not just dark brown, but the deep color of rich coffee. Pretty eyes—but even from here he could see the desperation in them.

(((● ●

"Come with me if you want to live."

Neva stared at the enormous hand the stranger extended to her. Her gaze followed the black leather–clad arm up to the massive shoulders, the strong jaw, and the thick lock of wavy blond hair hanging over his dark glasses. "You have *so* got to be kidding me," she said.

He shrugged. "I always wanted to say that line. Except I'm not kidding." With his other hand, the big stranger plunked a flower arrangement of purple irises and orange chrysanthemums on the bedside table. He yanked the tiny card off it and stuffed it into his jeans pocket, but not before she read, *To our valued employee, Bob.*

"You stole somebody's *flowers*?"

"Camouflage." He opened and closed the drawers and closet. "No clothes left, huh? Guess you'll have to come as you are."

"Why would I go anywhere with you? I know what you are." She practically spat the words at him, even as she grabbed the remote from the bed and poised her thumb over the red button for the nurses' station. "You're one of *them*."

"Yeah, well, I know what you are, too, sister."

Of course he would know, but it still stung. She didn't want to be like him or any of the rest of the damned creatures under Meredith's thumb. "Look, I know who sent you. And I can give you twice what she offered you."

He laughed at that. "Trust me, nobody could pay me enough to come *here*. It stinks."

"What about your pack leader?"

"I have no pack. I'm just here to spring you."

Something like hope stirred inside her, and she pushed it down hard. Not only was this a werewolf she was dealing with, but he had screwed up her plans once already. She wouldn't be fooled. "Meredith won't like it," she tested.

"Who?" He slid the sunglasses down his nose, revealing vivid blue eyes that studied her as intently as she was studying him. "Look, if you have a gripe with somebody, that's your problem. I'm here to get you out of here. Period."

From the set of his mouth, he looked like he was bracing himself for an argument. She was all set to give him one, too, then realized this was exactly the opportunity she needed. "Okay."

"Look, we both know you can't stay—*what*?"

"I said *okay*. I want to go. Go ahead, get me out of here. You messed up everything the other night and you're responsible for me being in this place, so you owe me, mister. Let's go."

"Wait just a damn minute." He pulled the sunglasses off completely then and pointed them at her. "I saved your frickin' life, lady. If anybody owes anybody, it's—"

"Just get me out of here and we're even." She started struggling to her feet as he opened and closed his mouth, obviously at a loss for words. He recovered enough to offer his big hand again, and this time she took it and used it to pull herself up, finding herself standing almost nose to nose with him. Or rather, nose to *chest*. Neva was tall herself, but this guy was huge. She eyed him warily. "No funny stuff. Get me out of here, and we're done."

He hesitated, his brow furrowed. "Anyone in their right mind would be happy to get out of here, but you're a little too keen. You thinking of trying to off yourself again?"

"That's none of your business. Are you going to help me get out of here or not?"

The frown deepened, but he didn't argue further, just put his sunglasses back on. "Can you walk?"

"Not fast, but yeah." Okay, technically she'd only shuffled around her room and limped partway to the nurses' station once. She had no idea if she'd hold up any farther than that, but she wasn't going to say so. Instead, she pulled the ties of her bathrobe tighter and grabbed her cane.

He placed himself on her left, her arm and leg casts against him, and threw an arm around her, his big hand curled around her waist. "What's your name?"

"Why's it matter?"

"Well, if we're stopped, it'll look pretty suspicious if I don't know my own *cousin's* name."

Cousin. Well, it was lot better than pretending to be his girlfriend—she wouldn't have to feign affection. After all, if he was her own cousin, Alec, she would have punched him rather than hug him just out of childhood habit. Before she could say anything, however, her newly acquired *cousin* picked up her chart from the plastic pocket on the door.

"Geneva Rayne Ross," he read.

"Just Neva."

"Christ, you used your real name? I thought you were trying to hide."

"Hey, I wasn't exactly thinking clearly when they brought me in here. So who the hell are *you*, the werewolf police? Why do you keep interfering in my life?"

He was silent for a long moment. "Travis Williamson. No. And goddess only knows."

She swung around and thumped the center of his chest with a right hook, which was all she could reach from the awkward angle. It was a point in his favor that he didn't let her fall—she'd overbalanced and would have done a fine face-plant if he wasn't hanging on to her.

"What the hell was that for?" he demanded.

"Luck."

"Must be *extra* good luck since you already stabbed me in the same frickin' spot," he muttered. "Lean on me," was all the warning she got before he abruptly propelled the pair of them sideways through the door and down the hall.

She'd been worried that she wouldn't be able to keep up, but there was no need. Her feet barely touched the floor at all. She couldn't be glued more tightly to Travis's right side if he'd used duct tape to secure her. And despite the strength of that big arm and its sizeable hand, he somehow managed not to squeeze her *too* hard. As for the effort required of him, she might as well have been a sack of groceries as he negotiated a path through the busy halls.

To her surprise he smelled good. Her senses were so much keener now, which was a real drawback in a place like a hospital, where most smells were repellent at best. Travis's scent was earthy and definitely *male*, but not in a stinky-gym-socks kind of way—instead, it reminded her of hiking trails in the mountains and summers by the lake. And it was strong. This close to him, the scent of him canceled out all the others around her, and she was oh so grateful for that little perk.

"My goodness, girl, where are you going?" It was Fern. Breaking away from a group of nurses by the elevator, she came over and looked like she was going to start examining her patient for damage. Instead she folded her arms and glared up at Travis. "This gal's in the hospital for a reason, mister."

"My cousin and I were just heading to the gift shop for a few minutes and then maybe the cafeteria," Neva said quickly. "I'm all right. I feel pretty good, and I'm really not putting much weight on my leg, see? Barely had to use my cane at all." She waved it and smiled.

Fern looked unconvinced. "You're going to wear yourself out."

"He promised to carry me if I got tired."

On cue, Travis swung her up into his arms. "I'll take good care of her, ma'am. We want her to get better." He leaned down to Fern and whispered, "Shopaholic. Neva won't be happy until she buys a few magazines and some knickknacks." Neva smacked him solidly, but he ignored it.

"Don't keep her too long," warned Fern. The frown was still there, but it had relaxed to two furrows instead of three. "I'm off shift now, honey," she said to Neva. "I've got three days off, but I'll check in on you first thing when I get back. I don't want to hear that they had to double your pain meds because of this little escapade." She patted Neva's good leg and headed back to her coworkers.

The chime of an elevator door sounded, and Travis turned and walked into the car with Neva still in his arms. Several people followed them on.

"You can put me down now," she whispered fiercely.

"Later," he said smugly. "The nurse was right. We don't want to wear you out."

"And what was that bit about me being a shopaholic?"

"You know you have trouble controlling yourself."

"I do not!"

"You can't be helped if you don't admit you have a problem." He smiled and addressed a couple who were staring at them. "She was injured at a shoe sale. Trampled when the doors opened."

"I am *so* going to hurt you," she muttered.

She repeated the phrase when they arrived in the parking garage. "A motorcycle? Are you crazy?" she said as he set her on her feet. "Nice bike, but I'm not getting on it."

"You'll be fine."

"No, I mean I'm not going with you. Thanks for getting me out and all, but we're done. We're even now and we're done." She dismissed him with a wave and headed toward the pedestrian exit. It would have been a much more dignified departure if her gait wasn't so awkward, if the floppy little cloth slippers offered a little more protection from the hard pavement, if she was used to using a cane, and if she wasn't dressed in a thin bathrobe with nothing but baggy pajamas underneath.

And if she didn't feel Travis's disapproving gaze drilling into her back every damn step of the way.

Forty-five minutes later she'd made it off the expansive hospital grounds and covered three city blocks. One block was with her own energy, and the last two were by sheer force of will. She was heading south, so the wind was at her back, but she was still freezing. Wasn't it supposed to be May? Neva collapsed gratefully on a bench at a bus stop, and she was even more grateful that no one else was there. She had to think, had to plan. At least she had a couple of pieces of ID in her bathrobe pocket. That was all she'd been carrying the night she'd jumped—just enough to identify her body.

It was still enough. She just had to figure out a way, and *fast*. With no idea what day it was—Tuesday? Wednesday?—she didn't know how much time she really had before the full moon turned her into something she couldn't live with.

A killer.

(((● ● ●

Travis was relieved when Neva finally sat down. She'd slowed considerably over the last couple of blocks, but he'd been afraid she'd collapse on the sidewalk rather than take a break. Stubborn woman, he thought, but he admired her spirit. She didn't rest long before forcing herself to her feet, however. He shook his head as she struggled down the sidewalk, determination in every limping step.

Of course, he'd been following her since she first walked away from him in the parking garage. He'd briefly entertained the notion of minding his business and riding away into the sunset, but he decided that just getting her out of the hospital building wasn't going to solve any problems. There was still the matter of a full moon to deal with, and there was no safe place for her to go. Nope, like it or not, he wasn't done—and besides, his inner wolf had kicked up hell from the moment Neva left his side.

He circled the Triumph around the block and came up alongside the blue-clad figure. Her pajamas were getting strange looks from passersby, or maybe it was the industrial-strength cane that she didn't really know how to use effectively. Whatever people were staring at, she was obviously struggling.

"Hey," he called out, but she ignored him. Her lips were pressed together in a straight line, and Travis had a sudden strange impulse to kiss them—and to smooth that little furrow between her brows with his lips, too. Shaking that image from his head, he tried again. "Neva!"

Her eyes darted in his direction, although her head didn't turn. She was still moving forward, but so slowly that Travis had to use his feet to coast the big bike alongside the curb. "What do you want?" she snapped.

"Not a thing. Just thought *you* might want a lift somewhere."

She stopped then and eyed him suspiciously, her arms folded in front of her. "Why?"

Why? Christ, he had no idea. "Why not?" he shot back.

The first tiny chink appeared in her armor. "It wouldn't work. My cast…" She shrugged.

"It'll work." He parked the bike and opened a saddlebag. Drew out a long leather duster, helped her to put her right arm into it, and draped it around the left. The shoulders of the coat sagged midway to her elbows and the hem reached the sidewalk. Her little fabric slippers looked ridiculous poking out from under the grainy brown leather. How the hell had she walked in those?

"It'll keep the wind off you and cover up that cast," said Travis. "You're going to have to sit on the bike first, though, so I can arrange the coat around you."

Easier said than done. There was some struggling and swearing before she was seated properly, during which time he was amazed they didn't knock over the bike. Travis settled in front of her at last, scooping up her casted leg and resting it on top of his thigh, tucking the leather duster all around it. She clutched him tightly with her good hand as he slowly wheeled away from the curb and merged into traffic.

The wind immediately snatched at Neva's hair. A few strands were tugged free, but most of it was tucked into the turned-up collar of the enormous coat. She wished she had a helmet, then snorted—it was a silly thing to want when her plans didn't include living more than a few hours at most.

She laid her face on Travis's broad back. Her pain meds had worn off, and she hurt everywhere. Her position on the bike felt precarious, as if she was going to tumble off and hit the pavement at any moment, but the creature within her had left her no choice in the matter. No choice in *any* matter, it seemed. She had to leave the hospital in order to carry out her plan, and once outside of the hospital, she couldn't get anywhere fast enough on her own. Therefore, she had no option but to trust this man. This *werewolf*, she corrected quickly. She couldn't let herself forget that he was the very thing she was running from.

Neva didn't have a clue what Travis's motives were. If he was the ax-murderer type, she supposed he'd already had his chance when he first found her. Instead, he'd helped her. He'd come back for her in the hospital, knowing what she was about to become. And all without ever knowing her name. Of course that didn't prove he didn't work for Meredith. And now? She hadn't even asked where he was headed, although she supposed it really didn't matter much. He was heading east, and that was good enough for her. Once there, wherever *there* was, it shouldn't be that hard to ditch him.

The hard part was going to be finding another way to do herself in, and fast. Before the animal inside grew strong enough to try and stop her. Or before she lost the will to carry out her plan. She closed her eyes as the stupid, useless tears started up again, and sobbed silently onto Travis's black jacket as the motorcycle carried them down the highway.

FOUR

"Where is she?"

The sharp voice rang out from the shadows at the back of the room, causing the three men who had just entered to stop in their tracks. Dozens of candles flared to life along the walls, revealing a strange series of symbols, shapes, and creatures, painstakingly drawn with black and gray powders on the moon-white marble floor. Dark spatters of blood gleamed wetly.

Another flurry of candles ignited behind an enormous velvet armchair with an ornately carved frame. The flickering light illumined the lithe form of a woman seated there and gilded the waves of her long blonde hair.

"You're hesitating—you haven't found her. Have you?" Meredith de la Ronde uncoiled from the armchair and stepped down from the dais like a model, pausing with each step for maximum effect in her thigh-high La Couturier boots. In lieu of the last stair, she planted her black suede heels with the bloodred soles on the naked corpse that was sprawled in front of it. To her satisfaction, not one of the three men facing her gave the dead man any notice at all. He might as well have been one of the marble floor tiles, even though he had worked alongside them until a few days ago.

If she'd been alone, she might have laughed.

Meredith had power, and she liked it. Not only did she plan to keep it, she was growing it by the day. Or rather, by the month.

The latest inductees to her pack were due to turn when the full moon reached its zenith this night. And as their sire, the one who had bitten them and shared with them the wolfen gift, she could draw energy from them, enough to fuel not only her dark spells but also her darker ambitions. Most of her pack members were mere thralls, toys and tools to be used up and discarded as Meredith saw fit. She stroked the exquisite pendant that hung between her breasts. The dark opal, set in silver, was the size of a raven's egg, and fire flashed in its depths; as long as she wore it, she owned nearly all of the wolves she'd created, mind, body, and soul.

Geneva had been among the few who were not so easily entranced, and to make matters worse, the stupid little bitch had the nerve to *escape*. Meredith had been sick with fury when she'd discovered it. She'd killed the guards, of course, then turned her rage on whoever was handy until the anger gave way to the grief it really was. Not for Geneva herself, certainly, or for any other person. No, Meredith mourned her greatest and most powerful spell. After years of research, of trial and error, pain and blood, it was her very best creation, her Sistine Chapel, her *Mona Lisa*—

And it had been totally reliant on a quality that only Geneva Rayne Ross possessed. Without her, it simply could not be employed. *Ever.* Meredith had first sent out most of the pack to recapture the little brat—or to recover the body. Meanwhile, she secretly went to one of her underground spell rooms and wept with frustration and disappointment until she had no tears left and no more things to break. Finally she found her equilibrium.

So Geneva had escaped. So what? *Let her try to manage a first Change all by her little lonesome. She'll die, and I won't have to kill her. Perfect.*

And if the bitch didn't die? Geneva couldn't hide forever, and once she was found, she would learn to do what she was told, at least long enough to serve Meredith's ends. And after that? *If you can't be a good example, then you'll just have to be a terrible warning.*

"Make yourselves useful and take that away." She waved her fingers airily at the corpse. The three men hastened to comply, giving the patterns on the floor a wide berth. Two seized the dead man and headed for the door. Meredith smirked and pointed an exquisitely manicured fingernail at the odd man out.

"You. Stay here."

((((( )

Never having had a passenger on the bike before, Travis had to admit there was something very appealing about having a woman pressed up against his back. And as he opened up the throttle on the highway, he felt Neva lay her head against him. Although he was certain it was just to shield herself from the wind, he still felt an unexpected surge of protectiveness toward her. But his wolf didn't have to be so damn smug about it.

That lupine smugness disappeared as the highway signs flew past them, and Neva began to sag. Her grip on his jacket loosened alarmingly, and for the last eighty miles, he drove one-handed in favor of holding her good arm tightly to him, willing her to stay upright.

While he would never have chosen cheap accommodations—his human side liked things clean and comfortable—he would have preferred something smaller and more out of the way. However, any port in a storm, and the Rocking Horse Casino was right on the highway and boasted an enormous hotel. He coasted into a quiet side lot with no small amount of relief. And in the heart-beat between bringing the bike to a stop and leaping off it, Travis used every ounce of his Changeling speed to catch Neva before she tumbled to the pavement.

Now what? Dressed like she was, she might attract attention if he took her along to the front desk with him. And her exhausted state might be interpreted as something else—drunk off her feet, at the very least. Worse, someone could easily suspect she was a victim of a date-rape drug and call in the cops. *No, Officer, everything's fine, she's just going to turn into a wolf soon.* Yeah, right.

There were no windows on this side of the building, and the one and only car parked here looked like it belonged to staff. He laid Neva carefully on a curved garden bench sheltered by tall, yellow rhododendrons, and tucked the heavy coat around her. "Stay here," he said, although it was unlikely she could hear him.

When he returned with the key card for a room, she hadn't moved a hair and was, in fact, snoring heartily. His mouth quirked when he picked her up and the snores failed to subside. Exhausted, he thought, and was glad he'd decided to stop to let her sleep for a while. She was going to need all her strength for later, when the moon was high.

Travis chose the side entrance to the stairs, where he was unlikely to encounter very many people. Humans preferred elevators as a general rule. He'd reached the third floor before Neva stirred.

"Put me down," she muttered without opening her eyes.

"In a minute." He found the room. Balancing Neva in his arms, he fumbled with the key card and cursed loudly as the lock rejected it twice. An old woman with enormous glasses poked her head out of a suite down the hall. He forced a smile for her benefit. "Newlyweds," he said and was relieved when the woman giggled knowingly, shook her finger at him, and withdrew. On the third swipe of the card, the door opened and he carried Neva inside.

"I don't feel good," was all she said as he stripped the leather duster off her and tucked her in one of the queen-size beds.

She looked colorless, even against the white sheets—until she opened her eyes. He could clearly see the green fire in their golden-brown depths, and he knew she didn't have much time. It was only about an hour till the full moon rose, and once it reached its highest point in the sky, Neva would shift form for the very first time and fully become what Travis had always been, or she would die trying. He shoved that thought away at once.

"Where the hell is your sire?" he burst out. "He should be helping you with this."

Neva snorted. "My *sire*? You make it sound like I'm a pedigreed dog. If you mean the monster that bit me, I'm several states away from her." She blinked. "At least I hope so. Where exactly are we?"

Travis was too busy digesting the previous sentence to answer her question. "Are you saying the gift was forced on you?"

"What gift?"

"Well, *the wolf*, of course."

She stared at him for several seconds. "A gift…What kind of a goddamn gift is *this*?" Neva struggled to sit up, fury in every feature. "Here, I'll make you into a creature from hell, and then you can show your thanks by murdering innocent people. Oh, and you can start with your family. You won't be needing *them* anymore."

Travis held up both hands. "Whoa there, you've been watching way too many bad movies. Changelings aren't like that at all."

"*Werewolves* are exactly like that. Don't try to snow me."

"I'm not a werewolf and neither are you," he said. "That Hollywood stuff is bunk. It pisses me off that they always show the gift as a curse. Some poor schmuck turns into a ravening animal when the moon's full, and can't remember what he did when he wakes up the next day…" Two and two belatedly made four in his head. "Is that what the cliff jumping was all about? You're not depressed. You think you're going to be some kind of monster, so you've decided to do away with yourself."

"You don't get it."

"I get it just fine. I get that you're still thinking about it, too, and that's why you were so gung ho about leaving the damn hospital."

She said nothing, just glared at him, and he knew he was right on the money. He glared back and pointed a finger at her to underscore his words. "Don't you try anything. I mean it. You give me the slightest reason to think you're going to do something stupid and I'll damn well tie you up."

"Oh yeah? Until when, exactly? You can't keep me leashed forever."

"*Until* you have a chance to experience what being a Changeling really means."

She rolled her eyes at that. "Going through screaming hell while an animal takes over my body? Oh, goody. And then afterward, maybe I can go practice my new skills by tearing the throats out of some homeless people."

"Jesus, it's not like that. A first Change can be pretty rough on you physically, of course. But this crazy notion about being a natural-born killer is just plain wrong." Guilt immediately punched him in the gut. He couldn't lie to her. "What I mean is, you'll have the power and the strength to kill humans, but you'll learn control, so you won't. You'll still be *you,* and frankly, you don't look like the homicidal type to me." *Unless looks could kill…*

"You're so full of shit. Or else you just don't get it. Once Meredith gets hold of someone, they're not themselves anymore. And her werewolves kill for her."

"That can't be—"

"*I saw them.* I watched them murder people. And I couldn't do a thing about it."

She'd pass any lie-detector test, he decided. She believed she was telling the truth, but he couldn't begin to fathom where she had gotten the strange ideas. Changelings had strict laws, and no wolf was permitted to run around killing people. *Usually...* He tried another approach. "Look, I don't know anything about Meredith's pack dynamics. What I do know is that once you learn to have control, you can have a great life."

Her face changed suddenly. "I had a great life," she said quietly, her anger displaced by enormous sadness. "At least, I had one planned." A tear caught on her lashes, and she rubbed it roughly away with the heel of her good hand.

Travis's heart clenched unexpectedly, and he lowered himself into a chair. "You still do," he said gruffly. "Nothing's different. You're not going to wake up tomorrow and be a different person. You'll just have a—I don't know how the hell to say it. It's like you'll have an extra *dimension* to you. You'll be *more.*"

"What I'll be is *useful.* To Meredith." She sniffed and wiped her nose fiercely on her sleeve. "I can't Change, don't you get that? You've got to let me go."

"Christ." He rubbed his palm over his face. "I'm getting tired of this argument. Last time: you *are* going to turn into a wolf, and you need to lie low till it's over. Case closed. So no, you're not going anywhere unless it's with me." He rose and pulled a large jackknife from his back pocket. "We need to take those casts off."

"What the hell?" Neva lurched backward until her back was flat against the headboard, clutching the blankets to her with one hand. "You're not touching these!"

"If we don't take the casts off now, it's just going to make it harder for you when you turn. Think about it—a wolf's leg doesn't bend the same way a human's does. Besides, I doubt that you still need them."

"Right, like I had them put on as a fashion statement."

"You walked three city blocks under your own steam, less than three days after a fall that would have been fatal to anyone else. You know full well your recovery's been faster than normal," Travis said. "I'll bet the doctors in the ER were amazed at how clean the breaks were and how aligned the bones were. That's why you have light fiberglass casts instead of heavy plaster, and I'll bet money there's no pins or screws either. In fact, by now your bones are probably knitted. You can thank the wolf for that."

"I'm not thanking it for a damn thing."

"Regardless, the Change will complete the healing."

"I'm not making the Change."

He rolled his eyes at that. "Whether you want it to or not, it's happening."

"I could kill somebody."

"Unlikely. But I'll make you a deal. If I promise to keep you from doing anything homicidal, will you promise to stay alive long enough to learn control?"

"I'm not promising anything."

He shrugged and took a step toward her.

"You touch my casts and I'll start screaming."

"No, you won't, because you don't want to attract attention."

"Yes, I do, and I'll attract a *lot* of attention if you come near me."

"You're a real pain in the ass, you know that? Have it your way, then, see how that works out for you." It was actually the tightness in her face that had stopped him—it was obvious that she was in pain. He folded the knife away and headed for the door. "Get some rest. I'll get us some chow and see what I can do about finding you some meds." He didn't bother mentioning that pharmaceuticals didn't work on Changelings and that she was probably too far gone for them to be of any use to her.

((◖ ◗ ●

The heavy door clunked shut behind him, and Neva blew out a breath. Her bruised and battered body was throbbing in a dozen places, and she wanted nothing more than to sleep for a week— but she didn't have the luxury of time. There was no telling how long Travis would be gone, and she didn't plan to be here when he got back.

She eased out of bed, her body shrieking silently in protest. Everything hurt, but she still wished she had some regular clothes she could at least *try* to get into. Travis hadn't brought in any luggage. He didn't appear to own much except whatever was in the saddlebags of his motorcycle, so she couldn't steal anything of his—well, except for the too-big coat. She slid on the stupid fabric slippers, then tried to adjust the pajamas and bathrobe that had twisted around her. It was frustrating with only one hand to work with, and for a moment she wondered if Travis had been right about not needing the casts anymore…She put it out of her mind at once. He was a *werewolf*, and he couldn't possibly be right about anything.

Neva struggled into the heavy leather duster and cautiously opened the door. Signs pointed to the elevators, the lobby, the bar, and the restaurant. The powerful smells of food made her stomach clench as if she hadn't eaten in days. She wasn't going to succumb, though. She had a mission. She shuffled as quickly as she could down the hallway in the direction of the back exit.

The stairs were pure hell. The curtains had been drawn in the motel room, and somehow Neva had missed the fact that they were three floors up. Leaning heavily on the railing, she finally came up with a strange lurch-step-slide-and-repeat that got her to the ground floor in one piece but with much of her energy spent. She stepped outside and sank to the concrete step as dizziness and pain overwhelmed her. It was fairly quiet here at the back of the motel. A dog barked in the distance, and the traffic sounds were muffled. She took several deep breaths of the cool air until the dizziness faded and her vision cleared. The sky was awash with deepening pinks and purples, and she gazed at the twilight colors with pleasure—until she realized that the moon would be making its appearance on the opposite horizon at any moment. And although a skyline of buildings blocked it from her sight, she knew that her body would be able to sense its rise. That realization sparked enough adrenaline to get her back on her feet, pain or no pain.

Heart pounding, she shuffled down a series of alleys until she found what she really needed—a car with a set of keys in it. It was a very old Toyota something or other with dented doors and ripped seats, but it would do for her last ride. At least it was unlikely that anyone would seriously miss it, and as she struggled to get into the little car, she wondered suddenly if anyone was going to miss *her*. To her dismay, her eyes teared up at once.

Shit. Don't think. Focus on what you're doing. Neva fumbled for the keys and prayed to any deity that might be listening that the vehicle would start. It coughed and complained, but the engine turned over. Suddenly a pair of headlights flashed in the rearview mirror, and bright light filled the car until Neva had to close her eyes. The downside of being in a small car became apparent anytime a pickup truck or other tall vehicle came up behind you at night. She waited for it to pass, which it did with painful slowness—and stopped directly in front of her. Her eyes flew open just as the door to the Toyota was ripped from its hinges and tossed to one side.

FIVE

Neva bared her teeth as Travis's big hands reached for her. "I'm not going with you."

"You *are* going with me, and you're going quietly." His voice was low, but there was no mistaking the underlying fury in it.

She opened her mouth to let loose a fire-engine shriek, but his iron grip covered it before she finished drawing the breath.

"You want to scream? Fine. But think it through, Neva. *The moon. Is. Up.*" He emphasized every syllable.

It was all too true. She could feel the lunar body pulling at her, tugging at some primeval instinct within in the same way that it drew the tides. Her gaze automatically shifted to the east. Blocked by tall buildings, she couldn't see the moon—but she knew its exact position in the sky.

"You start yelling and humans will come," he continued. "People who live here in this neighborhood, police, EMTs, you name it. And they'll all get to see you turn into something they won't understand. In less than a minute, it'll be all over YouTube, Facebook, CNN, the works. Live coverage of your Change—and of anyone you injure trying to escape." Travis released her and stepped back. "I'm your only hope, Neva. Quit fighting me."

For a brief, flickering moment, she wondered if maybe revealing herself to the whole world would solve her problem. If she proved that werewolves existed, maybe she could reveal Meredith and her gang for the evil they were. It could work, it—

Her eyes rested on the swing set and scattered toys in the yard beside her. *Not here, not now.* Travis, damn him, was all too right about the human witnesses and the possibility of innocent people getting hurt in this crowded neighborhood.

Neva glared up at her would-be savior. "What exactly do you want from me?"

He shook his head. "Not a damn thing from you personally. Only that it'll make *my* life a whole lot easier if the humans don't know about Changelings. Once you've turned, and shown that you're in control of yourself, I'll be glad to get out of *your* life. Deal?"

He struck that Terminator pose again, holding out his enormous hand just as he had at the hospital. What choice did she really have? She held up her casted arm and wiggled her fingers. In a flash he had scooped her out of the car and carried her to the truck. "Borrowed," he said in answer to her questioning look, and deposited her in the passenger seat none too gently.

When he slid behind the wheel, it was on the tip of her tongue to say something scathing about the oily stink of stale cigarette smoke and god only knew what else that coated every surface of the truck. But as she opened her mouth to speak, the powerful scent of fresh food slammed into her senses, overwhelming all else. A box with a large deluxe pizza dwarfed the dashboard, and bags of burgers and fries and pints of milk were stacked in the middle of the bench seat.

"Dig in," said Travis, slamming his door twice to make it stay shut. "Shape-shifting throws your metabolism into high gear, and you've got to have fuel in your system."

He was using his lecture voice again, but she wasn't listening. The sound of four hundred and sixty horses under the old truck's dented hood barely registered. She was *starving.* As if she hadn't seen food in days, she found herself alternately eating from a folded slice of pizza in one hand and a box of fries in the other. "Omigod," she said with her mouth crammed full. "This isn't like me at all."

"That's because it's not you. It's your wolf. Like I said, it needs fuel."

She stopped abruptly then and allowed the food to drop from her fingers to the floor. "No way. I'm not giving this, this *monster* one bit more—"

Her words disappeared in a huge gasp as every muscle in her body suddenly spasmed at once, then cramped tight as if she was being squeezed to death in a giant's grip. A long minute passed, then two, before it released her and eased away. Slowly she became aware of Travis's big hand firmly engulfing her shoulder.

"You're okay," he said. "Just breathe. The moon's getting higher, and you're going to Change soon, that's all."

That's all? Nooo, no, no, no, no, *no*! She wasn't doing this. She was supposed to end her life so she didn't end up a pawn of Meredith's, so she didn't hurt anybody, so she didn't savage the people she loved. She had to do something and do it fast. They were speeding down a dark highway, and she wondered frantically if she should jump—

She hadn't fully formed the thought before the creature, the *thing* within her, flat-out panicked. Like a captive animal scrabbling with its front paws in a futile effort to dig its way out of a cage, she could feel the entity struggling inside. Unconsciously, Neva thrashed and slapped at her arms, her legs, her chest, as she felt the creature fighting its way to the surface.

"Be calm!" Travis's commanding voice overrode the fearful thoughts scampering and clawing in her brain, and his comforting grip on her shoulder turned to iron as he gave her a teeth-rattling shake. "Nothing bad is going to happen to you. You're safe with me; I won't let you be hurt."

The terror—hers and that of the *thing* inside—eased away, and she took a full breath, finding her voice at last. "Nothing bad? I'm going to turn into what you are, and you say *nothing bad* is going to happen to me?"

Although he was driving, he turned his head to look at her, his blue eyes intent. "I wasn't talking to you, Neva. I was talking to your wolf. It'll make things worse if you frighten it."

If she frightened *it*? She had no idea how to respond to that notion. Nevertheless, the animal within her settled into stillness, and she could almost pretend it wasn't there. *Almost.* Except she could now view every detail of the countryside they were passing, each tree and house and fence line. If they slowed down, she knew she'd be able to see every leaf and blade of grass as well. Everything was vivid and distinct despite the time of night, and all silvered by the light of the full moon. Her hearing was keener, too, and she could hear insects, frogs, and night birds even over the sound of the truck's engine and the noise of the wheels on the road.

She'd run out of time. It was all Travis's fault, too. If only he hadn't interfered. If only he hadn't come back for her—

Neva sighed. She wasn't one for indulging in *if onlys*—if she did, the long, heavy list of *if onlys* in her life would weigh her down to her knees and she'd never get up again. No point in cringing in terror, either. The creature inside her had succeeded in weirding her out, but she wasn't going to let it pull a stunt like that again. And she was going to put up a helluva fight if the beast thought for one moment it was going to be in charge.

So. She was going to be a werewolf, and there wasn't a single damn thing she could do about it. Was there a bright side to this, any spark at all in the blackness ahead? *Maybe I could bite Travis…*

Travis had no idea what the woman seated next to him was thinking, only that she'd settled down and so had her wolf. It was unusual for Changelings to regard their alter egos as separate entities. He was one of the few who did. Maybe it was harder for him to reconcile the beast as part of himself because of what it had once done. For Neva, it was obviously tough to accept this new side of her because *she just plain didn't want it.* And what she was about to go through wouldn't make her any more fond of the wolf.

Telltale green fire was overwhelming the golden brown of her eyes as perspiration ran freely down her face. He had to hurry now and wished they'd left sooner. But she'd been so exhausted, so in need of rest in order to recover from the long ride, from her injuries, and to prepare for tonight. He let his foot get heavy, and the speedometer climbed—

And red and blue lights flashed in the rearview mirror. "Goddammit," he muttered and glanced at Neva. She was hunched over now, shuddering and gasping, and there was foam at the corner of her mouth. To human eyes, she'd look like an overdosed druggie—and an ambulance would be called, pronto. *Christ.* There was only one thing to do in a situation like this.

He floored it.

Travis had chosen the truck for some very deliberate reasons. One, the interior reeked like an ashtray, excruciating to Changeling noses. It was giving him a helluva headache, but it would help hide their scent from anyone—or any*thing*—that might be tracking Neva. Two, the truck had tires designed for off-road use and four-wheel drive. And three, there was a customized, big-ass engine under the hood that (hopefully) could outrun most things on the road. Even now the pickup was leaping forward like a cheetah on steroids.

Predictably, a wailing siren now accompanied the lights. Not so predictably, his pursuer was keeping pace with him. It wasn't gaining, thankfully—but not being shaken off either. If Travis slowed down enough to turn off onto a side road, the cop car might gain on him. If he turned at high speed, he'd roll the damn truck. If he stayed on the highway, sooner or later, another cop car—or even a chopper—would intercept him. And a long, low moan from Neva let him know that she could shift anytime now.

As Travis drove at speeds that would have done a moonshiner proud, he could swear that his inner wolf whined. Actually *whined*, as if in sympathy with the woman in the passenger seat. "Dammit, this is your fault," he said to his alter ego. "You wanted to save her, then you wanted to follow her, and then you *insisted* we had to go get her. Now look at the mess we're in. This is what happens when we get *involved*." A quick glance showed that Neva didn't appear to have heard him, and he told himself he didn't care if he did. She didn't want him around anyway, right?

Except he couldn't oblige her. He was involved *now*, dammit, and he'd see her through her Change no matter what. And somehow keep her from falling into human hands.

Suddenly, like a twig sprouting from a branch, a dirt road angled off sharply from the highway. Still, it took all his skill and a good deal of his Changeling strength on the wheel to keep the truck on at least two of its four wheels as he bore into the turnoff. In the rearview, the cop car fishtailed wildly from one side of the road to the other as it also swung into the turn. Still following them, but Travis was able to open up his lead. Suddenly, a huge black-and-white *something* appeared in his headlights, forcing him to veer off the road. He almost lost control then, plowing over stands of willow saplings that had overgrown the wet, shallow ditch, but somehow he managed to keep the truck level and get it back on the road.

Heart pounding, a glance over his shoulder showed Travis that the black-and-white thing he'd nearly hit was a frickin' cow—and a whole lot of its friends had joined it. The wandering herd was all over the road, standing squarely between him and the cop car, and even now, the flashing lights were diminishing in the rearview mirror.

Slowing to a mere breakneck pace, he thumped the steering wheel and laughed—until he got a look at Neva. *Oh, Christ.* Quickly he glanced around for another route, then turned off on an even rougher road, one that was probably little more than a goat path between miles of pastures. It took him as far as where the grazing land grew into forest, and he left the little road to plow the truck into the brush until he was satisfied that they couldn't be seen. Neva arched and flailed as he pulled her out of the truck. Her eyes were completely green now.

"Come on, honey, you need the earth's energy," he murmured as he carried her through the woods at a brisk jog. The brilliant moon dappled the entire forest with silver, and his natural night vision showed him every game trail through the thick underbrush. He followed one to a tangle of fallen trees that formed an arching shelter over tall grass that was bent and trampled—a large buck had probably bedded here during the day. He set Neva down on the thick cushion of grass, drew the heavy leather coat away, and then stripped the thin pajamas from her fevered skin. "You're going to kick my ass for this, right after you thank me."

He pulled his knife from his pocket and set to work on the casts.

SIX

Neva found herself in the midst of a nightmare—although she'd never felt such terrible pain in a dream before. She was trapped in her own body as it fought to become something else, something *other*. The bones in her face moved of their own volition, stretching, reshaping. Her back arched, and she screamed as her tailbone straightened and extended, as bone and muscle lengthened and shortened in her arms and legs. Her fingers released their agonized grip on the grass as they blunted and bound themselves into paws. Thousands of hot needles seemed to pierce her skin at once, and it crackled with static electricity as thick fur erupted everywhere. She felt all of these things and yet couldn't awaken, couldn't escape the nightmare. Couldn't escape the pain. She struggled against it, fought it, and the agony immediately spiraled upward beyond anything she thought possible, until she felt as if she were being torn in two from the inside out. Stark terror set in as her body stubbornly refused to pass out.

Don't fight it, you're making it worse.

In the midst of the hell she was in, Travis's voice was suddenly inside her head.

Stop fighting, Neva. Relax and go with it. It'll be over soon. Just hang on and go with it. You're safe, I promise you that.

Some of her panic subsided as she realized she wasn't alone, and she clung to his words like a lifeline. Still, it seemed like hours before the pain began to ebb. When it did, she wasn't certain where she was. It was as if the nightmare had eased into a dream, in which she stood in a forest clearing transformed by the moon's cold rays into a pool of silver light. Suddenly a large, dark wolf emerged from the foliage and pranced into the clearing with tail high. It was a beautiful creature—its legs and face were glossy black, but the rest of its thick, ebony pelt had dark-chocolate highlights in its luxurious depths. Still, Neva caught her breath as it turned and looked directly at *her*. For an instant she wanted to run away, but something in the wolf's body language calmed her. It bounded over to her, playful and friendly as a Labrador despite its much larger size.

Finished now.

Those words, triumphant and plain, were inside her head just as Travis's voice had been. Yet they were definitely not her own—were they? Neva frowned at the strange feel of them, their odd intonation, as if the words hadn't come from a human throat.

You and me. One.

Insight flashed—the wolf was speaking in her mind! She looked down into its joyfully grinning face, and she couldn't help smiling back. Then she noticed its unusual eyes.

"Omigod, those are—you are—*it's me!*" The word *one* echoed in her brain over and over as she flailed awake.

Neva found herself a wolf. And in the arms of the man who had helped her become one.

Travis's mouth quirked as Neva rolled upright and tried to stand, as wobbly legged as a fawn in her new body. She picked up a front foot and held it close to her eyes to examine it, splayed the clawed toes and wriggled them awkwardly. Then startled as her tail moved, and she turned to check it out as well. It eluded her at first, swinging away from her when she wanted to bring it closer, but eventually she got the hang of the muscles involved and succeeded in pinning her tail to the ground with a paw, long enough to nose at its long fur. She snuffled along the thick pelt that covered her ribs as well, fascinated by the strange tang of her new scent. Opened and closed her jaws a few times—and bit her tongue in the process, jumping backward in pain and surprise.

He laughed out loud then, and she chuffed out a breath in annoyance and bared her teeth at him. He didn't care. He needed to laugh at something out of sheer relief that she'd made it through the Change. She'd done well, too, in spite of having little or no preparation. In spite of her all-consuming fear.

"Guess we better take that body out for a test drive," he said. "Let's walk down to the lake."

As he rose to his feet, he was foolish enough to turn his back to her—and she seized his left butt cheek with very sharp teeth in very strong jaws.

The yell barely left his lips before instinct kicked in. In a heartbeat he shifted form, sending Neva flying into a thicket some twenty feet away in a shower of blue sparks.

A few scattered sparks fell around Travis as well and winked out as they came in contact with the ground. The static leftovers of a Change left a distinctive whiff of ozone in the air, as if lightning was about to strike. Travis trotted in the direction Neva had been thrown, his alter ego royally pissed at him. Hell, he couldn't blame the wolf for being upset—he was berating himself, too. Sure, a lot of years had passed, but how could he forget the hazards of being physically close to someone during the process? It was the first thing every shape-shifter child was taught. The build-up of energy could be downright dangerous, yet he hadn't hesitated to Change or spared a thought to warn her. Whatever pack she'd come from clearly hadn't bothered to tell her much of anything, either. He'd have something to say to them if he ever met up with them, especially her responsibility-shirking sire. For now, maybe he needed to find Neva a mentor or something…

He found her lying on her side, gasping for breath in a tangle of elderberry, its bluish leaves gleaming under the bright night sky.

I really hate you.

It was loud and clear in his brain. *Your first words. How sweet.*

Get out of my head. You're not invited.

This is how Changelings communicate as wolves. Get used to it. He picked his way through the bushes to get closer to her—although he was prepared to dodge if she decided to bite him again. *Are you okay?*

My head hurts. No thanks to you.

Yeah, well, my ass hurts. No thanks to you. Actually, it didn't hurt a bit—shifting forms healed all but the most serious wounds. But he made a mental note not to turn his back on her again. *Come on, let's head down to the lake now. You could probably use a drink.*

Only if you have something a lot stronger than water down there. Tell me how to Change back.

He stopped when he realized she wasn't following him. *What's the problem?*

I said I want to Change back. I want to be human. Tell me how.

Other than sapping most of her energy, there was no real reason she couldn't do it. Except Travis suspected she'd never Change again. Not voluntarily, and that was a problem. The wolf could be controlled but not denied, and if she suppressed it long enough, eventually it would burst through on its own—and not necessarily at a convenient time. With a mental picture of Neva suddenly shifting to wolf form in the middle of a shopping mall, he made up a bullshit story out of some partial truths. "You need to move around a bit first, flex and stretch those muscles after what they've just been through. If you don't, it could have a negative effect on your human body." She studied his face with skepticism, and he was suddenly glad for all the poker games he'd played over the decades. "Your body's got to have some time to recover, too, before you go shifting back to human. Not only did you just make your first Change, your injuries have healed up. That takes energy."

How long do I have to stay like this?

A few hours—three or four at the very least. Later, you won't need so much time.

The moonlight dappled the forest floor as Travis loped easily through the brush. He could hear Neva behind him, struggling as she tried to run on four feet. Everyone had trouble with that at first—mostly because everyone approached it like a bipedal human. *Relax and let your wolf take over.*

I'm not letting the damn wolf take over anything.

The determination in her words was underpinned by fear. Travis slowed and waited for her to catch up. He stepped off the trail, allowing her to go ahead.

She showed her teeth at him as she passed. *Don't you even think about sniffing my butt!*

Well, there goes all my *fun for the evening.* He allowed her a respectable lead, then fell in behind and studied her gait. It was smooth as running water for a few yards, using the effort-less ground-eating trot of natural wolves. It was obvious, how-ever, when Neva wrestled control away from her alter ego. One foot would get out of sync and the trot dissolved into more of a lurch. Like trying to drive standard after a lifetime of automatic vehicles, Travis decided. As long as she had time to think about it, she was never going to relax and enjoy being a Changeling. He launched himself forward and blasted past her, nipping her ear along the way. *Tag, you're it.*

I'm not playing, you jerk.

You're just saying that because you can't catch me. He stopped on the trail ahead, taunting her, wagging his tail and leaning over his front paws like a dog that wants to play. Neva might not want to join the game, but he was betting that her lupine side would love to.

I could if I wanted to—hey!

The dark wolf suddenly leaped ahead and charged straight for him. Travis barely had time to spin around and take off. To his surprise, Neva stopped fighting her animal persona and kept up with him. He dodged and feinted but couldn't shake her off. The pair of them raced through the forest and out to the grassy shoreline of the lake, where they splashed through the reeds and shallows. Away from the trees, the full moon was blindingly white in a clear sky, reflecting brightly in the calm waters, and every drop of water the wolves disturbed was a bead of purest silver. Time slowed down, and Travis gave himself over to running for the pure joy of it, jaws grinning, tongue lolling. Neva appeared to do so as well, giving up the chase in favor of loping easily beside him.

He'd forgotten what a simple pleasure it could be to have companionship. Without a pack for so many years, he'd denied himself any contact with his kind. It was better that way. Easier. Or so he told himself. Besides, there was always that little voice in his head telling him that he didn't deserve the comfort of a friend…or a mate.

Neva slowed, pausing to lap up water as she waded through the reeds. Travis's momentum sent him dashing ahead for several strides before he realized she'd dropped back. He came bouncing back, splashing her thoroughly, knowing that the guard hairs of her outer coat would repel most of the water. She gave him a look, but he ignored it.

She sniffed and sighed. *Glad that* you're *enjoying yourself.*

And you're not? He didn't believe that for a moment. A new wolf that was properly nurtured and protected through its first Change was an awful lot like a puppy at first. A brand-new world begged to be explored with senses far more acute than anything a human could imagine. *I'll bet you're afraid to enjoy it.*

I'm not afraid. I just don't want to get used to it. Tell me how to Change back now.

Why do you have to be such a control freak? Your wolf isn't out to run your life, you know.

Maybe, maybe not, but someone else is. And I'm not giving her any opportunity to take over. Now hurry up and tell me what to do.

Travis shook his big shaggy head. *So you're not afraid of your wolf, but you* are *afraid of your sire.*

Anyone with half a brain is afraid of her. Quit stalling and help me.

I am helping you. *If you think that your sire is any less able to command you when you're human, you're dead wrong.*

Neva stared at him with horror in her eyes, then suddenly struck out for deep water. Travis didn't even try to follow her. Instead, he turned and waded to shore, where he took his time carefully shaking out his fur. Finally he sat and watched Neva's frantic efforts, knowing full well what she was trying to do.

And knowing exactly how it would turn out.

Neva's mood was dismal when she finally clambered out of the water. It was further soured as she discovered Travis sleeping in a thick patch of clover. *Sleeping*, for heaven's sake. While she was out there, while she was…The truth abruptly dawned on her.

You knew, didn't you?

He yawned and stretched. *Yeah, I knew. I knew what you were trying to do, and I knew your wolf wouldn't allow you to harm yourself.*

It won't allow...hey, you said it wasn't out to run my life!

Under normal circumstances, it's not. But your wolf runs on instinct, and instinct programs every creature to fight to survive no matter what. And it won't make any difference if you're in human form when you try to off yourself—your wolf will not only take over, it will Change you no matter where you are and who you're with. Understand? If you're in the middle of Grand Central Station and your wolf thinks you're in danger, it will rise up and defend you. Even from yourself.

She sat abruptly. *You knew this would happen. You knew all along that if you could just make me turn—*

I'm a Changeling—of course I knew what would happen. But you make it sound like I planned it. I didn't make *you Change.*

Yes, you did. You kept me alive. I had everything under control until you *came along.*

Since when does jumping off a fucking cliff mean things are under control?

He was on his feet now, tawny fur bristling, broad head lowered and lips pulled back to expose his long, sharp teeth. It wasn't so long ago that Neva would have been terrified to be up close and personal with a seriously pissed-off wolf. Now it just irritated her.

Don't you dare growl at me, mister. I'm the one who has to spend the rest of my life in hiding, thanks to you. And right now, she had no idea where on earth, literally, she could hide. South America? China? How big was Meredith's network? It already seemed like her spies were everywhere.

Travis shook himself hard. *There are no wolves in South America. You'd stick out like a sore thumb there. Why don't you tell me about this sire of yours and maybe we can figure something out.*

Hey, what's in my head is private! Quit listening!

Quit broadcasting. It's one of the things you need to learn, especially since you're convinced that someone's looking for you.

Great, just great. The good news just kept rolling in. Neva flopped onto the ground, not even bothering to shake herself off, and watched the moonlit water drip like jewels from her coat to the clover leaves. She glanced at the big, tawny wolf, which was busy rolling on its back with its paws in the air. *What planet are you from?*

Why?

Because you might be a werewolf, but you sure don't know very much about them.

Travis rolled upright and curled his lip at her. *And you think you do?*

Look, I've seen somebody die during their first turning. And I think maybe he was the lucky one. Because everyone who succeeded became a stone-cold murderer. I can't do that. I won't do that. Not for Meredith, not for anybody. I'm not a killer.

The tawny wolf gave a derisive snort. *Everyone is, given the right circumstances. But once you learn control—*

Neva sighed deeply, then drew in air along the olfactory glands that lined her muzzle. The lakeshore was rich with scents—each plant had its own. She could scent that there was a bird sitting in a nest suspended in the taller reeds nearby. A small furry mammal—maybe a raccoon—was hunting along the shore where she and Travis had emerged from the forest and—

She could smell a Changeling. She couldn't fathom how she knew what it was, but her wolf had snapped to attention.

Travis was already on his feet. *Say nothing, think nothing*, he ordered. *We've got to get the hell out of here. Now.*

SEVEN

Neva followed close behind him as he arrowed up the bank and into the cover of the forest. *How are we going to get the truck?*

Travis dove into a narrow game trail. Thick brush arched overhead, barely allowing any moonlight to spill through to the dark forest floor. He ran full out, grateful that Neva was able to keep up, at least for now. *We'll find another truck.*

There was a pause. *You stole it, didn't you?*

No more talking. I'm not the only one hearing you.

He figured her question was better left unanswered anyway. How could she understand the kind of life he'd lived, the lengths he'd been forced to go to in order to stay off the grid? He had no bank account, no credit cards, no driver's license—at least, nothing in his own name. He dared leave no trail that would lead to him, paper or electronic. The only ID he'd ever had was a church baptismal certificate for Travis Williamson—from 1920. Tough to present *that* to the DMV.

In fact, it had become downright difficult to be a long-lived Changeling in a human world. If he was still with a pack, it would have been different. Most packs these days either cultivated contacts or had a couple of their own members who were computer savvy enough to create a lifetime's worth of human records for each of the pack's members. Illegal, of course, but only according to human laws. For his kind it was a matter of basic survival. Besides, most Changelings now hid in plain sight by living as humans. They had jobs and paid bills and went to school and mowed the grass and did all the everyday things that humans did.

A lone wolf, without access to pack resources, had a harder time of it. Survival depended a helluva lot on "borrowing"—cell phones, vehicles, credit cards, you name it. And in Travis's case, it also depended on staying clear of other Changelings. He wished he knew if the creature that was following them was after Neva.

Or after him.

It was dawn before Travis let them stop for more than a few minutes. They settled into a stand of brush near a highway. Neva's paws were raw and sore, and she was starving again, but she had to admit they'd covered a lot of ground.

Almost forty miles.

She made a derisive noise in her throat. *I'm not falling for that. I might be new, but I'm not gullible. No way did we run that far.*

Have it your way. I guess the highway sign is just plain wrong, then.

What sign? She stuck her head up and looked around. A green sign in the distance spelled out Idaho Falls—153 Miles in big white letters.

We drove about two-thirds of the distance before we lost the truck. We ran overland the rest of the way.

Yeah, but forty miles?

Look it up. Natural wolves can cover fifty miles or more in a day while they're just looking for food. Changelings can go farther and faster—and we had a lot more motivation.

Four-legged motivation, she thought, and automatically looked behind her. *Do you think he's gone?* She hadn't sensed the werewolf that was following them for hours.

I don't know. Did you recognize the scent at all?

No.

Then maybe we blundered into someone else's territory and they were just checking us out.

Someone else's territory. Neva hadn't given much thought to the existence of other werewolves, other packs. But here was Travis, and somewhere in the miles behind them was another creature like themselves. A *Changeling*. She'd never heard that word outside of storybooks, where it usually referred to the creature left behind when a fairy stole a human child.

One word can have many meanings. Travis rolled in the dewy grass, jaws grinning, tongue lolling. Changeling *is the closest human word to our name for ourselves, our people. Our kind.*

Your kind, not mine. Neva looked away from him. *I didn't sign on for this.*

That might be, but you're one of us now.

I'm not! I'm nothing like you! She jumped to her feet, baring her teeth at him and growling low in her throat. *I'm not a mindless slave, and I'm not a murderer.*

Travis rolled over and regarded her coolly. *Do I seem like a mindless slave to you? Do you see anyone pulling my strings?*

She didn't know how to respond to that. Sure, Travis seemed independent, a rebel, a real lone wolf—and she nearly groaned at the pun—but what if it was just a very good act? Maybe he was really a hit man or some kind of enforcer, someone the packs hired to handle troublemakers. Like herself.

A hit man? Really? Travis rolled his eyes.

Actually, more like a goon or a thug, she thought at him deliberately. Of course, if he was really out to kill her, why save her from herself? Why not just let things run their course? She thought briefly of the battered Toyota in the alley. If she'd found it just a little bit faster, she wouldn't be here.

You didn't really want to die.

So what? She furrowed her wolfen brow, hoping that created a frown. Travis certainly seemed to frown as much in lupine form as he did as a human, so she knew it was possible. *Sometimes what you want and what you have to do are two different things.*

For the briefest of seconds, surprise flashed in his eyes. It was shut down almost immediately, however, and his frown deepened into a glower.

Why are you by yourself? she asked suddenly.

What the hell kind of question is that?

You seem to know all about packs and sires and the whole werewolf-slash-Changeling routine, yet here you are all by yourself. Where's your pack?

Maybe I like being by myself.

She snorted. *If that was true, you wouldn't be grouchy all the time.*

I am not grouchy. He was silent for a long time after that, resting his chin on his paws with his eyes closed. Neva didn't believe for a moment that Travis was really sleeping—more likely, he was ignoring her—but there was no denying that the need for rest was a heavy weight pressing down on *her.* She gave in and stretched out under a low-hanging sumac shrub. How odd to be so comfortable lying on the ground, she thought. Didn't werewolves get cold?

One of the perks of being a Changeling—you can camp anywhere. Travis's voice in her head sounded far away.

Werewolf. And get out of my head.

Changeling. You're the one who's thinking too damn loud.

See? Grouchy. If there was a reply to that, she didn't hear it before sleep claimed her.

(((● ●

The full moon's light turned the fifty-foot circle of smooth white stones to glowing silver orbs. The flattened grass within the circle gleamed, too, liberally coated with white ash and pale corpse powder. Nine naked humans, the latest inductees, had been thickly painted with a mixture of the noxious stuff as well. They stood huddled together in the very center, not knowing what was about to happen to them but not willing to make a break for the thick, dark forest beyond the bright ring, either. Not with the cold light reflected in the eyes of several dozen wolves.

Her wolves, Meredith thought with satisfaction. She owned them, all of them, and after tonight, she'd own the ones in the circle as well. Of course she'd enjoy having more servants to order around, but that was simply a nice perk. The real prize was power, and while all living creatures produced energy, werewolves produced it in spades. With the level of magic she now commanded, she could draw raw power from all of them. And they wouldn't even know what was happening.

Meredith's pack stood as silent sentinels as the moon reached its highest point and the magic infused in the ashen mixture was activated. Miniature whips of red lightning crackled along the pale ground within the circle, licking at the feet of the captives. Most, however, weren't paying attention. Instead, some clutched at their heads or their stomachs, some fell to their knees and retched, one slapped at himself as if bees were attacking him.

It wasn't long before all were writhing on the ground.

One after the other, most of the humans in the circle began to scream. As their bones reshaped themselves, as their skin stretched, as their muscles tore and reformed. Meredith didn't need to use her preternatural senses to hear the wrenching and popping of joints over the hoarsening cries of her victims, all signs of the shift progressing nicely. She still wished they'd hurry the hell up—she was anxious to get to the next part, *her* part.

At least a ninth conscript had been found in time for tonight's turning. The guy didn't have much between his ears, but any port in a storm. The circle now contained six men and three women. Numbers were as powerful as words, and Meredith had been concerned that she'd have to make do with an inconvenient *eight* instead of a potent *nine*. She put aside the fact that there could have been *several* more if she hadn't been so distraught over Geneva's escape and killed them. Three times three would work well enough, however. No volunteers, of course, but that was immaterial. By this time tomorrow, they'd believe they'd signed on of their own volition.

They'd believe anything she told them.

Meredith rubbed her finger over a tiny snag on one of her freshly done nails, and hoped the nail would hold out for a little while longer. Not that she minded the cost of the exquisite black-diamond polish, but the manicurist was presently on her hands and knees in the middle of the circle. What if the woman hadn't recovered sufficiently to redo her work tomorrow? Meredith could attempt a binding spell on the nail, of course, but magic was so very difficult to finesse on teeny-tiny things—it didn't have the laser-like precision to work only on her nail without affecting the finger.

Finally the dark blush of fur covered the contorted shapes, and a few moments later seven new wolves stood on shaky legs. Two lay motionless, however, and Meredith cursed viciously as she crossed the ring of stones and strode over to her new wolves. She toed one of the unmoving heaps of fur and spat on it, furious that she'd have to find someone else to do her nails. The other body she ignored entirely in favor of looking over the new crop. Five gray wolves, one black, one rusty cream. All cowered before her but one, one of the grays, Riley something or other. He'd been nearly as much trouble as Geneva from the very beginning. A big wolf, his ears flattened against his broad skull and he snarled as he glared hatefully at his maker.

He actually had the temerity to challenge her? Meredith couldn't be more delighted. Her exquisitely shaped lips parted in a model-perfect smile—

Just before they curled back to reveal the fangs of a monstrous silver wolf.

(((● ●

His eyes were closed, yet Travis was far from asleep. Neva hadn't noticed his ears, erect and angled to catch the faintest of sounds, his nostrils flared wide and facing the slight breeze in order to detect any scent of their pursuer. It appeared the stranger had given up hours ago, but Travis was vigilant just the same. Neva, on the other hand, had zonked out mere seconds after sprawling beneath a sumac bush. She deserved the rest, too—although she'd kept up with him, he knew it had been hard on her. He'd set a fast pace and headed directly downwind, keeping their scent away from the unknown Changeling they'd detected in the distance. There was nothing Travis could do about the truck, however. The stranger would have had ample time to study it with his nose and learn plenty about them. Any shape-shifter worth his salt would discern that a female was making her first Change, and Travis's inner wolf snarled at the thought of anyone knowing anything about Neva. It pissed off his human side, too (and for reasons he didn't want to examine too closely). Could her pack have found her already?

Or was Travis himself the target? *Just because you're paranoid doesn't mean they're not after you.* Eventually he dismissed the idea that it could have been someone from his old pack. Not only had it been decades since he'd seen any of them, Travis didn't recognize the scent at all. And he seriously doubted that any-one who didn't know him personally would be following him. No, either the Changeling was after Neva, or it was a random stranger just checking them out.

Travis was personally rooting for the random-stranger the-ory, because the wolf would have memorized *both* their scents and tracked them like a bloodhound. Sure, Travis and Neva had played and run through the lake shallows for a considerable dis-tance before returning to dry land. The stranger would have had to circle the lake, casting back and forth to find the place they'd left the water. But he would find it. And follow. Their trail would be as plain as a four-lane highway to Changeling senses.

Yet the wolf had apparently given up the chase. If the Changeling had truly been after either one of them, he would even now be breathing down their necks—or attempting to tear out their throats. Except that no sane wolf would tackle a shape-shifter of Travis's size and experience alone.

Which means there's a chance he's fallen back to wait for reinforcements.

Travis opened his eyes and heaved himself to his feet. He hated to do it, but he nosed Neva awake anyway. *Come on. We have to get moving.*

EIGHT

Neva wanted more sleep—about a week's worth—but if there was any chance they were still being followed, it was a luxury she couldn't afford. Meredith's wolves were certain to be hunting for her. *Or for my body.* For the first time, she realized that their crazed leader probably didn't expect her to survive a first Change by herself. A new question surfaced almost immediately: If she died, would Meredith have cared at all? Would she have been the teeniest, tiniest bit sorry? Neva shoved that question away, tried to deep-six that whole line of thinking, and only succeeded in diverting it somewhat.

There was no guarantee Neva would have survived even if she'd stayed. No one in the pack received any coaching or comfort during their initial shift. Pain and shock combined to overcome some of the newbies, more so if they fought it. Resistance was, indeed, futile. There was only death or enslavement to Meredith's warped magic.

Neva had managed to create a third option: escape. She was still amazed she'd pulled it off, but she hadn't had any faith in her ability to elude Meredith for long. Her whole plan had been to die before she could be forced into standard pack initiation: the slaughter of a human being. Every member had to prove their absolute obedience and loyalty to Meredith through murder. At least that's what she said—Neva suspected that Meredith somehow used the deaths to power some of her horrible spells.

And every pack member would hasten to comply. Neva knew she would have, too, had she stayed. Not because she wanted to, not because she feared whatever punishment would be meted out if she didn't (although that was certain to be ugly and painful). No, it was because the magic Meredith commanded usurped the will of every member of her pack. Once they made that first Change, they were hers.

If that's true, why am I not running back to her?

Why indeed? Travis's words popped into her head. He was about twenty yards ahead of her as they raced along a small river valley where the foliage was dense. She thought she detected a note of amusement in his "voice"—he probably got a kick out of annoying her.

Have you been listening all along? she demanded.

Have you made any effort to keep your thoughts to yourself?

She ignored that. *Look, when can I Change back to human? I've had enough of running around on four feet. Tell me how.*

When we get to a town.

We've bypassed three towns, a truck stop, and a fruit stand already. You're not my boss. It should be my decision when I Change, and I want to Change now. For all I know, you could be trying to keep me like this so you have somebody to hang out with.

Despite their ground-eating gallop, Travis stopped so suddenly that she had to swerve to avoid crashing into him. She tripped over her own feet and tumbled down a brushy slope, where she lay with the wind half knocked out of her. Stiff-legged, he stalked after her, and from her prone vantage point, she appreciated anew that not only was he a helluva lot bigger than she was as a human, he was also damn huge as a wolf. His tawny-gold ruff stood out, and the ridge of fur along his spine rose as well. His muzzle was wrinkling with suppressed fury, although he was keeping his sharp teeth covered for the moment.

It was *his* fault that she fell, and *he* was pissed? It was all she could do not to growl at him. *How sweet of you to come and see if I'm all right.*

He ignored the remark. *Number one, I don't need anyone to hang with. Number two, if I did, I wouldn't choose a green wolf because it's a helluva lot harder to keep a low profile. And number three, this* I-don't-trust-you *shit is getting old.*

You think I should trust you? You're a werewolf!

It's not a character defect.

For a split second, the anger in his gaze gave way to something else. Sadness? Pain? Before Neva could decide which, however, Travis's usual glare returned full force.

You wanna walk on two legs? Fine. Let's do it.

Now they were getting somewhere. Neva stood up and followed Travis's terse instructions: *Picture yourself as a human. Close your eyes so you can concentrate—you have to hold the image until you feel your human body. Call it to you. Not like that. Okay, that's better. Now let go.*

There was a strange sensation over every square inch of her, as if she'd suddenly drawn in all the essence, the energy, even the air from all around her. Soaked it in like a dry sponge pulls in water. And her hearing, her sense of smell—all of her senses, in fact— were abruptly dulled as if she really *was* underwater. She opened her eyes in a panic, but realized she was in her human skin—and her senses were naturally blunted as a result. Neva heaved a sigh of relief and turned to say something to the tawny wolf, who was sitting and staring at her with his head cocked to one side. He didn't look angry anymore. In fact, his lips were drawn back in a wide lupine grin. Obviously he was pleased that she'd managed to—

Omigod, I'm NAKED! Neva tried to cover herself with her hands and finally dove behind a tree. "Where the hell are my clothes, you bastard!"

Probably back by the truck. That's okay, you look fine without them. Better, in fact.

She looked around the tree trunk and bared her teeth at him. "What didn't you tell me? What did you leave out? You're fully dressed when you shift back into human form. I've seen it. So why aren't my clothes here?"

Probably because you're new at it. Most Changelings have to learn to bring their clothes along during the transition. It takes practice, that's all.

Great. So how do I get my clothes back? Where the hell do they go while I'm a wolf?

You can't now, and nobody knows. Travis turned and trotted back up the slope.

Whaddya mean, nobody knows?

Exactly what I said. Changelings have been trying to solve that one for eons. Current thought says they go to a different dimension or something. Whatever. The big tawny wolf did a passable imitation of a shrug. *We've hung around here long enough. It's time to get going.*

Neva realized with a start that she had no idea where *here* was. She made her way awkwardly up the bank, slowed down by the uneven stones. *Wait, I can't travel like this. I don't even have shoes!*

You wanted to be human now, *remember? And you seem to suspect me of goddess knows what every time you don't get your way. So deal with it. If you don't like being human, Change back.*

She cursed him out soundly as she stumbled along. The easy, ground-eating pace of her wolf had now given way to painful, awkward plodding. The game trail they were following had seemed like a smooth, green tunnel before, a perfect little highway through the brush. Now she stood a lot taller on two feet than on four, so what had once been an overgrown ceiling of shady foliage was now a hellish wall of scratchy branches and itchy leaves. And *bugs*, dammit. She couldn't even see through the bushes to know where she was stepping. The ground felt rough under her feet now, the soil hard-packed and crisscrossed with tree roots. *I don't know how to shift back, you jerk!*

Then figure it out.

And just like that he was out of sight.

((((●

Meredith licked the blood from her lips, then resumed her human form in a shower of blue sparks. She spared a glance at the folds of her Grecian-inspired gown and was satisfied that it remained pristine. The feather-white fabric glowed flawlessly in the moonlight.

It would have been more fun to kill the upstart wolf, but she was already short on initiates. As it was, Riley would be a long time healing and was useless in the meantime—except for the example she'd just made of him. "Take him back and throw him in the pit," she ordered and turned her back to look at the other new wolves. She didn't need to watch to know that she'd be obeyed instantly.

The gray mixture beneath her feet crackled with energy. Tiny veins of red lightning shot through the ash, charged further by the spilling of living blood within the circle. She felt tingly all over, but not half as good as she would a few moments from now. Meredith drew the pendant from between her breasts and held it aloft. Immediately the black opal flashed in the moonlight and began to pulse with crimson fire like the beating heart of a dragon. The energy in the circle built, and the six new wolves stood motionless, their gaze fixated on the opal in her hand and their eyes reflecting its light. Meredith laughed as she felt their living energy join with the magic, her magic, in the circle.

The collective power grew, swirling around her, faster now. It surrounded her, ascended her legs like a living thing, caressing, scintillating, arousing as it rose higher. And higher still. Her breath came in short, sharp pants, and her nipples thrust at the fabric that imprisoned them until they were sensitized beyond bearing. Finally she yanked the dress away from her with her free hand, tore and clawed at the fabric until she stood naked in the moon's light. Her long blonde hair fell loose around her hips, wild tresses glowing nearly white. One hand still held the opal high above her head; the other cupped her mons as she began to thrust her hips in time to the gem's fiery pulse. She chanted out the words, the dark, power-rich words, as the wild energy built to a crescendo and erupted through every molecule of her body in a tumultuous rush of sexual and magical release, turning her last word into a scream of raw triumph and pleasure.

((((● ●

It felt like she'd been walking for hours, and Neva was no less furious with Travis. The big werewolf had interfered in her original plans with his self-appointed mission to save her, forcing her through a Change she hadn't wanted, and now leaving her in the middle of nowhere, naked.

Angry as she was, however, her sense of fairness nagged at her. He'd saved her life, coached her safely through a process that might have killed her, and had taught her how to return to her human self. The problem was, she'd demanded the latter knowledge *right now.*

Swell timing. She really should have thought that one through.

And he hadn't exactly left her on her own, either. Although Travis was out of sight, her newly heightened senses told her he was little more than a couple hundred yards ahead on the narrow game trail. Obviously he'd slowed his pace to match hers—and hers was worse than pathetic.

Fighting for every step, she was making poor headway through the brush in her human form, and her bare skin was scratched and insect-bitten everywhere. Her feet had finally gone somewhat numb, but they began throbbing the moment she stood still. She had to admit that her lupine form had been a swift and efficient method of traveling, yet she certainly wasn't about to resume it again—even if she could figure out how. Come to think of it, she wasn't sure why she was still following Travis. Or why he was bothering to stay with her—after all, she didn't need his help anymore. And he'd made it plain that he didn't need anyone, especially not someone like *her*.

She considered her options.

The stony hillsides on either side of the wide valley seemed inhospitable to all but a mountain goat. The banks of the trickling creek they were following were the only places where trees and thick brush grew lushly. The rest of the land was a sea of tall, dry grass and sage, occasionally crisscrossed by ancient wire fencing. *And wherever there's fencing, there're people. Somewhere.* Neva stopped and looked back over the path she'd already traveled. Off to the west at the base of the hill was what seemed to be an abandoned barn. She hadn't paid attention before she passed it, but she could remedy that now. Maybe she could find something in the old building she could use.

Neva began to trudge back along the path she'd already traveled, then left the cover of the trees and struck out across the field.

NINE

What the hell? Travis had been stewing in his own thoughts when his wolf stopped dead in its tracks and refused to move an inch. Immediately his senses discerned that Neva was much farther behind him than she had been. He chuffed out an impatient breath—how much slower did he have to go just so she could indulge her bullheaded determination to walk on two legs instead of four? He'd been so damn certain that she'd soon be begging him to tell her how to return to her lupine form. *Ha.* He should have known better. He couldn't be that lucky. Instead, he'd spent the last few hours trying not to think about the naked woman on the trail behind him.

The *gorgeous* naked woman. He'd gotten a look at her when he was taking off her casts and clothes, but he hadn't had time for admiration with her Change imminent and her eyes glowing green. His concern for her had somehow overridden the impulse. But now—dear goddess, when she'd returned to her human form, it was like he'd been slapped in the head with a two-by-four. He didn't see stars, but he did see that her nipples were the exact color of caramel and appeared just as luscious. Her skin was unusually fair, a delightful contrast to the rich brown hair that tumbled in waves to her shoulders—and the freckles on her shoulders matched the ones that dusted her nose and cheekbones. It was all he could do not to resume his human form as well. His paws twitched as he yearned to glide his hands over her curves, memorize her enticing shape by touch. Worse, his human self definitely had a hard-on. That didn't translate well to the wolfen body he was currently in, and it wasn't long before the acute discomfort had forced him to leave the scene.

He'd been keeping his distance from Neva ever since. Physically, at least. Mentally, it was a near-impossible feat, which made his current mood irritated with a chance of insanity. Although his wolf clearly wanted to go back for Neva, Travis was in no hurry to be knocked off-kilter again by her powerful appeal. He plunked his butt on the trail and waited for her to catch the hell up.

And waited.

Finally his senses—and maybe his *sense*, period—kicked in: the woman had not stopped to rest or slowed her snail's pace. She was heading in another direction entirely. *Oh, for Christ's sake.*

With difficulty, Travis retained control of his wolfen self and kept it from dashing after her. If she wanted to go somewhere else, then maybe she *should* go. After all, it was probably past time they went their separate ways. He'd gone above and beyond by saving her life, springing her from the hospital, and helping her through her first shift. What else was he supposed to do for her? It was obvious that she wasn't very interested in being a Changeling like him anyway.

Bad sire, said his wolf. *Frightened.*

I didn't ask you. He wasn't about to start conversing with his alter ego, but his animal persona had a point. What little Travis knew of Neva's history wouldn't make him excited to be a Changeling, either. He'd hoped she'd have a little fun when her wolf first emerged, enjoy the freedom and the sheer joy of existence that came with it. Instead, she'd actually tried to drown herself.

Bad sire.

Travis's lupine brows furrowed. Despite her actions, he knew full well that Neva never had a true death wish—it was all an effort to keep her sire from using her. She was convinced that this Meredith woman would force her to kill. And admittedly, a sire had the power to compel a new Changeling, at least at first. But what Changeling would demand murder? True, her sire didn't seem to take her responsibilities very seriously, but *kill a human on purpose*?

No, it was plain that Neva hadn't been taught the first thing about Changeling law. She was mistaken, had to be. She didn't even know that her sire's influence would eventually wear off. So who would tell her the truth about her new life if Travis didn't?

Shit. With a very human sigh, he leaned his forehead against a tree, and considered banging it there a few times. Although he'd like nothing better than to ride off into the sunset—and maybe find another Triumph Thunderbird to do it with—it looked like he was going to be babysitting a while longer. The decision prompted a burst of excitement from his wolf, and his tail wagged involuntarily.

At least one of us is frickin' happy about it.

((((● ●

Baker couldn't believe his luck. She hadn't looked. *The cold bitch hadn't even looked.*

Meredith had been so annoyed at the demise of her manicurist—Tina, he reminded himself. *The poor woman's name had been Tina*—that she hadn't bothered to examine the second body. His. Baker lay as still as death, and Meredith had been further distracted by Riley. Damn him for standing up to her, for not playing along to preserve his own life. Sometimes you had to pick your battles, fight another day and all that shit. But not

Riley. After Meredith chewed his ass, literally, the guy had been more dead than alive, and the devil only knew where he'd been dragged off to.

Baker had maintained his corpse act even when the bitch queen had performed her perverse ritual. It had been damn hard. Just as he'd expected, she drew power from her initiates as surely as a fucking spider sucked the life from its prey. He'd felt the fingers of bloodred light crackle and hiss through the ash in the circle, felt the light crawl over him, invade him. It had pulled his energy from him as if it were a plant torn from the soil, its long, living roots extracted from every corner and crevice of his being. It was terrifying and painful, and it took everything he had to calm the animal he'd become, to explain to it that *real* death awaited if it so much as twitched. Afterward Baker didn't have to feign death. He was a hollowed-out husk, passing in and out of consciousness.

During his last snatch of awareness, Meredith had become a great silver wolf again and led her mindless pack into the night. He had no idea where the zombified creatures were going, only that it was certain to end in innocent blood being spilled.

There was nothing he could do about it. His job was to make sure his own blood stayed right where it fucking belonged, and to do that, he had to get the hell out of here. Baker opened his eyes and blinked a few times before trying to sit up, which took a few tries. Discovery number one was that a wolfen body didn't operate the same way—jeez, it didn't even *bend* the same way—as a human body did. His head pounded horribly, and the world spun for a long, sickening moment before righting itself. He tried to get the ghastly taste of the thick white ash from his mouth, but that didn't work. Discovery number two was that wolves couldn't spit.

Dammit, he thought. *There'd better be fucking something a wolf* can *do, like get my hairy ass out of here.* He staggered over to where Tina's body lay rigid. The dead wolf's eyes were wide and staring, her head pulled back and the jaws frozen open as if she was howling. Saddened, Baker sighed and moved on, crossing the blackened border of the circle. On the other side, he shook the foul ash from his coat as best as he could and headed into the darkness on uncertain feet.

((((● ●

The dirt floor was black with decades of old motor oil and sawdust, but it felt cool to her abused feet as Neva crossed the threshold. Soft shadow enveloped her body, soothed her sun-reddened skin, and wrung a sigh of relief from her.

Otherwise, the barn looked nothing like the oasis she'd imagined it would be.

No livestock had ever been tucked in here at night. There were no stalls, no harnesses, no grain bins. More importantly, no horse blankets, no feed sacks—nothing she could use to cover herself with, and that was what she'd been hoping for most.

An ancient orange tractor with a flat tire slumped in a corner, next to a long row of rusted implements. Benches and shelves lined another wall, piled with tools and strange metal parts, ancient coffee cans, and endless jars filled with nails, screws, washers, etc. Thick cobwebs draped everything, and Neva jumped as one brushed her arm. Immediately her entire body broke out in goose bumps, and she swore vehemently. She'd seen people *die*, for heaven's sake, and here she was still afraid of stupid spiders.

The ladder to the loft seemed solid, and she risked climbing up for a look. No sweet smell of hay greeted her, only the mustiness of decay and countless generations of mice. She could see a tangled mess of old furniture and car parts, even a collection of birdcages, and daylight shone through several sizeable holes in the sagging roof. Disappointed, she returned to the ground floor and sat on a rickety piano stool by the workbench.

Now what? Why couldn't the guy who owned this old building have left a spare pair of coveralls hanging around instead of the badly stained denture uppers she'd spied amid the tools on the bench? *Yuck.* Plainly, she'd have been better off following the game trail by the creek. She was hungry, exhausted, sunburned, and thirsty, and her feet were bruised, cut, and bleeding. She had no idea where she was or where Travis had been taking her. And oh, by the way, she was still naked. *Damn that big werewolf.* She'd already reconciled herself that none of it was his fault, but right now she needed something, someone, to blame.

Why don't you blame your sire?

Neva threw a hand across her breasts and crossed her legs as the enormous tawny wolf filled the doorway. "What do you want?"

I came to see if you're okay. And I want to know why you aren't ragging on your sire instead of me.

"It's complicated."

And I'm handy, right?

"Maybe," she admitted. She could feel color flush her cheekbones.

The big wolf chuffed and wheeled to leave. *Whatever. Let's get going.*

"No."

Why the hell not?

"Look, I'm tired, I'm thirsty, and I'm hungry. So I'm staying here to rest."

There's no water, food, or anything else here. Travis came back, stuck his big-maned head through the doorway, and looked around. *It's nothing but a damn garage. So unless you're a frickin' car, you're not going to find what you need here. Now come on.*

Of course, he was right. Hadn't she just come to the same conclusion herself? But the thought of trudging barefoot back across that field on the harsh stems of the stiff, dead grass just made her want to lie down and bawl. Damned if she was going to do *that* in front of Travis. She wasn't the teary sort even when she was alone. With a deep breath, Neva stood up—and stumbled as soon as she tried to walk. Pain shot through her bleeding and battered feet and surprised a yelp from her. She stifled it almost immediately, but the great tawny wolf was by her side in a heartbeat.

Sit down. Travis's voice was loud in her head. *Let me see your feet.*

She didn't sit, but leaned wearily on the workbench and held up a foot behind her. The wolf sniffed it, then did something totally unexpected. He licked it.

"Ew! What are you doing?" she said, yanking her foot away. "I don't want dog germs!"

He snorted. *FYI, Changelings don't have as many germs as humans. In fact, our saliva has healing properties. So why don't you just sit the hell down and let me look after this?*

Neva hesitated, then finally shrugged. At least she'd get to rest a little longer. She returned to the piano stool and rested her feet on a milk crate, one hand in her lap hiding her mons and the other arm folded across her breasts. Mentally she braced herself for smart-ass commentary on her nakedness, or perhaps criticism of her decision to return to human form, but there were no words in her head but her own. The great wolf seemed completely focused on her feet. She was certain it would tickle unbearably or hurt like crazy. Instead, its tongue was like a warm, wet washcloth and soothed wherever it touched.

Its tongue? Strange—maybe it was her imagination or maybe it was part of her newfound Changeling abilities, but Neva sensed that Travis's inner wolf was fully in charge of this procedure. Did he trust the creature that much? Was she safe with it? Usually Travis was front and center while in his lupine form, but at the moment he was definitely submerged within the animal persona. No sooner had she finished the thought than the *animal persona* looked up at her and slowly winked one vivid blue eye, as if they were sharing a secret. She relaxed and winked back, although she couldn't help wondering exactly *where* Travis was. Asleep? Aware? Could he hear and see what was going on? Just in case, she repositioned her hands to make sure she was covered.

TEN

Travis lay in the tall grass, alert and watchful. With his golden tawny pelt, he was as perfectly camouflaged as a lion on the savannah. Behind him, the barn cast a long, dark shadow as the sun dipped toward the horizon. And his Changeling hearing could easily pick up the soft sounds from inside the building: Neva's breathing, slow and even.

She'd fallen asleep with her head resting on her arm on the workbench while he (or rather, his alter ego) had bathed her injured feet. Travis had buried himself as deep as he could within the animal, hoping to be less aware of how appealing she was. Hoping to dampen the effects on him. But when her hands had relaxed and slipped from what she sought to hide…Well, better to just get his butt out of there.

Damn stubborn, obstinate, bullheaded woman. He should never have listened to her, should never have given in to her demands. He should have known she wouldn't voluntarily shift back to wolf once she was human again. And he wasn't her sire, so he probably couldn't force her to Change either. He sighed heavily and rested his chin on his paws. Her poor feet had been a frickin' mess, and he was forced to admire the grit and determination that drove Neva to keep walking on them—although goddess only knew how she'd managed it. It was a helluva lot easier to travel cross-country as a wolf than a naked human, yet she'd persisted in her chosen course. She'd neither complained nor asked for help. He snorted—hadn't she decided it was *his* fault and that he was a jerk? Travis told himself he didn't give a damn what she thought, although somewhere deep inside it bothered him. A lot.

All he could do now was hope that if Neva got some rest and regained some of her strength, she might be willing to listen to reason. *And I might learn to frickin' fly.*

He sighed heavily, and in the very next breath detected a faint, nearly imperceptible trace of new scents in the breeze. Travis was on his feet in a heartbeat, peering over the top of the tall, dry grass and angling his ears toward the trees and brush of the distant creek. Changelings were on the game trail that he and Neva had left. Through a break in the foliage, he counted five wolves, moving fast. *Shit.* They would follow until the scent of their quarry ended abruptly…and then it was only a matter of time before they figured out that he and Neva had doubled back. He'd left the path exactly at the point that Neva had, by a fallen-down fence that practically pointed the way to the barn. *We might as well have put up a goddamn neon sign.*

Cursing himself, cursing Neva, and cursing whoever the hell was following them, he charged into the barn.

Trying to shift to her wolfen form was like trying to coax a flame from a temperamental lighter. It was even harder while trying to scale a rocky hillside naked. Neva tried to keep close to the scrubby bushes, even though her unprotected skin bore fresh scratches and scrapes in several places. Above her, the big golden wolf led the way, choosing the path that would be easiest for her.

They'd run out the back of the barn, wedged a heavy wooden pallet against the door behind them, and headed straight up the hill, keeping the tall barn between them and their pursuers' line of sight. Neva hoped that their enemies wouldn't pick up their trail too quickly but—

Travis's voice in her head was urgent. *For Christ's sake, Neva! You have to Change now! Call your wolf!*

"I can't," she panted. "I can't find it."

Neva climbed up on a small shelf of rock and knelt behind an ancient, stunted pine that was more bush than tree. Its needles jabbed at her mercilessly, but she was past caring about present pain. She peered through the green branches and saw exactly what she didn't want to see. Five wolves loping over the field, heading for the barn. Natural wolves would yip hunting calls to encourage each other and to frighten their prey into running blindly. The five Changelings, however, were silent as death itself.

Except it wasn't death she was afraid of. No, instead of killing her, they'd drag her back to their leader, and she knew what that meant. Meredith would delight in making Neva do unspeakable things just to demonstrate her insane power—

Neva jumped as a great furry body suddenly squeezed in beside her. The great tawny wolf peered through the branches and snarled silently at their hunters. *Neva, we've only got minutes at most before they find us. Get with the program!*

"I'm sorry I pulled you into this," she whispered, more calmly than she felt. "It's me they want, and they won't kill me." *Unfortunately.* "There's nothing else you can do here, Travis. You can still get away if I'm not slowing you down."

Fuck that. And fuck you, too, for even suggesting it. The wolf turned its head, and its blue eyes, Travis's eyes, flamed with fury. *If you can't make yourself shift, then we have to try something different. I'm not your sire, but maybe my wolf can talk to yours.*

She sensed, rather than saw, Travis fading deep into the animal, and she was left alone facing his great golden wolf. To her shock the formerly gentle and protective creature bared its long fangs at her.

"What the hell is your problem?" She planted her back against the stunted tree, heedless of the abrasions to her unprotected skin. Bark and pine needles just didn't compare to monster wolf teeth. "You were licking my feet a little while ago!"

Danger now. Be wolf.

"I can't, I don't know how."

Danger. Be wolf now. The *now* was punctuated by a sudden, sharp nip to her arm.

"Quit that!" The skin wasn't broken, although she could feel the scrape of teeth, but it still hurt like hell.

The wolf ignored her, and she held up her hands to fend off the big animal. Again and again, the tawny muzzle dove past her puny defenses to deliver another hard nip. "Dammit, I said quit!" she shouted, and punched the wolf full in the nose. Its answer was a bite to her fist that drew blood—

That's when she felt the stirring inside, the all-too-familiar lupine presence, the *other*. The big tawny wolf sat back, apparently satisfied that it had succeeded in rousing its counterpart in her. Her wolf. Fear rose in her throat, threatening to choke her, but Neva wasn't going to succumb to it this time. Without even looking, she could sense her enemies getting closer. Her choices had narrowed to exactly one, and she was going to take it. She'd become a goddamn *giraffe* if it meant escaping Meredith. "Okay," she murmured, closing her eyes and reaching deep. *Here wolfy, wolfy. I know you're in here somewhere. Come and play.*

There was a lightning-quick flash of recognition as she suddenly made contact with the animal that lived within her. An eruption of light and energy shot through every nerve fiber, every cell, followed by a curious inside-out sensation, as if soul and body had just switched places—

And just like that, she was wolf. Wolf was her. Scattered blue sparks fell to the ground, making tiny hissing noises as the remains of the enormous static charge winked out amid the dry grass. Neva staggered a little and nearly tripped over her own paws, then realized she wasn't going to get anywhere as a human trying to manage the finer points of four-legged locomotion. She addressed her lupine self: *All right, here's the deal—as long as you don't do anything weird, you can be in charge for a while. So how about getting us out of here?*

Without hesitation, the slim, dark wolf sprang forward on sure feet and raced swiftly up the rocky slope as if it was level ground. Neva's initial surprise was followed by relief, and then she allowed herself to feel honest-to-god *exhilaration*. There was simply no comparison between the effortless strength and agility she now had at her disposal, and the miserable struggle it had been to cover the same terrain as a human. Well, to be fair, she'd been a *naked* human. She might have done better with hiking shoes and—oh, what the hell, this was downright *glorious*.

The tawny wolf closed the gap between them, and they crested the hill together. They'd barely started down the opposite side, however, when a long, lingering howl sounded from the valley they'd just left.

The hunters had found their trail.

(((● ●

Neva's wolfen form was as fast and as agile as it had been at the lake, and she seemed to keep pace with Travis without effort. He just wished she had given up the *I-don't-wanna-be-a-wolf* crap a helluva lot sooner. They were in serious trouble. A Changeling could elude almost any other creature on the planet—but escaping from other Changelings posed a huge challenge. Although Travis surpassed most shape-shifters in strength and speed, and had the experience to employ cunning and strategy, Neva didn't.

She was keeping up with him now, but he knew it couldn't last. They needed an edge, a human one, and fast.

Wheels.

Travis went over his mental map, trying to figure out where the hell they were. Not only was this a different valley, he could tell by the sky that they had veered off from his original direction. Their pursuers hadn't topped the hill yet, but it was only a matter of time before the wolves picked up Neva's trail from the barn. He was certain now that *she* was the quarry, not him. He'd like to believe it was a rescue party coming for her, but Neva's story made that unlikely. At first he'd thought she'd been misinformed about "werewolves," or perhaps misconstrued something she saw. It ran against everything he'd ever been taught to think that a pack would allow harm to come to humans, never mind cause that harm. He was much more inclined to believe Neva now. There was no denying that his own wolf was openly hostile toward the strangers. Even his human side was forced to admit that something about them felt just plain *wrong*.

The mounting number of *why*s was giving him a headache. Why send *five* wolves, for Christ's sake? Why spend so much effort on a newly turned Changeling? Why was it so damn important to chase Neva down at all? He grumbled to himself that if Neva's sire had wanted her, she should have taken more responsibility in the first place, spent some time teaching Neva about her new life. At the very least, Meredith could have assigned somebody to see Neva through her first shift if Meredith wasn't interested in doing it herself. It would have been far more efficient than sending out five Changelings now.

Travis chuffed out a breath in disgust. None of it added up. And he *hated* things that didn't add up.

There were farms now, green and gold and brown fields patchworked across the valley floor with a scattering of tiny bright squares that were houses and barns. As a wolf, Travis would normally stay as far away as possible from human habitations, silently skirting the properties like a ghost. Now he headed straight for the little farms, and for the beaten-dirt road that wound through them like a dusty river.

Shit. A quick glance behind showed two of their pursuers topping the hill. It was going to be a race now, and he hoped like hell that Neva could keep up. Ahead, Travis scanned the farms for anything that might be useful. Hefty grain trucks, rusted pickup trucks, and egg-shaped minivans that had seen better days seemed to be the only choices, and none of them were likely to outrun a pack of motivated Changelings. Or withstand an assault by them. Then a glint of polished chrome caught his eye...

What the hell are you doing? I thought we were supposed to hide from humans! Neva tried to look in every direction at once as she followed the big tawny wolf across an open farmyard. Luckily no one appeared to be home, and even the dogs were strangely quiet, slinking away from the Changelings that had invaded their territory.

Move back from me.

Neva dropped back barely in time before Travis resumed his human form on the run. She dodged the trail of sparks he left as he headed straight for a very shiny, very new, and very large vehicle. To her surprise, he jumped up and flung open the door.

"Get in, quick."

She pulled up abruptly. *You gotta be kidding. A dump truck? Really?*

"Never mind what it is. You wanna live, get the hell in."

All too mindful that Meredith's wolves were behind them, Neva leaped into the cab of the truck and paced the bench seat. *There's no keys!*

Travis slid behind the wheel and slammed the door behind him. "Push-button start." The diesel engine suddenly thundered awake, and he threw it into gear. Gravel flew as they erupted from the farmhouse laneway in a cloud of black smoke. In the side mirror, Neva saw something else fly, too. Strange bright-pink pebbles pinged off the dirt road behind them.

"Goddammit, it's loaded," Travis said without even looking, and shifting gears as quickly as he dared. "We'll never get up enough speed if I don't get rid of whatever's in the bed."

Looks like bubble gum.

"What?" He glanced at his mirror and pounded the steering wheel in frustration. "Christ, that's all we need."

Why? What is it?

"Seed. It's frickin' treated *seed*. Coated with fungicide, fertilizer, whatever."

The implications were clear. It was like leaving a trail of fluorescent-pink breadcrumbs for Meredith's enforcers to follow—assuming the truck could manage enough speed to get out of sight. *Can't we just dump it?*

"It takes time, and we don't have any." He frowned as he drove, and Neva wondered if that was his natural expression. It seemed to her that his brows were furrowed more often than not. Maybe his face was just naturally fierce, but she knew it was capable of displaying other emotions—when she'd come to her senses after her first Change, he'd been holding her and laughing as if she'd just done the most fantastic thing ever. And when he'd been carrying her into the elevator at the hospital, he'd been downright charming even while annoying the hell out of her. In spite of the fact that he lived in a near-constant state of being pissed off, and insisted on trying to boss her around at every turn, part of her had noticed from the beginning that Travis Williamson was a very attractive man.

And what a completely *stupid* thing to think about when five of Meredith's mindless wolves were on their trail and—

A gigantic gray wolf leaped up at Neva's window, and the impact caused a starburst of cracks in the glass before the creature fell away.

"Shit!" Travis yelled as he swung the wheel and the heavy truck wobbled crazily. He punched a button on the dash. "Get down on the floor and brace yourself, *now.*"

Not sure what to expect, Neva complied, tucking herself tightly beneath the dashboard and shielding her face with her tail for good measure, although she peered at Travis with one eye. He gripped the wheel tightly, and she could feel a new vibration thrumming through the steel frame of the truck all around her. Belatedly she realized he was raising the truck bed. *Are you crazy? We're going too fast!*

"No choice. Hang on!"

Neva closed her eyes. The truck groaned throughout as if protesting the speed, too, but Travis didn't slow down in the least. She heard the loud *hiss* and scrape of the load as it began to shift and slide from the steel bed, and she tried to imagine the cascade of pink bouncing onto the road—no way was she going to climb up and look. As the vehicle swayed and shivered, Neva shivered as well and scrunched farther under the dash until the glove box popped open and made her jump.

A huge crash against her door nearly gave her heart failure, and the inside panel bulged inward.

"One of them's fast. Hope he got a headache that time. Just stay down."

As the hissing of the sliding load became louder, the vibrations got worse. She imagined the dump-truck engineers—*Hey, let's design a truck that can be unloaded at fifty miles per hour.*

Not.

Her heightened senses told her that the truck's weight had shifted dramatically and the front wheels weren't as firmly on the pavement as they had been just a few moments ago. What if they tipped over? Could werewolves survive car wrecks?

Even as the monstrous vehicle rattled and shook, the irony didn't escape Neva. Once desperate to end her life, she was now hoping like crazy not to die. And if she did, she was *so* going to haunt Travis to the very end of his goddamn days.

A loud yelp emerged above the noise of the groaning hydraulics and sliding grain.

"Eat that, you son of a bitch," Travis said through gritted teeth.

The loud *hiss* of the seed leaving the truck tapered off at long last and finally ended. She dared to open her eyes just in time to see Travis reach for the dashboard controls. The hydraulics protested even louder, and the tone of the vibrations changed. She could feel the center of gravity shifting, feel the truck wanting to fishtail. Travis strained to hold the wheel steady, and a moment later, there was a huge, teeth-rattling *thump* as the steel bed returned to its rightful place on the truck, followed by a deafening clang as the tailgate swung shut.

They weren't dead. Not even trapped in a flaming pile of twisted steel.

Neva allowed herself the luxury of a real breath as anger rushed in to replace her relief. If she was in human form, she'd verbally chew Travis a new one for his insanely risky stunt. Of course, the downside was that she would be naked again, hardly a position of strength. As she climbed back into the passenger seat, she concluded that mental shouting would just have to do—until she looked at him. Travis was frowning, of course. He was also sweating. His powerful hands were clenched hard enough on the steering wheel to whiten his knuckles, and she watched as he slowly relaxed them and slid his palms up and down the wheel. The wheel that was no longer round.

You were scared, too.

"Hell yeah," he snarled at her. "Only a lunatic wouldn't be scared shitless. But we had to do something fast."

They didn't even slow down as they ran the stop sign. The big dump truck rolled straight ahead, picking up speed. She risked a look in the mirror in time to see a minivan fishtail crazily and skid sideways into a deep pile of bright-pink seed. *Omigod, you've caused an accident. What if they're hurt? What if they have kids in the car?*

"Look again," said Travis, shifting gears.

Four men leaped from the van and charged over the heaps of seed. In the blink of an eye, they were no longer running on two legs but four. A fifth wolf shook itself free of the enormous pile of grain and joined them. The pack was still following the dump truck, but now that it was empty, they weren't fast enough. As Neva watched in the mirror, the creatures became smaller and smaller until they disappeared from sight entirely.

She breathed a sigh of relief. *They're gone.*

"Good. Because we're nearly out of fuel."

You stole a truck without gas in it? Are you kidding me?

"For Christ's sake, the gauges don't work until you start it up, you know. And I was a little preoccupied with saving our asses—which I managed to do, but don't bother thanking me or anything."

Neva sighed, and the sound was almost the same from wolfen lips as from human. Travis was right. Again. That grated, but not as much as it once did. How could she be irritated with him when he'd managed to outmaneuver Meredith's wolves? Neva had been scared, and even now she was nauseous and shivering, partly because her body was dumping the excess adrenaline, but mostly at the thought of what Meredith might have done to her—and surely would have done to Travis. *Thank you. It was a close call.*

He was silent for a long moment. "You're welcome," he said at last, so quietly that only her Changeling senses could pick it up.

ELEVEN

Baker was surprised that a hunting party hadn't come after him. Surely whatever wolves had been assigned to cleanup duty had noticed they were one body short in the ashen circle. Perhaps they decided to keep it quiet—the devil knew *he* would. No one in his right mind would volunteer that kind of information to someone like Meredith. It reminded him of his dad's old adage on the ranch when wolves began targeting the calves in the high pasture one summer—*shoot, shovel, and shut up.*

He grimaced. What would his dad say if he knew his own son was now one of the hated predators? Hell, what would his dad say if he saw a wolf, any wolf, that was this fucking big? *That's how you tell the werewolves from the natural wolves, Dad.* Of course, Baker didn't plan to tell his father anything of the sort. In fact, unless Baker found a way to return to his human form, he wasn't going to be doing any talking at all. Right now, however, he figured his best bet was to use his new four-legged body to get gone, as far and as fast as he could in case anyone did decide to follow him. He'd figure out how to stand on two legs again later.

And somehow he'd figure out how to save Riley. There was no way he was leaving his best friend in Meredith's bloodstained hands. For shit's sake, he and Riley had done everything together since second grade, and now they were both fucking grade-A werewolves. It was just like something out of a horror movie, but they'd deal with it together. If Riley was still alive. Baker shook his head, making the thick gray fur around his neck stand out like a mane. He wasn't going to think like that. Not about Riley.

Hold on, buddy. Just hold on.

(((((● ●

The moon was blotted out by an overcast sky, a lucky break as far as Travis was concerned. Break number two was a narrow steel bridge over a shallow creek. The fuel gauge was on empty when he deliberately skidded the truck and wedged it sideways between the girders, blocking both lanes. If the hunters had managed to obtain another vehicle, they'd have to abandon it here.

Neva thought they should wipe down the cab of the truck before leaving, but there was no point. Local law enforcement would most likely chalk up the whole incident to joyriding teens. He had no record, as he'd never been foolish enough to get arrested, and he doubted that Neva's prints were on file, either.

As wolves, they splashed through the cold water of the creek for more than fifteen miles. The first ten, Neva kept up with him readily. The last five, she was cold and exhausted, and he'd had to all but bite her to keep her going. The frigid water would hide their scent. Another town had been much closer, less than two miles away from the bridge in the opposite direction. But their pursuers would *expect* them to go there.

When the fugitive pair finally emerged from the water, they were at the edge of the Crossford industrial park, with an entire county between them and the abandoned truck.

The darkness was deep and soothing, a velvety blanket to hide them from human sight. Lights were few and far between here, and simple to steer clear of. Travis led the sagging Neva through a maze of warehouses and compounds until he saw a small, rundown building without any lights around it at all. It looked like it might have started its life as a car parts dealership, but a big wooden sign now read, "Brother's Keeper Secondhand Store," and in smaller letters under it, "Food Bank." Break number three, he thought.

He resumed his human form and pulled some slim tools from the inner pocket of his leather jacket. The lock was a simple one. "Food, clothing, and shelter," he announced, holding the door open for Neva. He expected her to make some smart-mouthed comment about breaking and entering, but the dark wolf was silent as she crossed the threshold. He'd pushed her hard and far, but he couldn't be sorry. It very nearly hadn't been far enough. After they'd rested and eaten, he was going to push her into moving on again. At least for a while. If he got her to a safe location—and gave her the rundown of the basic rules of Changeling life—surely he would have more than fulfilled his responsibilities. She could manage on her own from there.

His wolf didn't seem to like that idea at all, but too frickin' bad. Travis figured it was way past time he gave up babysitting. Time to hit the open road. He'd done his good deed and then some, so surely he deserved to resume his complication-free existence where he only had himself to worry about. The little voice in his head scoffed at him, *That's all you deserve.* He sighed and turned his attention to Neva.

A blue glow in the clothing section of the thrift store—and a few errant sparks that Travis hoped wouldn't set the place on fire—signaled her return to human form. He could only see her head and bare shoulders above the garment racks, and a fleeting glimpse of more as she passed from one aisle to another. There was something teasing and erotic about it, although he'd seen her completely naked more than once now. Changeling senses allowed him to hear the soft susurrus of fabric as it brushed over her bare skin. His cock hardened until he had to readjust his jeans to accommodate it, and his mind had a sudden clear picture of laying her down atop an enormous pile of soft clothing and—

She emerged wearing a truly hideous tentlike dress in a loud red, purple, and orange tropical fabric that no self-respecting islander would be caught dead in. Not only was it at least ten sizes too big, it covered Neva from neck to ankle. As he watched, she belted it casually with a fuzzy pink chenille tie that looked stolen from some grandma's bathrobe.

He couldn't help it. "What the hell is *that*?"

Neva shrugged. "I think they call it loungewear. I don't see any point to wearing clothes that I actually like, since I'll just lose them the next time I turn into a wolf. This way I'll be *glad* they're gone."

A dress like that would have to be burned to make sure it didn't come back from the dead, he thought. "I'll teach you how to keep your clothes, how to bring them with you when you're ready to take on human form," he blurted. *Oh, for Christ's sake.* There was another promise, another commitment, another responsibility. But, god*damn*, it would haunt him for the rest of his life if he left such a beautiful woman to dress like a—

She *was* beautiful, he realized. Even in that monstrosity of a dress, she looked utterly appealing. His cock certainly hadn't relaxed one bit, but the rest of him was fully focused now. And it wasn't just her looks that intrigued him. He'd never met a woman with more grit and determination, and while she drove him crazy with her stubbornness and her irritating refusal to trust him, he admired her.

And he wanted her.

"Good. When do we start?" she asked, but he didn't answer. Instead, he found himself trailing his knuckles along her jawline. He lifted her chin with a finger and traced the outline of her lips, then touched them with his own. And there it was, just as he'd imagined—a taste to match her scent, sweet and tart at the same time. A hint of apple wine, a scattering of spice. For a moment he wasn't sure if she would respond in kind or try to deck him. She didn't seem sure at first, either. Then something abruptly changed, eased, and gave way. Her lips were full with arousal as she poured herself into the kiss, and just as suddenly, he couldn't get enough of her.

Travis savored, tasted, inhaled, devoured. Rained kisses on her lips, her face, her ears, her throat. Tore away the gaudy fabric to feast on those caramel nipples, and the feather-soft breasts that filled his hands oh so perfectly.

The last thing he expected was to be interrupted by his inner wolf. It whuffed its concern, not for him, but for Neva. Startled, his wits returned, and he took a hard look at the woman in his arms. The overbright robe she wore failed to lend any color to her lovely face, and there were deep shadows under her eyes.

"Mmm, don't stop," she murmured, gliding a hand through his hair. He grabbed her wrist and could feel the faint tremble in it. Neva was exhausted. In fact, if he wasn't holding her, would she be standing at all?

"How many times have you Changed recently?" he demanded, trying to come up with that number himself. Two? Three?

"Don't know." She tried to press her face close for another kiss. "Doesn't matter."

He gave her a shake. "Wake up. It matters plenty."

Neva frowned at him. "You kiss me, then you yell at me. You really need to join an anger management program, you know?" At least he thought that was what she said. The words were slurred together as if she'd been drinking. She shoved at him, but succeeded only in pushing herself off balance.

Oh, for Christ's sake. Travis caught her before she fell and simply picked her up. Her protest was cranky but mumbled, and that fact alone showed she was in rough shape. It also told him he was a complete idiot and a jerk and everything she'd ever accused him of being. Shifting form took enormous amounts of energy. Even though Changelings could draw most of that energy from the earth and the air around them—hence the static charge that accompanied the transition—*new* Changelings weren't practiced enough to do that. The energy they spent on a first Change was usually all their own. While he was old enough and experienced enough to shift two or three times a day if the need arose, Neva was definitely not. It would take rest, and plenty of it, plus major calories, in order to rebuild her reserves.

Well, at least he didn't have to go hunt down a moose for her. Cradling Neva to his chest, he strode to the back of the building, where endless shelves of auto parts had been supplanted with food bank items. The assortment was somewhat odd (an entire pallet of canned sardines in mustard sauce?) but plentiful. There was an aisle of canned Asian vegetables with names he couldn't read. There were cases of sports drinks that promised electrolytes, and he nabbed a couple of bottles. But it was protein he was looking for, and he really didn't want to go back for the damn sardines unless he had to. Finally he found some ancient refrigerator units on the very back wall that boasted six cartons of milk, some cheese, and a few packages of something he didn't expect from a place like this—real meat. Raw animal protein was a new Changeling's best friend.

Neva just wanted to sleep, but someone kept waking her up. *Swallow this. Eat that. Chew that some more. Just another bite. Drink this.* Tiny bits of food were placed in her mouth, cups were held to her lips. No sooner had she drifted off than the whole cycle started again. She wanted to push it away, tell whoever it was to stop, to leave her alone, but she couldn't seem to muster the anger or the energy. Or the will—in spite of her exhaustion, she was aware of a monstrous hunger, almost like a living thing. A great, gaping void in her midsection that could not be filled. As if the person feeding her understood her need, the pea-size bites of food came faster, especially the meat.

Good. Her inner wolf was awake and eager. *More.*

Neva's eyes remained closed, but she would have rolled them if she'd had the energy. In her previous life, she'd been extremely health-conscious and tried to limit her consumption of red meat. She'd even considered going vegan, but right now meat seemed like the most amazing substance in the world, a perfect anti-dote to the vast hunger that had taken her over. It was delicious, soothing, succulent, and—

Completely raw.

Someone—Travis, of course, she could smell him now—was feeding her *raw meat* like she was a goddamn dog. Her hands lay slack in her lap, only because she lacked the strength to move them. Otherwise she'd be throttling him. With a supreme effort, she managed to glare at him through slitted eyes, but within a few seconds her weary lids drooped shut. Exhausted and resigned, she accepted the next bite, promising herself to exact revenge as soon as she was herself again. Or as close to being herself as she was ever going to get, now that she was a full-fledged were—

Only the fact that she was freezing kept her from plunging headlong into asleep again. Despite the blankets tucked around her, she shivered like a clockwork toy—until she felt herself drawn into Travis's lap and held close against his broad chest by strong arms. His body radiated heat, a delicious, life-giving heat that gradually seeped inside her and warmed her very bones. Vaguely she remembered that he'd done this for her before. Just as she relaxed into dreamlessness, she thought she saw a big golden wolf curled around her, sheltering her, protecting her. As before, as if they shared a great secret, it winked one of its blue, blue eyes…

The next time Neva awoke, it was on her own. No one was urging food on her, although she could see a carton of milk, a box of crackers, some cheese, and a jar of peanut butter with a spoon in it, all gathered on a small table near her hand. She blinked the sleep away, ran a hand through her hair, and focused on her surroundings. Furniture of every shape, size, and vintage surrounded her. Bookshelves lined the walls, and dining room chairs hung from the rafters. Buried in quilts up to her chin, she was ensconced in an old, overstuffed recliner. So comfortable, in fact, that only the desperate need to pee provided any motivation to move at all. She struggled out of the chair and stumbled her way through the furniture maze and the labyrinth of used-clothing racks until she found a washroom.

When she emerged, Travis was standing there with an assortment of jeans and T-shirts over his arm.

"Try these on or go find some on your own. You need clothing—*real* clothing so you won't stand out—and then we've got to get out of here."

Neva looked down at herself. She was wearing a simple cotton nightgown. "I didn't put this on."

"What you *did* put on has been staked, salted, and buried."

"You had no right to dress me. I'm not a Barbie doll!"

"I figure since I sat up all night feeding you and keeping you warm, I definitely had the right."

She pointed an accusing finger at him. "*You.* You fed me *raw meat!*"

"Yeah, I did, and it's done you a world of good. By rights, you shouldn't be on your feet yet. You wanna yell at me about it, fine. Just do it after you get dressed—it's already past dawn, and this place opens at eight. I want to be long gone before any conscientious volunteers decide to come in early."

Dammit. What she really wanted to do was go back to sleep. She snatched the clothes from his hands, plus a proffered pair of sneakers, and stalked off to the thrift-store dressing room. Travis's selections fit surprisingly well, and the colors and styles had obviously been chosen to suit her. Either he'd gained tremendous experience in stealing women's clothing over the years—and she'd make sure she gave him a hard time about that notion—or he'd measured her. *He's so going to die if I find out that he did.*

"Threatening me again?" he asked as she made her way to where he was straddling a wooden chair.

"How many times do I have to tell you to stay out of my head?"

"And how many times do I have to tell *you* to quit broadcasting? I didn't measure you. I didn't even peek—*much.* For your next question, I've arranged transportation and packed a lunch. Let's get the hell outta here."

That hadn't been her next question at all, but he was gone. There was nothing to do but run to catch up.

TWELVE

The little bitch was *alive*? Meredith paced her elegant bedroom, which encompassed the entire top floor of the cliffside mansion overlooking the Pacific. She passed by the window through which she'd tossed the bearer of the news, her platinum-blonde hair and gold satin robe fluttering as the sea breeze rushed through the shattered pane.

Alive? Perhaps she had misunderstood what she had seen in her silver scrying bowl. But what other conclusion could she have drawn from viewing Geneva leaping off a high cliff? The image had gone cloudy then, and Meredith had assumed the outcome. In a frenzied rage, she'd torn Geneva's guards to pieces, then turned her wrath on the other prisoners. Several had been slaughtered in their cells. By the time the day of the full moon arrived, she'd been almost too exhausted to kill the wolves that had been forced to admit that they hadn't found Geneva's body. Even the initiation of the newest wolves—those that were left—and the energy Meredith gained by their transformation had failed to cheer her for long.

Alive. Meredith had tried hard to take comfort in the certainty that even if she could survive such a fall, Geneva would die slowly and painfully during her first shift. Apparently the bitch was made of stronger stuff than previously suspected. No. No, not *strong*, just obstinate and uncooperative as usual, Meredith corrected herself. As a werewolf, Geneva might be a little harder to capture, but she *would* be captured.

Meredith drew a long, cleansing breath of salt air, then another, feeling the dreadful tension leave her lithe body. There was a reason for actual cheer. Her darkly beautiful spell she'd grieved as lost to her was now resurrected, her plans restored, because Geneva lived. Soon, perhaps even by the next full moon, it could all come to fruition.

Of course the little bitch's crime would have to be dealt with first. Geneva had done what no one had ever dared to do: not just defy Meredith, but escape. That could *not* go unpunished. Meredith had already made an example of that upstart Riley, which couldn't fail to make an impression on the pack. She'd won their battle in the ash circle, leaving him severely wounded and only half-conscious. But the next day when she'd demanded his sworn fealty, he'd spit at her. *Spit. At. Her.* Meredith had immediately bound the great wolf with magic so he couldn't return to human form, then had him flayed in the courtyard until gobbets of bloody fur had sprayed the marble walls as well as the faces of the onlookers.

Really, he should have had the courtesy to die right then and there, but that was a werewolf for you. The animal nature was tough and resilient. However, it also seemed to be unpredictable, and that factor was keeping her up at nights in her spell room. Meredith's magic was potent enough to dominate almost any human or werewolf, body and soul.

Almost.

Over the years, the meticulous records in her grimoires showed that approximately 1 percent of those she turned into werewolves were like Riley and Geneva, completely unaffected by Meredith's forceful efforts at mind control and magical possession. She could control their bodies to a degree, prevent them from shape-shifting—or force them to do it. But that was about all. It was a constant frustration to her. Recently she'd had great hopes for some ancient Peruvian spells using blood and thorns, but the subject's temperament had failed to change in the slightest. She assuaged some of her disappointment by watching her pack tear him to pieces.

Now she had to contend with Riley. He'd been dumped in a cell, where he would either live to be useful eventually, perhaps as hunting practice for her wolves, or die. Of course, even the dead had their uses. *Waste not, want not.* The weaklings who hadn't survived their first Change had been gathered up and burned to ash by now, and that ash was a highly potent ingredient in many of Meredith's spells. She sighed at the thought—she still hadn't found a suitable replacement for her manicurist. A small mistake, that one, made in her eagerness to build up the numbers after killing several of her other conscripts.

Fortunately she didn't make many mistakes. She ruled by strength and power and cleverness, none of which could be matched. It didn't hurt to hammer that home as often as possible, but truth be told, it wasn't the pack she wanted to impress this time. It was Geneva herself. She'd have to think of something truly special to inflict on her. It was pure bad luck that she turned out to be one of the recalcitrant few that couldn't be controlled. *Yet.* Meredith was determined to find a way. If she had to keep the little bitch locked up for the next twenty years, *someday* Geneva would be forced to acknowledge Meredith's complete superiority in all things, once and for all.

So. Where was Geneva now, and who could she send to track her down? The messenger had said the brat was being helped— some big werewolf had been spotted traveling with her. Obviously it was someone with age and experience, or they wouldn't have been able to elude Meredith's wolves. No matter. *If you want something done right, you have to do it yourself.* Meredith glided to an elegant marble table that held a wide, silver bowl, and began slowly stirring the cold water inside it with delicate fingertips. As the spell left her lips, the water clouded and bubbled, then cleared to reveal a lovely but strange image...a natural bower of evergreens in a forest. She studied it for a long time. Scrying was a difficult art, and not only did it take skill to discern *what* you were seeing, but *when*. Past, present, or future? Was she looking at a place Geneva had been, or was going to be?

Perhaps she and her wolves should pay a visit.

((((●

You can't go home again. High on a hillside, curled in the hollow beneath a thicket of junipers, Baker rested his chin on his paws. His dad's ranch spread out over much of the valley. He'd sat on this hill a lot as a kid—it was his favorite place to think—but he'd never enjoyed the view with such incredible clarity. The night sky was clouded over, but the darkness provided no barrier to his sight. The daytime colors were gone, replaced by a whole new palette, beautiful in its own right.

On the homestead far below, Benner and Jack, the ranch dogs, were silent. In fact, over the many miles he'd traveled, no dogs had challenged him or sounded the alarm. Maybe they knew he wasn't an ordinary wolf. Maybe it spooked them. Hell, he knew *he* was spooked. Probably why he came here—where else did you go when you were scared but home? Baker hadn't lived here for years, but somehow his feet had found the way even though his brain hadn't been thinking about it. Instinct, he supposed.

Instinct wasn't doing a fucking thing about turning him back into a human being, though. And until he was on two legs again, he'd find no welcome at his family home. Nor would he be able to help his friend Riley. Somehow there had to be a way, and he was gonna find it. *Somehow...*Baker closed his eyes, and exhaustion claimed him.

((◖ ◗ ●

"At least it's not a dump truck."

That was all Neva had to say about his latest choice of ride as she threw in her backpack and got in. Travis had been sure she'd approve of the four-wheel-drive pickup he'd appropriated—okay, it was old and rusted, but it ran and wouldn't attract attention. Of course she'd still be pissed at him about the raw meat thing, and especially for replacing her nightgown while she was asleep. He should probably just be glad she got in the truck at all.

He wasn't much for explaining things, so he didn't even try to tell her that the clothing switch had nothing to do with the hideous dress—much—and everything to do with the fact that he'd ripped out the front of it during their impromptu make-out session. And later, half asleep, she'd turned her head at the wrong moment and the cup of milk he'd been trying to get her to drink had soaked her to the skin. Not good for someone who was already chilled. He'd cussed himself out as he sought something simple to put on her.

He'd held her for a while then, so his naturally high body heat could warm her. That's the story he was going with, anyway, the fact that he'd enjoyed the closeness notwithstanding. *Christ, I'm telling myself a helluva lot of lies lately.* Or maybe the lies were to appease that little voice in his head, the one that told him he had a lot to make up for, to atone for. To pay for what could never be repaid. The voice that said he could never have what he wanted most...

Travis glanced over at Neva. She was resting her stubborn chin in her hand, looking out the window. Deliberately not looking at him. Did she remember last night at all? Did she remember the kisses and caresses that she had returned? Did she remember sleeping in his arms? In that moment he'd felt as close to *home*, to truly belonging, as he had since—

Hell, it didn't matter how he felt. Getting close to anyone was a serious mistake, and getting close to Neva was an even bigger mistake. She was tough and smart and beautiful. And she deserved so much more than *him*. He'd had no right to kiss her last night, no right at all. If he was lucky, she'd have no memory of it. If she did, he'd have to play it down somehow, maybe pass it off as a dream, or just downright piss her off. *Ha. That shouldn't be hard.* The fact that it would be hard on *him*, he ignored.

His wolf was suddenly present. More than present, more like a scant layer of skin cells away from the surface. *Mate.*

No. No way. Don't you pull that shit on me.

Mate. Mine.

NO.

Not only did the wolf retreat, Travis could swear it left in a huff. The wolf was part of him, but it was unusual for it to display human emotion. *Weird.* Maybe it was just horny—goddess knew *he* was—and it was likely due to Neva's presence. Had he ever spent so much time around a woman, especially one he was attracted to? It was probably driving his animal persona crazy.

Apple wine and spice... Now that he knew what her lips tasted like, he seemed to catch the scent of it everywhere, and it was making him more on edge than his wolf. Still, he was determined to ignore it or fight it. He had to. He had to teach Neva a few more things and then leave her. That was the plan. Only now, instead of looking forward to being on his own again, he thought the plan sucked.

Big time.

"So, what's the deal with this Meredith bitch?" he asked, partly because he wanted to know but mostly for a distraction. "What the hell did you do to make her send out the goon squad?"

Neva was silent for so long that he thought she might not answer. Then she shrugged as if it didn't matter. "I didn't *do* anything, at least not anything in a sane person's books. Meredith's always liked things to go her way, and I didn't play along. I didn't want to be a werewolf, for one thing."

No shit, he thought, but wisely kept it to himself. "You've known her for a while then."

"Yeah. I hadn't seen her for nearly six years, though—she'd been traveling, and I didn't hear from her much. Don't know what she was doing or who she was with. But when she came back, she moved into this big-ass property on the coast. Expensive and utterly gorgeous, like something a movie star would live in," Neva said, and shifted in her seat. "She called me, invited me to come and visit, said she wanted to *reconnect*, and I stupidly said okay.

"That was before I realized how isolated it was. She e-mailed me a map, but I got lost more than once. The road was damn scary—it turned into one lane, then gravel, then it was practically a goat path through a redwood forest. I *wanted* to turn back, but I didn't want to be chicken." She closed her eyes for a moment. "Maybe it was intuition warning me. I should have listened."

Yeah, and I should have done a lot of things differently in my life, too. He shook his head as he drove. "Most of us don't recognize intuition until after the fact. But you can't go back and fix the past."

"Isn't that the truth?" She sighed. She fiddled with the laces on her backpack, as if she needed to channel nervous energy. Sure enough, she talked faster as she continued. "There was some kind of party going on when I got to the house, a big one in the upstairs reception room, and Meredith said it was all for me.

Kind of in my honor. She talked nonstop, gave me the grand tour, and introduced me to tons of people. I was actually having fun, and it seemed like we were really getting along well. I probably had a couple drinks, but not too much. We were laughing and giggling and—well, *girl stuff*, you know?"

No, he didn't, but Travis recognized his cue to nod as if he did. She nodded back, and he noticed she was hugging her backpack.

"Then everyone was standing back, forming a circle around us and looking expectant. Meredith said, 'As you know, this little celebration is for Geneva. It's been years since we've gotten together, she and I, and may we never be far apart again.' It was kind of an odd little toast, but everyone raised their glasses and clapped, and then she suddenly started to laugh. Not like before, though. This time she was laughing at *me*—and everyone in the room started laughing, too, like they were all in on some big joke.

"That's when she turned into a wolf." Neva was staring out the windshield, but Travis guessed she wasn't seeing the road ahead. She was back in that room, in the middle of the crowd, watching the impossible happen. Growing up Changeling, such things were the stuff of daily life. Growing up human was different.

"Must have scared the hell out of you."

She made a disparaging noise. "I was beyond scared. One minute Meredith was human and the next she was a wolf, a huge silver wolf. Just like that. Jesus, I thought I was hallucinating. I screamed and wanted to know what the hell had been put in my drink. And then she turned back into Meredith like nothing had happened. I wanted to leave right then and there, but she grabbed my arm."

Still staring out the windshield, Neva rubbed her left biceps. Travis wondered if she was even conscious of it. "I couldn't believe it. She was so strong—so powerful," she continued. "I couldn't pull my arm away, and I thought for a minute she was going to break it in two. That's when I lost it. I punched her, and kicked and fought to get away, but nothing worked. Nothing I did had any effect on her at all."

That would be a shock by itself, Travis thought. A human's strength was puny compared to a Changeling's. And even in two-legged form, a Changeling could take a punch that would break bones in a human being.

"'Time to join the party, Geneva.' That's what she said to me, and she was still laughing. All of them were. There was this smell then, this thick, ozone-like smell like you sometimes get after a thunderstorm. My hair suddenly stood on end, just floated up around my head, and so did hers, that's how much static there was. The lights flickered out and the air was suddenly filled with tiny blue sparks, the kind you see in a dark room when you scuff your feet over the carpet. It was just a minute or two, that's all—but when the lights came back on, all the people were gone. Meredith and I were completely surrounded by enormous wolves."

"Jesus."

"I quit fighting then. Froze. There were close to fifty of them, all snarling and showing their teeth. I was afraid of setting them off, afraid they'd tear me to pieces if I so much as breathed wrong. Meanwhile, Meredith's going on and on about how great it is to be a werewolf. 'We're stronger, faster, smarter than humans. We can take what we want. And you have something I need, dear Geneva.' That's what she said just before she bit me. She wasn't even a wolf when she did it. She lifted the arm she had hold of and bit my wrist to the bone. I—I—"

"Take a breath there, you're safe." His first instinct was to reach out a comforting hand, but he quelled that notion at once. Something told him she wouldn't appreciate being touched just yet.

"I know that. I know I'm safe with you." She looked at him for the first time since she began her story. "Which makes no sense to me. I mean, you're a werewolf, too, but it's not the same. You're—well, you can be a real jerk sometimes, but you're *decent*."

He didn't know what to say to that. It was probably the best compliment he'd ever received. He shrugged, and Neva looked out the window again as if embarrassed by her admission.

"It's Meredith I can't ever get out of my head," she said at last. "If you'd seen her in that moment—dressed up like a Hollywood diva, all white silk and golden hair. And then she looks up from my arm and smiles, with my blood smeared on her teeth and dripping from her bright-red mouth. That's the image that wakes me up in the night. Well, one of them…but hey, I've had enough of traveling down memory lane for one day."

"Christ, no wonder. That's a nightmare and a half," said Travis. And that was only *one* of her memories? How did she manage to sleep at all? "So you were right, the gift of the wolf was forced on you."

"Hell yeah. You said that was against the rules, right?"

"The highest Changeling law is *never harm a human*. The second is *never turn anyone against their will*."

"You gotta be kidding. Meredith breaks both of those rules before breakfast. So what's supposed to happen if you do turn somebody? Is there some sort of penalty? What if you kill somebody by accident, like hit them with a car?"

Such simple questions. Just a few little words, yet they kicked off a sudden roaring in his head. "Depends on the circumstances. If it was accidental, you could be banished from pack territory," he said roughly. "And other packs are unlikely to take you in."

Neva snorted. "Meredith's pack isn't about to kick her out. She controls them. And believe me, there's nothing accidental about what she does." She was quiet for a moment. "Other packs don't accept a banished werewolf?"

"No, not usually."

"That must be why Meredith is able to recruit some of her wolves. Most of the werewolves in her pack were turned by her, but not all of them. There's some that joined up—werewolves traveling alone, just like you. That's why I was so sure you worked for her."

"Wait a minute—I've been around a long time, and I've only met one other loner like me. And FYI, I don't work for anybody."

"I get that, Mr. Independent. I don't know where the hell she finds them. I'm just saying that there's no way that Meredith's wolves—the ones she recruits or the ones she makes—are going to get rid of her."

He shook his head. "It wouldn't be the pack she's created that would be responsible for dealing with the problem. It's the founding pack, the pack she came from, that would most likely make a judgment on her crimes."

"Yeah, but she doesn't have a *founding pack*. She wasn't born a Changeling like you. She was turned. So who's in charge of her, then? Isn't there anyone who can stop her?"

"Maybe her sire, if they're still around," said Travis. "But for such serious offenses, any pack that knows what she's been doing can take action against her. She'll be killed if her actions are shown to have been deliberate and—"

"No!" Neva shouted suddenly. "You can't!"

"For Christ's sake, what's the problem? You've told me she's a murderer and she wants to kill you, too. What do you *think* a pack is going to do with her? Put her in *werewolf jail*?"

"You can't kill her. I won't let you."

"I never said I was going to—"

"She's my sister!"

THIRTEEN

Travis nearly drove off the road. At the last moment he managed to steer unsteadily to the shoulder, and threw the truck into park with a jerk. "Your own *sister* turned you without your consent? Why the hell didn't you tell me this before?" he demanded of Neva.

She folded her arms over her backpack. She wasn't going to be intimidated, even though he looked like he was ready to break something in half. "I'm telling you now."

"Now?" He left the truck and stalked across the dry shallow ditch to the grassy embankment shaded by a thick stand of trees, where he paced back and forth like a caged lion. "Well, big fucking thanks for telling me *now*. I've been working my ass off to keep you safe since I met you. Don't you think a little information like that might have been useful to know? What other little details are you keeping to yourself?"

"Give me a break, you're a *werewolf*. You're the first one I've ever met that didn't work for Meredith, remember?" She slid from the truck and stomped in his direction, dragging the backpack with her and half wanting to hit him with it. "How was I supposed to know I could trust you?" He kept walking, and she was wondering just how far she'd have to chase him when he suddenly whipped around to face her. Neva teetered on her toes for a moment, off balance from the abruptness of the stop.

"I'm no werewolf, and I'm tired of hearing the word. I'm a *Changeling*, okay? And either you trust me or we call it quits right here." It was his turn to fold his arms, as if he was daring her to convince him.

Right then and there she decided to take on that challenge and dropped the backpack in the grass. "I already told you," she said as she approached him. She ran her hands over his leather jacket, feeling the muscles beneath it, the wide shoulders, the thick biceps, and broad chest. "Yes, I'm sure. I trust you, Travis Williamson." She teased her fingertips over the ever-present furrows in his brow, then circled her arms around his neck and drew his face down to hers, brushing the corners of his lips with hers. Gradually his angry expression softened, until finally his arms wrapped around her and their mouths met hungrily. Cars whizzed by on the highway, some honking at the sight of them wrapped around each other. One slowed down, and the passenger leaned out the window.

"Hey, get a room!" the young man shouted. His laughter lingered in the air as the vehicle sped away.

"You heard him," Travis murmured against her lips.

"There're no rooms around here," she managed. His answer was simply to lift her in one arm and, scooping up her backpack with the other, carry her up the slope and into the woods beyond, kissing her soundly along the way. She had no idea how he could see where he was going while his lips were so busy, but not so much as a single twig brushed against her. "Where the hell are you taking me?" She laughed when she came up for air.

"To a room, of course." He set her on her feet with her back against his powerful frame. An enormous fallen tree had bent several others to the ground years ago. The living ones curved and struggled their way skyward once more, but not without forming a thick, fragrant bower of evergreen branches that swept the ground. A part between them formed a narrow doorway, and Travis led her inside.

"This is pretty amazing," she said, admiring the thickly interwoven limbs above and around them. The shelter it formed was roughly bowl shaped, with the center ceiling over seven feet tall. The floor was a mix of dry grasses, strangely flattened and stirred into odd spiral patterns. She frowned then. "Hey, does something live here? I'm not staying in a damn Sasquatch hotel, buddy."

"Nobody lives here," said Travis. He pulled her tight against him, the bulge in his jeans pressing into her backside. His big hands cupped her breasts as he bent to nuzzle her hair. "Deer bed down in here in bad weather because it's dry and protected. Nothing else."

He planted soft, open-mouthed kisses along her neck as he unbuttoned her jeans, and she shivered with pleasure as he slid a hand inside. Questing fingers stroked the soft mound of her vee, and she rocked her hips, wanting, needing *more*. A wave of heat flushed the delicate skin above her breasts and up her throat, and her clothes seemed cumbersome and heavy. In a single smooth movement, she pulled her T-shirt over her head, taking the tiny scrap of a bra with it.

The blood pulsed in his veins, in his ears, his head—and especially in his cock. The throbbing drowned out every thought, every sense of caution, every hesitation he might have had. And when Neva began to undress, he was utterly lost, swamped in deep water by a wave of sheer want. Travis shrugged out of his jacket and shirt in a heartbeat. Groaned as his hot skin came in contact with hers, as she rubbed herself like a cat against him. Turning her, he held her tightly, reveling in her firm breasts and erect nipples pressing into his flesh. And when he could no longer stand it, Travis seized her by the waist and lifted her straight up so he could taste those luscious caramel-colored nipples. Neva squealed and kicked as her head brushed the ceiling of tree limbs, but he held her there firmly, effortlessly, and feasted on her breasts until his cock threatened to burst from its denim prison.

As if she sensed his need, she reached for his zipper as soon as he set her on her feet. He groaned as he sprang free, but his relief was incomplete. He had to have more, and he had to have it with the woman who was in his arms. No one else would do, came a new thought. *No one else would ever do.* He wanted, needed, yearned, ached to have her. Nothing in his world, in his entire long life, had ever been so important, so imperative, as being skin to skin with Neva Rayne Ross...who was even now kicking free of the last of her clothes.

In a flash he was on his knees, clutching her hips as he kissed his way down her belly to the dark, delicate curls of her vee. Her hands tangled in his hair, and her breath came faster as he slid his arm between her knees and planted his hand at the small of her back, pulling her tight against his mouth as he began to lick where her clit lay hidden. With the other hand, he thumbed aside a soft fold, exposing it to his tongue. Writhing against him, she moaned as her breath hitched with pleasure, her clit beginning to swell against his lips like a smooth round pearl. He took turns bathing it with his tongue and suckling it ever so gently, like a nipple. He could feel her excitement climbing, her hips instinctively arching into the sensation, and he reveled in heaping pleasure upon pleasure. She gasped as he slipped a finger inside her, as he began to stroke the velvety heart of her core, as he continued to flick his tongue over her clit.

The orgasm screamed through her like lightning, raw and powerful.

The wildness rose in Travis, too, and he stood, lifting her until he could settle her velvet sheath just above his cock. She grinned at him and clutched his shoulders as he allowed her to hover there for a breath, then two, letting her moisture tease the head of his penis, letting the tip tease her soft folds apart. "*Yes, yes, yes, yes,*" she chanted, and wriggled in an effort to get what she wanted. The movement teased him unmercifully until finally he released her...

She orgasmed again as she slid down his cock to the hilt, clawing at his back as if trying to pull him in even farther, even as he fought to remain still...Ah hell, three seconds of stillness was long enough. He began to pump his hips, and she matched his rhythm, wrapping her legs tightly around him, rubbing her breasts against his sweat-slicked chest. He rolled to the ground with her, moving with her, breathing with her. They gasped and clutched at each other until he couldn't tell where he left off and she began. Two universes merging, colliding—

Exploding into one.

They reached for each other twice more before collapsing in the grass. Every molecule seemed utterly spent, and Travis wondered if his brain had leaked out of his ears. He couldn't seem to put together a single coherent thought. What he *felt*, however, was plain. More than merely sated—more like *complete*. He closed his eyes, enjoying the simple sweetness of the sensation, with Neva's head nestled on his shoulder and her body draped like a rag doll across his.

He was almost asleep when a single word drifted across his mind, a word that didn't come from his human self at all.

Mine.

Go away, he thought. He didn't feel like dealing with his alter ego right now. He'd rather nestle down into blissful sleep, breathing in the warm fragrance of Neva's skin and the satisfying tang of recent sex.

Mate. His wolf was insistent. *Mine.*

Give it up, will you? It's been the best afternoon of my god-damn life. Don't spoil it with your bullshit.

Mate. Mine. Ours.

We can't do that, and you know damn well why.

It did. He had a mental image of the wolf pulling back, bowing its head a little as if ashamed. But instead of retreating to wherever it lived inside him, the wolf suddenly came roaring up to the surface, snarling and clawing as if it would tear him in two. Travis managed to fling Neva to one side just as he Changed form. The massive tawny wolf leaped from the shelter and hit the ground, running hard.

What the hell? Neva was in no mood to be awakened, especially not so abruptly. She sat up from where she'd landed, but there was no sign of Travis, only a pair of sparks that slowly floated down to the dry grass and sizzled there. She grabbed one of her shoes and beat them out, then brandished the shoe as if looking for something else to pound with it. Nothing appeared, however.

Where had he gone? Her hair crackled with static as she pushed it out of her eyes, telling her that he'd taken on his furry form, but why? And why the hurry? Were they in danger? Had someone found them? Just in case, Neva got dressed, although her body was slow to obey her commands. It was still in that delicious state of languor that followed satisfying sex—and the sex had been utterly incredible.

She certainly had no regrets. She'd been attracted to Travis for some time now, maybe even from the very beginning. And she'd finally decided to act on the attraction—*oh, hell, I did way more than that.* Neva had discovered a wildness in herself that both startled and excited her. She'd indulged herself thoroughly in exploring, rubbing, touching, licking, tasting this man…and enjoying all those delicious things in abundant return. Travis had given her everything she ever wanted and a few things she hadn't even *known* she wanted.

As she tied her running shoes, she wondered if perhaps Travis was having second thoughts. *Is that why he left?* Naw, that didn't make sense, she chided herself. If the guy wanted to leave because he was uncomfortable with the inevitable after-sex interaction, he would have just walked. After all, the door was literally open, right? Why shove her to one side and go all *Wild Kingdom* inside this small space?

Speaking of which, what about his wolf? During the first round of sex, she'd spotted the great tawny creature lingering like a golden shadow behind Travis's features. She'd been too preoccupied, too aroused to give a damn, of course. So the wolf wanted to watch? So what? She'd heard it howl in her mind, too—not the mournful howl of wild wolves, but a throaty roar of triumph that echoed through her own orgasm. It was a wonder she hadn't joined in.

During rounds two and three, however, Travis's wolf had been strangely absent. Maybe it had gotten its fill the first time. Maybe it had just been curious. After all, one of her friends had a black Lab that was forever sticking its nose into her physical relationships—literally—if she forgot to shut the bedroom door. The fact remained that Neva had never had sex with a werewolf before. Was it supposed to be like that? She hadn't been a werewolf before, either. Had Travis seen *her* wolf as well?

There were no answers, just more questions. Like, did Travis expect her to just wait here or what? Well, she certainly didn't need his permission to head for the truck—but she *would* approach it cautiously just in case any of Meredith's minions were in the area. She'd keep her head down and recon the area from the cover of the woods before she walked out in the open.

An hour later, Neva was still in the bushes at the edge of the tree line. The truck was in plain sight. Travis, however, was not, and it was really starting to piss her off. Geez, had he bailed on her? She felt more than a little foolish for declaring that she trusted him, and yet she'd only told the truth. *Get a grip, girl.* Wasn't it more likely that he just didn't know how to handle things between them, postintimacy? She pictured his characteristic frown, imagined him struggling to think of something to say. *Ha.* Maybe he thought she'd be looking for some sort of commitment from him. Sure, she was warming up to the idea of building something between them, but she was going to let that happen—or not—at its own pace. Whatever his issue was, there was no sign of man or wolf anywhere, and she had no idea what she should do. She did know that she'd had enough of waiting around. What if she just started driving until he caught up to her?

Assuming he planned to come back at all, said an unwanted voice in her head.

Shut up, she told it, even as she shouldered her backpack. After being chased by Meredith's enforcers, she didn't feel like hanging around any one place for very long—and she didn't even know where the hell she was. Travis could damn well find her later if he was so inclined. And if not, well, she'd be pretty disappointed, but at least she didn't need his help anymore.

At an abandoned garage that morning, he'd spent an hour demonstrating what he called Clothing Retrieval 101. Of course, he made it look easy—one minute he was a wolf, the next, a hot guy who rocked an old leather jacket and jeans. Then he did it twice more. He talked her out of trying it herself, citing that she needed more rest before she shifted form again, but she thought she had the basic points down. In case she didn't, she'd filled the backpack full of clothes at the thrift store. *Best to be prepared*. Hopefully, if she practiced enough, her human form would one day be fully dressed when she was finished running on four feet.

Funny how things changed. Originally, she'd determined to *never, ever* take on animal form again. Yet she knew darn well she couldn't have escaped Meredith's servants yesterday if it hadn't been for her powerful and agile lupine form.

And Travis.

At least she'd had the chance to ask Travis about the were-wolf—correction, *Changeling*—laws he'd spoken of. He'd insisted that Changelings like himself followed a strict code. They weren't supposed to force others into becoming like them, and they didn't believe in harming humans. Was it possible that not all were-wolves were the brute animals she'd come to hate? She certainly didn't hate Travis—although his disappearing act wasn't winning him any points, and she was *so* going to kick his ass if he showed up again. (When. *When* he showed up again.) If there was such a thing as a good guy among werewolves, it was probably Travis Williamson. He'd assumed responsibility for her when he didn't have to, and he'd managed to take pretty good care of her. He was a thief, certainly—something that still puzzled her—yet he had chosen not to be a killer.

He wanted to kill my sister.

Obviously that code of nonviolence didn't extend to Changeling justice. A sudden chill made her shiver as guilt pointed an accusing finger at Neva. She'd just had sex with some-one who wanted to sentence her only sister to death. Not that Meredith didn't deserve it—after all, she murdered people regu-larly without a second thought. Her followers did, too. But there had to be another way. Had to be. Meanwhile, Neva was left with a question—were all werewolves natural-born killers, just as she had thought? What about Travis?

Hell, what about me? Neva was a werewolf now, too. Could she trust *herself*? Was her judgment influenced by the creature that lived within? Would her basic nature change, making it only a matter of time before she took someone's life? She hadn't fallen in line like the rest of Meredith's victims—but was that only a matter of time, too? Would she one day run back to her sister, as anxious to please as the rest of the mindless followers—and just as willing to murder for her?

Neva's head hurt from all the answerless questions. Her only chance was to avoid Meredith, and that meant living out her days on the run or in hiding. There was no hope that her sister would either forgive her or forget about her. Not because she missed her or anything like that, of course. There was no love lost between them, and hadn't been since day one. Meredith would take tremendous pleasure in humiliating Neva and forcing her to do everything she could think of that was against her nature. *Especially* hurting people. And Neva had no doubts that remaining family members would top the list—Meredith had hinted at that more than once.

The one thing her sister wouldn't do was kill Neva, at least not right away. At the fateful party where Neva had been bitten, Meredith had let slip that she had a starring role for her, a key part of some great, grand plan that only her little sister could help fulfill. Neva didn't know what it was, only that it couldn't be good. All she'd been able to glean since was that her role involved magic, a truly terrifying prospect. When she was a child reading storybooks, magic had seemed like something wonderful, and hey, wouldn't it be cool to possess it? From what she'd seen since, the magic possessed Meredith utterly and completely. Her power and her spells were as addictive to her as any drug. Added to her cruel and self-centered personality, it was a marriage made in hell. Whatever Meredith's great and grand plan was, Neva couldn't allow herself to be part of it.

Another reason for her to have quietly committed suicide. She'd much rather have given up her own life than risk killing another. Or giving Meredith any more power. Travis couldn't possibly understand what he'd done by saving her. But it was too late now.

She left the cover of the bushes and walked to the truck, then thought better of it. The vehicle was stolen, for crying out loud, and with her luck, she'd be pulled over for some minor traffic infraction and the theft discovered. Instead, Neva walked a couple hundred yards down the highway and stuck out her thumb. There wasn't a lot of traffic, but she only needed one sympathetic driver.

Where should I say I'm headed? Travis hadn't mentioned a destination. They'd simply been heading straight east because Meredith lived on the West Coast. Why not angle a little to the south? Winter was coming, and she hated being cold. Florida sounded good. From there, she could even leave the country altogether. South America? Maybe Brazil. They spoke Portuguese, and she knew basic Spanish, which was similar, right? Or maybe she needed an entire *ocean* between her and Meredith's pack. She'd always wanted to experience the culture in Hong Kong—

No, no, and no. I'm thinking like me! Surely Meredith would guess what kind of choices she might make. And what she didn't guess, she might be able to divine through magic. Meredith was forever creating spells, and the level of power she'd achieved was truly terrifying. Who knew what she could do? Was she watching Neva right now?

"Get a grip," Neva scolded herself again, and made herself feel better by flipping a finger at the air, just in case her nemesis *was* watching. She needed to do something completely out of character, pick a location that Meredith would never associate with her. *Greenland, maybe. Oh, goody.*

A few minutes later, an eastbound eighteen-wheeler began to slow and move to the shoulder of the highway where she stood.

((((● ●

The big tawny wolf ran full-out, its belly low to the ground and its tail streaming straight behind it like a golden banner. Jaws gaped wide to gulp air, and its ears were flattened to its broad skull. Inside the powerful lupine body, Travis wrestled with his animal self as if it were a runaway horse, one that had seized the bit between its teeth so that no amount of tugging and sawing at the reins would sway its course. Of course if it had been a horse, he would have sold it on the auction block in a New York minute.

As for the wolf, he was stuck with it.

As his lungs burned, he finally seized control from his animal persona—and promptly tumbled down a steep embankment, bouncing off the loose soil and gravel until he landed in the oily water at the bottom of the reed-filled ditch. Pop cans, beer bottles, and fast-food wrappers bobbed around him as Travis rose slowly to his feet and shook himself. He picked his way through the distasteful mess until he could climb up the bank and into the cover of the forest beyond. There he plunked his furry ass beneath a tree and berated his animal persona.

What the fucking hell was that about?

His alter ego snarled and snapped its teeth together with an appalling ring that would have chilled the blood of anyone close enough to hear it.

Travis was simply pissed. *You don't get to come out of nowhere and take over, not unless my life's in danger. So what the fuck is the problem?*

Mate.

No, no mate. Not for you or me. I had sex. Just nice, ordinary, human sex. Hell, there had been nothing ordinary about it, but he wasn't about to discuss it with his alter ego. *So get over it already.*

Mate. Mine. Ours.

Some long-ago memory niggled at Travis's brain. He remembered his grandfather instructing him, "The wolf within has its own primal rules. If a Changeling's life is in danger, the wolf will emerge to defend it. It will also rise to the surface, unbidden, to defend a mate at all costs. And like our brothers, the wolves of the forest, Changelings mate for life."

Travis slammed that mental door shut and barred it. *She isn't. No way. She can't be. She doesn't even like us all that much.*

The wolf made a noise of derision. *Likes* very *much.*

Natural wolves were adept at reading the most subtle of cues in body language, expression, etc. Changeling wolves were even better at it. Travis found himself both elated and annoyed by his wolf's certainty. *So we like each other, so what? We're two consenting adults who got it on. That's what humans do. And that's the end of it.*

Mine. Ours.

You're not even listening. You can't choose her. I won't choose her.

No choosing. Is.

Is. That one tiny word carried an enormous amount of information, and Travis felt the weight of it as surely as if he'd shouldered an elephant. *Is.* With that single word, the wolf was telling him that the choice wasn't arbitrary, or a matter of convenience, or anything else that Travis had foolishly hoped. The bottom line was that Changelings recognized their true mates.

And the wolf had recognized Neva, probably from the very beginning.

Between one breath and the next, a number of puzzle pieces snicked into place. Travis realized that it was the wolf that had found Neva in the first place. The wolf had saved her. In fact, the wolf had been leading him every goddamn step of the way to the final act.

Changelings not only recognized their mates, but claimed them in true primal fashion. *Through sex.* Nothing could break the bond once forged. But Neva was blissfully unaware of what had just happened. Maybe he should just shut up about the whole thing and hope that the relationship would progress naturally and she'd want to stay with him. There was only one little problem, one little detail he hadn't told her and hadn't planned on *ever* telling her—or anybody else. But he'd have to.

And what were the chances she'd want anything to do with him *then*?

Travis wanted to shriek curses, but the best he could do in this form was howl like an anguished soul in hell. Loud and long, the ululation rose from his throat again and again until he couldn't utter another note. And still the truth stabbed him viciously, the truth that his wolf was a fucking loose cannon. It could rise of its own free will and there wasn't a goddamn thing he could do about it. Yeah, sure, it was supposed to do so only under extreme circumstances, as if the wolf was a wise weapon that knew best how to defend him or another Changeling. Well, his idiot wolf had taken over once before—and the tragic consequences had changed his life forever.

He screamed silently at the animal within. *This is how you damned us in the first place!*

FOURTEEN

Baker had tried since dawn to resume his human form. Nothing had happened except he'd given himself a pounding headache from the mental exertion. His lupine body, however, was considerably refreshed after a night's sleep. Best to get gone while he had the energy to do it. Not knowing if he'd ever see it again, he left his family's land and struck out in an easterly direction.

Miles later, he still had no idea where the hell he was going. He needed help, but had no fucking clue where to find it. Only another werewolf could tell him what the damn key was to Changing his form, and where was he supposed to find one of those?

As if in direct answer, his nostrils detected a scent just south of him. A werewolf, but not one he'd encountered before—so maybe it didn't work for the bitch queen. That didn't necessarily mean it was friendly, of course. In fact, the way his luck was running these days, it would probably try to kill him.

It was a chance he was willing to take, however. He ran in the direction of the scent.

((((● ●

Private planes were such handy little things, Meredith thought. The nearest airport to her destination had been ridiculously small, of course, but in this case it was an advantage. No one was checking cargo. Not that they'd have seen anything, anyway. From a tiny glazed clay pot, Meredith had dabbed a finger's worth of greenish-black ooze the consistency of old honey on the forehead of each of the dozen werewolves she'd brought with her. Humans were easy to fool, and with just a few words, the substance enacted a veiling spell that would hide them from mortal eyes. Despite the fact that it was broad daylight, the wolves would be nothing but a blurred shadow, a mere gust of wind as they passed. Meredith rubbed some between her breasts and assumed her own lupine form, feeling both the tingle of the spell and a swell of pride at her own skill and craftsmanship—the concealing charm was of her own clever design.

She leaped effortlessly from the aircraft door and bounded over the tarmac and into the fields beyond, with the pack following at a respectful distance. Thanks to her magic, the location shown her in her scrying bowl was fixed in her mind like the North Star, and her cross-country path was a nearly straight line.

Secure in her preparations, Meredith was exhilarated. She loved her lupine self. She adored her luxurious silver pelt, of course. What if she'd been drab gray or brown like so many of her pack? Her hairdresser changed the color of her hair easily, but changing the color of her fur? Dye wouldn't work, and the magic required would be complicated. Thankfully, she was spared those concerns since her wolf's unique beauty completely suited her regal station. Elegant looks aside, however, what she loved *most* was the raw power of the animal persona: teeth and muscle and speed. Endurance, too—natural wolves could run nearly forever, and werewolves, even longer.

Still, as swift as she had been, no one was in the evergreen bower when she arrived. Sending her wolves downwind into a thicketed gully to wait until she called for them, Meredith paced carefully around the natural shelter. Her acute senses immediately told her that Geneva had been there, and so had a male werewolf. The scent of sex hung heavy in the air, plus something more—

The unmistakable smell of bonding.

Meredith resumed her human form in a fury, and birds fled from the surrounding trees. "How dare he try to claim her?" she screamed in the empty bower. "She's *mine!*" As a leader, she actively discouraged sex of any kind between the wolves in her pack—it wasn't a difficult spell—because pair bonding bordered on magic, a natural earth magic that was at odds with her own. It set in motion powerful forces that could possibly disrupt her control of her servants.

Meredith's hold on Geneva had been tenuous to start with. *Now this!* And what if this new bonding affected the elaborate spell she'd labored so long and hard to create? "No. No, no, no, no, *no!*" Having almost lost the chance to enact her masterpiece once, Meredith wasn't going to stand for anything interfering with her plans again. Not her brat sister, not a bonding, and certainly not the werewolf who had stuck both his nose and his dick where it wasn't wanted. With rage and frustration mounting, she began mouthing the words that would eventually set the bower and all the trees that surrounded it on fire—

And stopped in midsentence as the breeze brought her new information. Her fiery rage gave way to icy calculation, and a sly smile parted her red, red lips. Someone was coming—and she was *so* going to enjoy making his acquaintance.

((((● ●

Travis loped toward the bower, all too aware of how long he'd been gone. He'd have a lot of explaining to do—assuming that Neva was even still there. Goddess only knew what she thought of him taking off in such a hurry. Regardless, he had things to tell her, things that couldn't wait. He should have told her first, of course, but who knew that things were going to get physical so fast. Not like he'd made any frickin' effort to slow it down or stop it...

Hell, might as well have tried to stop an avalanche with a bucket. The intensity of the attraction, and the raw need, coupled with the lupine instinct to lay claim, had simply overwhelmed all else.

Now, however, his thoughts were clear as crystal. He couldn't continue, he *would not* continue, without telling Neva what she needed to know about him. It was the right thing to do, even if it meant she never spoke to him again. Funny how doing the right thing often resulted in unpleasant consequences. And these would be soul damaging. *Good thing my soul is ruined already.*

He yearned to catch her scent, pull it deep into his lungs until it became part of him, but with the wind behind Travis, it wasn't going to happen. She would sense his approach, of course. Would she be excited, glad, relieved that he was back—or just annoyed by his disappearance? If he'd been in his human form, he might have laughed a little at that. *Of course* she'd be pissed at him.

Moments later, his heart leaped as he caught a glimpse of her in the bower. Relieved that she was still there, he slowed his pace and shifted form before he approached the part in the trees. "We have to talk, Neva," he began. "I have things to tell you." She stood on the far side, facing away from him, hugging herself as if cold. His first impulse was to go to her and wrap his arms around her, but he had things to say, difficult things that he dared not risk being distracted from.

"I know I told you that Changelings don't kill humans, that it's our highest law," he began. She nodded without turning around. Was she mad at him? Jesus, she wasn't crying, was she?

He hurried on, determined to get the words out. "But that doesn't mean it never happens. I didn't tell you about me and my brother. My younger brother, Jackson. Hell, we were both young—I was maybe twenty in human years, he was fourteen." Travis took a deep breath and tried to steady his voice, but it was so damned hard to talk about this. Hard to even *think* about this, after spending decades trying to avoid the wretched memory. Maybe it was a good thing after all that Neva wasn't looking in his direction. He might never get the words out if she did. "We were running as wolves, just messing around, you know? Wrestling, fighting, seeing who could jump the farthest, who was the fastest, that kind of shit. And we started chasing a deer, a *mulie*, the biggest buck we'd ever seen.

"It would have all been fine, except we weren't supposed to *be* wolves. Everyone in the pack was on high alert because it was hunting season. Everyone was supposed to stay on two legs, but when you're young, you think you're going to live forever. We thought we were so damn clever that nothing would happen to us. We could outsmart any stupid human hunters."

"What happened?" Neva asked, her voice soft and quiet.

"We ran straight into a party of hunters. Three were in the trees, just waiting for deer to walk under them. We didn't even know they were there until the deer went down. We didn't even hear the report of the rifle until the damn buck just dropped right in front of us. And then Jackson—Christ, my little brother, Jackson—he was taken down, too. One shot, one stupid fucking shot." Travis's voice shook, but he kept on going. "I felt it before I saw what happened, as if the bullet had gone through my own heart. I was behind a ways because I was going to let him catch the damn deer—you know, so he'd feel good about himself. Two hunters were already moving in to claim the trophies when I came out of the brush."

"You must have been wild."

"I lost it. I don't even know where my human side went, but my wolf took over. There were three hunters in the trees, two on the ground, and four back at their camp, and I killed every last one of them. Tore them to pieces—young, old, it didn't matter to me. I don't remember doing it, but I did it. I came to myself in the middle of the mess, after they were all dead." The tinny taste of blood had been on his tongue, dripping from his jaws and staining the golden tawny fur of his chest, but there was no point in relating such gory details.

"The bottom line is, I'm a murderer, Neva. I broke the highest and most absolute law that Changelings have." He paused for a long moment. "I buried my little brother far away from that place, and then I left. I never went back to the pack or to my family. I've never seen them since, any of them, and that was a long time ago."

"You banished yourself?"

"Yeah, I guess I did." He sighed. He hadn't known what else to do. He couldn't change what had happened, couldn't make it right or make up for it, no matter what. The fact that his inner wolf was responsible for the deed hardly mattered. Lives, once taken, could never be restored. He wished Neva would turn around now, and yet he dreaded it—surely there would be disgust and revulsion, the same things he felt toward himself and his wolf. There might even be fear on her beautiful face. It would devastate him, but it was no less than he deserved. He squared his shoulders and waited for her reaction. For his sentence.

Neva said nothing, and then he saw her shoulders shaking. Christ, not tears, please, anything but tears. "Neva, honey, don't," he said gently and reached out to her, stroking her hair and running the long, dark waves through his big fingers.

Abruptly, the hair in his hand became bright gold. "What the hell?" He dropped the suddenly blonde tress as if it were a rattlesnake. Neva turned around then, allowing the icy laughter she'd been suppressing to peal through the bower. Her exquisite face was oh so familiar and yet completely alien to him, and his blood chilled with realization.

It wasn't Neva.

(((● ●

Baker hugged the ground beneath a nearly impenetrable thicket of hawthorn and prayed that he wouldn't be detected. His muzzle and ears were badly cut by the long thorns that adorned the branches, but this inhospitable hiding place was his best and only hope. If any of Meredith's wolves realized he was there, they'd damn well have to come in here after him.

So far they were too busy watching the fun to notice that there was another player on the field. A battle royal raged between the golden wolf he'd been following and the fucking bitch queen herself. Gold and silver fur flew as they spilled out of the shelter of evergreens, biting and clawing, each vying for a throathold. Silently he cheered on the big male, even as he knew it wouldn't be a fair fight. Sooner or later, just as with Riley, Meredith would pull some of her damned magic out of her ass and gain the upper hand.

This time, however, she simply called in her minions. A dozen powerful werewolves took over what she started, and bore the golden wolf to the ground under their sheer weight alone. It was like watching linebackers dog-piling on a quarterback, but there was no referee to drag them off. Meredith sat back and licked her wounds, and Baker was glad to see that the tawny wolf had managed to do some damage before he went down. Still in lupine form, the bitch somehow managed a bored expression, as if the outcome of the struggle meant nothing to her. Baker wasn't buying it. She was a long way from home, and she'd brought twelve goons with her. Not only that, but she hadn't killed the guy with some scary-ass magic when he'd made her bleed. So whoever this big gold wolf was, he must be important.

Baker shook his head as his earlier prediction came true. The bitch queen lifted a paw, and a thick coil of slender scarlet cord simply appeared at her feet. He squinted to make out details. The cord was thicker than string and thinner than rope—and there was a strange sheen to it. Meredith bent her silver muzzle and daintily picked up the coil in her teeth. With a jerk of her head, she tossed it straight into the midst of the snarling pack.

Although Baker knew the struggle had been futile, he still felt a twinge of disappointment when the thugs stepped away to reveal the tawny wolf lying on the ground. Red blood stained his golden pelt, revealing slashes and bites in countless places, but it wasn't the wounds that kept him down. The strange red cord bound and muzzled the big werewolf. *Shit.* Not only had Baker wished the guy well, he'd hoped for some information from him. And he wouldn't mind shaking hands with him either (if either of them *had* hands). Golden Boy had held his own against impossible odds. Despite their size and muscle, several of his opponents were lame and bleeding far more profusely than he was.

Suddenly a voice reverberated in his head. It was anguished and desperate, yet potent enough that Baker winced and his brain recoiled at its strength. Unconsciously, he put a paw over his head.

Neva! Stay away from here—

The words were cut short, and the tawny wolf exhaled as if for the last time.

FIFTEEN

Neva wandered through the truck stop, wondering if she should take a chance on the busy diner that took up one side of the building, or if she should just grab some prepackaged snacks and get back on the road. The driver who'd given her a lift had been kind, but talkative. *Way more than talkative.* More like evangelistic. He'd called himself a "prepper" and advocated learning survival skills for the coming apocalypse. By the time they'd crossed two state lines, she knew more than she'd ever wanted to know about which bugs were edible, how to filter urine for water, and what everyday items could be turned into weapons.

In the end, she'd lied about her destination and bailed when he stopped for gas. Part of her—okay, a big part—wanted to wait around in hopes of Travis showing up. The more sensible side of her said that was a dumb idea and she ought to keep moving.

Her wolf had a whole different take on the subject. Neva could swear it was pacing inside her, more like a caged tiger than a wolf, and had been ever since she'd left Travis behind. It didn't like being away from him one bit. She supposed he was the only werewolf that her alter ego had met so far—and since he'd been there when her inner wolf was, well, *born*, so to speak, maybe it had imprinted on him. She didn't know.

Mate. Ours.

Neva stopped dead in the middle of reading a package of granola bars. *No,* she said to her wolf. *We had sex. That doesn't mean we're automatically mates.* She sensed confusion from her animal persona—and from herself as well. She'd never indulged in gratuitous sex before. It wasn't really in her nature, so why was she trying to pretend that's all it was? Of course, a lot of things had happened in that forest bower that she hadn't thought were in her nature. She'd felt incredibly wild and free, and yet deeply intimate. She'd chalked it up to being a new werewolf. Now she wondered: Had she really hitchhiked out of there to flee Meredith, or to run away from Travis? And to avoid what sex with him might mean for their relationship?

Oh no. She'd used the *R* word. Not out loud, but she'd *thought* it, dammit. She didn't have a *relationship* with Travis, did she? Wasn't she just a pain in his ass until he was satisfied she'd been properly introduced to the Changeling world? Hadn't it been his plan all along to leave her after that? Plans could change, though. So could hearts. She'd told herself repeatedly that her feelings for Travis were perfectly normal, red-blooded attraction to a big, strong, good-looking man. Emphasis on *normal*.

Now, however…if it wasn't love, it was suspiciously close to it. And Neva didn't know if that was good or bad or both. Pairing up with a werewolf had certainly never been in her plans. Of course, neither had becoming a werewolf herself. So if she really did have feelings for the guy, what was she doing alone in a truck stop, miles down the road?

The pain in her head erupted so violently that at first she thought she was having a stroke. It took her to her knees, gasping for air and holding her skull with both hands in case it blew apart. Travis's voice echoed loudly in every cell of her body—

And then it was gone. Just *gone*.

Shaking, sweating, she allowed herself to be helped to her feet by a purple-uniformed waitress and a trucker with a long, braided beard. "I'm okay," Neva said, although she wasn't convinced of it herself. "Just a sudden migraine—makes me lose my balance sometimes. It's already fading."

"You better sit down for a bit, hon." The waitress guided her to a booth and held her arm until she was settled in. "My cousin Ethan gets those, says they're a real bugger. Now can I bring you something, or do you want to lie down for a while? I got my RV out back if you need some peace and quiet. It ain't tidy, but it's clean."

"Thanks, that's really kind of you. I just need a glass of milk, and maybe some aspirin. I'll be okay if I just sit still." At least Neva sincerely hoped that was the case. At least the pain was gone—except for a residual ache as if she'd been banging her head on the nearest wall. "I guess I probably should eat, too." She thanked all her stars that she had a well-washed twenty in her pocket, courtesy of her jeans' previous owner.

The waitress smiled and left her a menu. Neva could hardly read it. Not because there was anything wrong with her eyes, but because it was pretty damn distracting to get a full-volume warning from somebody inside your brain. *Stay away from here.* Away from where? Tough to tell when she didn't know where the hell the guy was. She didn't know which bothered her more: the way he was able to connect with her so suddenly or the fact that his voice cut off so abruptly. Was he in trouble? What should she do now?

The waitress zoomed by and left a tall glass of milk and a small blister package of aspirin. "It's off the shelf in the store. Just pay Raymond at the till before you leave, hon," she called over her shoulder as she filled coffee cups at another table.

When the woman returned, Neva ordered the double bacon cheeseburger special with fries *and* onion rings, plus a milkshake. The waitress's eyebrows rose, but she didn't say a word as she wrote up the order and headed for the kitchen.

Stay away from here. Travis's words had been clear but not the meaning. Where the hell was *here*? Was it wherever he had disappeared to in such a hurry? Or was it the last place he'd seen Neva? Jeez, what if Meredith's gang had tracked them to their little love nest in the pines? That idea repelled Neva on several levels—it seemed like a violation to have their enemies trampling on the grass where she and Travis had come together so powerfully. A soft clenching at her core let her know that her body hadn't forgotten a single detail of that encounter.

The waitress brought her order just as Neva sighed heavily, and mistook the sound for approval.

"Looks good, don't it, hon? My husband, Carl, he's the cook, and he does a fine job, if I do say so. Lots of truckers come here just for his burgers. But if you have room afterward, you have simply *got* to try his rhubarb pie."

"Thanks," Neva said as the waitress breezed off to another table. She picked up the monstrous burger with both hands. She didn't know if there'd be any room for the pie afterward, but she was definitely going to devour every last grease-soaked calorie of the food before her. Not because she was starving (although she was) and not because she didn't know where her next meal was coming from (she didn't). She was going to eat this so her inner wolf was fully fueled, and *then* she was going to go looking for Travis.

(((● ●

Naked, Meredith inspected her image in the full-length mirror and noted with satisfaction that her skin was once again perfect in every way. The wounds she'd received from the golden wolf had vanished into nothingness as soon as she'd resumed her shapely human form. She drew a finger around one breast idly as she considered her newest prize, currently locked in a basement cell. The big werewolf's color wasn't the only unique thing about him. He was a true shape-shifter, born to a dual existence. Nearly every creature in her pack had been human until she made them otherwise. Those few she hadn't Changed herself, the werewolves she'd recruited here and there, had been transformed by someone else.

Just as she had been.

Meredith had traveled the country, studying magic in New England, New Orleans, and the American Southwest, experimenting and blending, until she'd developed a discipline that was uniquely hers. That was when she'd decided it was long past time to visit Europe in hopes of adding something new to her already formidable skills. But *new* didn't begin to describe what an attraction spell brought within her reach. Andrei de la Ronde was thin, white-haired, and quiet, easily mistaken for an aged librarian rather than the wealthy and powerful man he was. But that wasn't all that swam beneath the surface. If it wasn't for the psychic discernment she'd cultivated since childhood, she might have missed the shining blue aura that marked him as an honest-to-god werewolf.

Andrei hadn't known a thing about Meredith's talents and abilities, of course. Only that a striking blonde American appeared on his arm at a party and dazzled him with a whispered invitation. She'd learned a lot that first night in his arms. One: werewolves had incredible stamina—even if their human side appeared long in the fang. Sex created energy, and energy powered enchantments. This was a union that could fuel far greater spells than she had been able to accomplish with mere human males.

Two: Andrei was wealthier than most small countries, and he moved in powerful circles. There was very little knowledge and very few places he could not help her to access. And three: he was single, his wife having died some years back. There were no children, no exes, no relatives, *nobody* with whom she'd have to share all that money and power once she got her hands on it.

As always, Meredith carefully weighed effort against reward. She had no love for him, of course, but Andrei was remarkably easy to tolerate because he made few demands. It took very little to keep him happy, and he was a busy man, so she'd have ample time to pursue her one true love, which was magic. So really, the decision was a no-brainer. Once made, it was a simple matter to convince him that he wanted to marry her. She thought about weaving a potent little truth spell to make him reveal his lupine nature to her, but it proved unnecessary. He volunteered the information on his own—and, right on cue, she announced that she loved him anyway. The results were classic. Just like the old beauty and the beast story…

They wed according to her plan, traveled around the world according to her whim, and took up their main residence in Monaco, according to her taste. She thought she had it all. *And then he told her the rest of the story.* There was a way for beauty to become a beast as well! Shape-shifting spells were the most difficult to master in any magic culture—and to be able to change form at a moment's notice was beyond anything she'd ever read about in the most ancient of grimoires. And there was one more incredible perk: werewolves were extremely long-lived. While Andrei appeared to be in his seventies, in reality, he had already surpassed the life spans of several humans combined. With virtual immortality, what levels of power and spell craft might Meredith be able to reach?

Her generous new husband handed it all to her by simply biting her little finger. Dear Andrei—he actually shed a tear when he did it, fearing he might hurt his fair-haired girl, as he called her. Really, it was rather a shame that he was killed by a wild animal less than a year later...

Meredith sighed and turned her attention to her newest toy. The golden wolf was the first natural werewolf she'd met since Andrei—and a much more impressive specimen than her husband had been. Curious, she wanted to see the massive creature's human side. She'd tried to order the animal out of the way, like a lion tamer driving a wild beast back. Her magic was stronger than any whip and chair, yet the tawny animal did not budge. Instead, she could feel the great wolf calmly testing her, studying her. She was accustomed to instilling fear in others, but this creature regarded her with calculation instead of terror. And for the briefest of moments she'd felt a tiny thrill of fear herself—

She, Meredith de la Ronde, who feared no one.

To her surprise, it was exciting. She watched in the mirror as her nipples became erect, just from the memory of that brief flicker of fright. Her fingers brushed over them ever so lightly, and with lightning quickness, the delicate nerve endings fired the sensations through her entire body. Moisture appeared between her legs at once, and she scented the warm tang of her own arousal.

Interesting.

The wolfen persona had not fled, but departed from her view as casually as if it had turned its back on her and sauntered away. The message was very clear: not only did the animal have no fear of her, it was wholly confident that she would not harm the human that the wolf was leaving in its place. In its vivid eyes had been the promise of sudden and immediate retribution. Meredith chose to be amused by its threat. She would teach the foolish creature some respect—and fear—later.

While the werewolf's lupine form had been interesting, its human side was nothing short of fascinating to her. Andrei's fine features had seemed rather elegant, but this male? Definitely mountain-man material. Not only was he physically strong, but she'd admired the mental power he'd mustered to try and warn Geneva. None of Meredith's pack was so adept at telepathic communication, a frustrating lack when she wanted reports from the field. Was the ability more pronounced in a natural werewolf? And his force of will was evident when fighting against the spell that was dragging him into unconsciousness. The spell won, of course. *Magic always wins. And so do I.*

Someday Geneva was going to concede that fact. Someday soon the stupid little bitch was going to be on her hands and knees before Meredith, admitting at last that her big sister was superior in every possible way, and confessing her utter and complete loyalty. And then she would receive the opportunity to prove that devotion by facilitating Meredith's greatest magical accomplishment.

But right now, she had to find the brat.

All the trackers had been able to glean was that Geneva had gotten into a vehicle headed east. The scrying bowl had shown only the interior of an unknown truck stop, which was no help at all—they all looked alike. Meredith moved from the mirror to one of the glass walls overlooking the ocean. She adored the view. There was a forest of redwoods on three sides of the property, a paradise of delights when she ran on four legs. But it wasn't enough, nothing she had was enough compared to the powerful magic she craved. And she would have it, with or without her sister's cooperation.

Effort versus reward. Meredith had spent far too much time on her troublesome sister already. There was work demanding her attention in her spell room, crafts and incantations waiting to be finished, including her beloved pet project. Fortunately, although she'd been enraged by the discovery at the time, the unmistakable scents of recent sex and bonding in the pine grove had an upside: any further labor to capture Geneva was unnecessary. She couldn't imagine why Geneva had left the scene—the pair shouldn't have been out of reach of each other, never mind out of sight—but it made absolutely no difference. Even if Geneva hadn't been a willing participant, the brat's inner wolf would be drawn back to its new mate, whether she liked it or not.

So all Meredith had to do was wait for the little idiot to show up.

Meanwhile, she was going to test out some of her theories about born werewolves. Blood from her pack acted as a catalyst in some of her spells. Did the new werewolf's veins contain something stronger, more dynamic?

"Frederick," she said. Her voice was barely above a sultry whisper, but a balding red-haired man appeared at once in the doorway of her sprawling bedroom. Save for his pupils dilating ever so slightly, he didn't react at all to her nakedness. He wouldn't dare. "Have Zarita get a blood sample from our newest guest. No, better make that a pint."

"Would you like it delivered it to your workroom or to the kitchen, Ms. de la Ronde?"

"Workroom, of course. I have things to do." He disappeared, and she considered his odd question. Perhaps it wasn't so odd… After all, she often drank small amounts of human blood, taken from new recruits before she turned them. Usually she called for it to be added to a snifter of brandy or cognac when she'd been on a project in her workroom for hours. Spell casting was a nuanced art, and once started, had to be carried through to its natural end, even if that took *days*. You didn't take coffee breaks or naps or punch out at a certain hour, no matter how exhausted you were. Real magic couldn't be hurried or interrupted.

During one of her sessions, she'd discovered that a small taste of human blood gave her an enormous rush. In fact, it was enlivening, renewing not only her energy but often her enthusiasm. Further experimentation showed that a *full* glass would deliver a burst of amazing power and strength. The kitchen staff would bring it to her in a large crystal goblet as if it was the finest of liqueurs. Only *she* knew that it was much, much better than that. Ingesting blood had helped her to carry her latest spellcrafting project over the finish line more than once.

Sadly, the incredible effects were short-lived, lasting but an hour or so. And as soon as her human conscripts made their first shift to werewolf, their blood became utterly useless to her as a restorative. It was as if the transformation of the body's shape transformed the blood as well, permanently.

But the blood of a *natural* werewolf...Meredith made a thoughtful little moue at the mirror. That just might be worth sampling. She'd planned to utilize it in tonight's spells, but it wouldn't hurt to have a little pick-me-up while she worked.

SIXTEEN

Beneath his prickly fortress of hawthorn, Baker's sense of security evaporated when one of Meredith's trackers picked up on his presence. A grizzled black-and-gray wolf was close, so close that Baker could see its nostrils flare as it studied his scent—and he was certain the creature must be able to hear his heart hammering. Strangely, however, it didn't raise the alarm. Instead the tracker moved on to cast about for smells elsewhere. *Must be searching for someone else.* Apparently, trussing up the golden wolf like a holiday turkey wasn't enough for the bitch queen.

Baker didn't move, or even take a full breath, until his senses told him that all the wolves had left. And then he waited a long time to make damn fucking certain they were gone. Finally he crawled out from the thorny thicket, slowly and painfully. It was going to take some work—and no doubt some bizarre contortions with this animal body—to draw out some of the spines that were embedded in his hide, but the task would have to wait. *Better to get the hell out of here first.*

He'd taken note of the direction the bitch queen and her horde had gone, and he made sure to head the opposite way. Baker decided to shadow the highway from the cover of the woods that lined it. There was plenty of brush to hide him, but not so much that he had to push his way through. Which suited him fine, since it was a toss-up as to whether he had more hawthorn spines in his ass or in his muzzle.

He passed a pickup truck, abandoned by the side of the road. Too bad he couldn't figure out how to return to his upright-with-thumbs form. Unless the truck was out of gas, he could fix almost anything, and he wasn't above borrowing the vehicle. Strange how his priorities had shifted. It wasn't like he'd made a habit of stealing other people's cars in his past life—in fact, he'd have never done such a thing.

Now, however, everything was a matter of survival. His and Riley's.

Leaving the pickup behind, Baker followed the highway for another couple of miles until a flatbed rig hauling a pair of muddy backhoes slowed to a stop. Since it was headed the opposite way, he gave it only a fleeting glance—until the passenger door opened and it appeared that someone got out. Baker could see nothing with the truck between him and the passenger, and for reasons he couldn't identify, he stood still until the rig pulled away. Just before the person was revealed, a strange new sense hit him between the eyes. Or rather, between the *nostrils*. Conditions had combined—wind, temperature, hell, even barometric pressure, probably—to bring him a single scent. Werewolf, like him. In human form. And female.

More important than any of that, he knew exactly who she was before his sight confirmed it.

(((● ●

The truck slowly sped up and reentered its lane on the highway, but Neva watched it disappear without really seeing it. Her animal senses were on hyper alert, reaching out for any sign of Meredith and her thugs. Neva could definitely smell them, but only faintly. Of course, the wind was from the wrong direction—and Travis had lectured her on staying downwind of enemies.

Unless she wanted to broadcast her own presence, she needed to make her approach from a slightly different direction. At least she'd had the sense to ask the truck driver to drop her off a couple of miles from the pickup that she and Travis had left behind. If she crossed to the same side of the road as the vehicle and walked down to it using the cover of the woods, then she wouldn't be detected by her enemies. She hoped.

It was a longer hike than it looked, however. Thankful there wasn't much traffic at this time of night, Neva crossed the four lanes of pavement without encountering any vehicles. She had to veer around a flattened raccoon on the center line, however. The *ew* factor was bad enough, especially with a Changeling's intense sense of smell, but she had to admit that the creep factor was worse. The spillage of blood and guts reminded her too much of things she wished she could unsee from her time at Meredith's mansion.

The gravel shoulder led to the steep edge of a wide ditch, and *of course* there was water at the bottom. *Crap.* She was soon picking her way through cattail clumps and starting every time a frog jumped out of her way. She'd soaked her shoes for the third time when a car slowed down. It sped away quickly after she gave the driver a smile and a thumbs-up. *Probably didn't reassure them,* she thought. *I'll bet they left because I look like a crazy woman.* Heaven only knew when she'd last brushed her hair.

Above the rotted-vegetable smell of stagnant water and the tangy mix of rubbery asphalt and fuel and dead raccoon from the highway, the scents of Meredith and her pack continued to dissipate. Her sister had definitely been in the area, but she had just as definitely left. Neva thought she could detect Travis's scent, but it, too, was faint. Why?

Neva slogged up the opposite side of the ditch in squishy shoes and set out for the forest beyond. Road maintenance crews kept a hundred-foot swath cut down and cleared along this section of highway. The stiff, dry stubble of brush was maybe six inches high—enough to stab mercilessly at her ankles—and she remembered when she'd foolishly insisted Travis help her Change back to human form. She'd ended up shoving her way through the bushes that lined the trail, naked and barefoot. He'd been pissed at her, but he hadn't left. Instead, he'd stayed just out of sight, only to come running when she needed him. And his wolf—the great tawny wolf that lived within him—had been oh so gentle with her poor bleeding feet.

It'd be great if Travis popped out of the brush right about now. She'd be genuinely glad to see him, even if he was a pain in the ass at times. She trudged into the cool, dark shelter of the trees with relief. A well-worn game trail beckoned, undoubtedly smoothed by countless herds of deer over the years, and she took it gratefully. Her thoughts were divided between missing Travis and contemplating removing the wet shoes that were even now rubbing blisters into her feet. Suddenly the path before her sprang to impossible life. Heaving up from forest floor, the path buckled and shed leaves and earth as if a full-grown tree was emerging. Instead, a huge wolf shook itself free of the debris and faced her, its drawn lips exposing merciless teeth that gleamed in the shadows.

(((● ●

Travis's stomach lurched as dizziness threatened to send him reeling back into unconsciousness. He held himself motionless, breathing through his mouth, fighting to stay awake as if trying to keep his head above water. Finally the vertigo receded and his equilibrium settled. He opened his eyelids to scant slits in case he was being watched, and heaved a sigh when his wolfen senses assured him that he was alone.

There wasn't else much to be relieved about.

Travis was lying on a metal bench in a smooth concrete cell. There were no windows, only a small grate set at eye level in a heavy steel door. A tiny fluorescent light buzzed and flickered in a cage set into the twelve-foot ceiling. He didn't know where he was, but he was certain of who was responsible for his captivity. Neva's crazy-ass sister, Meredith, was behind this.

Christ. The only way this could be worse was if Neva was a prisoner, too. Just as he'd gone down beneath the hostile pack, Travis had tried to warn her. He had no idea if the message had gotten through before he'd been hit with—

He frowned. *Magic.* He'd been hit with the genuine article, impacted as surely as if someone had clubbed him with a fence post. And it certainly wasn't the clumsy work of an amateur. Just another little detail that Neva had failed to mention. In a world where true magic had become scarce, her sister wielded a stunning quantity of raw power with ease and finesse. *Might have been good to know.* That, and one other tiny piece of info that hadn't been revealed to him:

Meredith wasn't just Neva's sister. She was her fucking *twin*.

He'd made the biggest confession of his life, laid his soul bare, not to the woman he was falling hard for, but to someone who was most likely his worst nightmare. Goddess help him, not only did it turn his stomach to think of this vicious lunatic knowing his most intimate secrets, but he knew damn well this was going to bite him in the ass one way or another.

He had to get out of here.

As he sat up, another wave of dizziness washed over him, and he gripped the edges of the bench until his knuckles whitened. Eventually his head cleared—then a new realization had him ice cold and sweating at the same time.

I was a wolf when I passed out. Why the hell am I waking up on two legs?

Changelings didn't revert to human in their fucking sleep—that only happened in old B movies. His wolf wouldn't leave him vulnerable like this, even if it could. In fact, he had the opposite problem, a wolf that was too damn protective. Travis reached deep, searching, calling. The creature he'd shared his existence with since he was born was AWOL.

((((●

The threat hadn't fully registered in Neva's mind before she was baring her own fangs at the giant wolf. She hadn't called on her alter ego, but in the face of danger it sprang instantly to rampant life. In less than a heartbeat, she was on four feet, her dark fur bristling to make herself look larger than she was. Her human side was incensed at the intruder, and shouted at him as loudly as she could in mindspeak: *What the hell do you want?*

To Neva's surprise, the big wolf looked uncertain of himself, although he was far bigger than she was. She waited, but he gave no answer, only continued to snarl and growl at her. Her heightened senses told her that, thankfully, the creature was alone—and *holy crap*, she'd met him before.

She snapped her teeth in his direction. *You. You're one of Meredith's new batch, aren't you? Barry? Barney?*

He shook his head, opening and closing his mouth. Faintly, tentatively, a word sounded in her head. *Baker.*

Okay, Baker, you can stand down now. What's up with scaring the bejesus out of me? To her surprise, the big gray wolf again showed his long teeth, the heavy ruff around his thick neck and the fur along his spine standing on end.

I know who you are. You're the bitch queen's sister. I should kill you right now. His words were more confident now, stronger, as if he was just getting the hang of talking mind to mind. *But you're useful, so you're gonna come with me.* He took a menacing step forward.

Neva was shocked even as a long, low growl escaped her throat. *Me? What the hell did I ever do to you? I just escaped from my lunatic sister myself!*

Only her wolf's instinctive reaction saved her from Baker's sudden lunge. As it was, she left a mouthful of fur in the savage teeth as she dove right between his front legs, spun out to the side, and ran for her life.

(((((●

Travis supposed he should be flattered that Meredith sent no fewer than a dozen guards to fetch him. And even without his alter ego's help, he managed to bloody a few faces before they drove him to the floor and shackled him hand and foot. Walking was more than a little awkward after that, but he had burly guys on either side of him holding him up, their meaty hands hiking his armpits to his ears. Seemed familiar—he was fairly certain he'd allowed a couple of bouncers to escort him from their club like this once.

Key word there—*allowed.*

This was different. He didn't know where he was going, and he certainly didn't have any choice in the matter. The cuffs and ankle restraints he should have been able to shatter with little effort were holding him fast. Even the links of the chains had no give at all in them. Had his Changeling strength failed him? What had happened to his wolf? With difficulty he brought the cuffs near his nose as he shuffled fast to keep from being dragged by his captors, but his senses detected no silver in the dark metal.

What he *did* detect was the faint but unmistakable mingled scents of blood and death.

Magic.

Not the earthy kind that his grandfather had practiced with gratitude and reverence all his long life. Not the happy *greet the dawn* and *make offerings to the four directions* and *build bonfires to celebrate the turn of the year* kind of stuff at all.

Travis was well and truly amazed now that Neva had ever managed to escape her sister's grasp. Because what Meredith was practicing was deep, dark, and dangerous. His stomach turned over as he realized exactly where she was getting all her power. His grandfather had warned him about such things. But he had been a stupid kid at the time and thought it was just a scary story, the kind you tell around campfires and then everybody screams and laughs and passes the s'mores.

He *so* did not feel like laughing.

They came to a stop in front of a glass elevator just off a massive circular lounge. The room was centered around a fire pit big enough to roast an elephant. The entire house was on a scale that boggled Travis's mind—and filled with sumptuous furnishings, exquisite artworks, and everything a millionaire (better make that a *billionaire*) could possibly want. It was obvious that Meredith already had a great deal of money. Nobody bought this kind of stuff with a garden-variety plastic card. She had followers and supporters—willing or not. And if she was a Changeling, then she already had a fountain of youth, so to speak.

So what's the end game? What the hell else could she possibly want?

Travis was shoved into the elevator and his face pressed against its back wall by the guards. Through the transparent material—acrylic, he thought, not glass—he watched three more floors glide by. The fourth was an architect's dream, a penthouse with floor-to-ceiling windows offering a 360-degree view of old-growth forest and restless ocean. The ceiling had a central skylight the size of a helicopter pad, and he caught a quick glimpse of afternoon thunderheads rising high into the blue expanse.

He was hauled out of the crowded compartment and thrown to his knees on pure-white, deep-pile carpet. Two guards roughly shoved his head down and held it there so he could only see the floor—until finely manicured toes sporting brilliant red polish came just within his line of sight. The guards stepped back, and Travis looked up into the face of a Marilyn Monroe wannabe—platinum-blonde hair, red lipstick, perfect complexion, and round breasts threatening to spill from a slinky white dress. Only the eyes were wrong. They were dark, and harder and colder than the diamonds that dripped from her ears. Nothing like the warm come-hither expression of a Hollywood goddess graced Meredith's flawless face, even though she smiled radiantly.

Sharks can smile, too. Still, despite his dangerous circumstances—and he did not doubt he was in extreme danger—Travis felt strangely relieved. It came from the fact that he could see nothing of Neva in the face of the monster in front of him. Bone structure, yes, but nothing important, nothing that counted. Neva and Meredith were as different from each other as angels and demons. Only one had a soul. Meredith's humanity was long gone.

She played with the wavy hair that always fell forward over his right brow, twirling it around her finger and tugging on it playfully. "You look like a fair-haired Elvis." She laughed. "No wonder my silly little sister was infatuated with you. But you'd look *so* much better," she purred in a deeper tone, stroking his hair back and bringing her face close to his, "with *me.*"

She kissed him then, and swirled her tongue over his mouth before drawing back. Repulsed, his first impulse was to spit at her, but he decided that wouldn't be smart given the current situation. He settled for a total lack of response. It seemed she wasn't overly bothered by that…until she Changed and tore the throat out of the guard next to him. Arterial blood spurted onto the snowy-white carpet as the man's life pumped away. And he didn't utter a sound or lift a finger, or even change expression. Just died at the feet of a silver wolf.

The creature was big, almost as big as Travis's wolf. Wagging its plume of a tail, it grinned widely at him with bloody fangs. But it was the overbright eyes that arrested his attention. Travis could see plainly that the animal was as insane as a rabid dog. His grandfather had spoken once, in hushed tones, of Changelings whose inner wolf had gone completely mad. According to the ancient stories, there was only one cause for the dreaded and incurable condition—the continued ingestion of human blood over a long period of time. It was the unspoken subscript to the highest Changeling law. Not just *don't kill*, but *don't drink*.

Travis's face must have registered the horror he felt, because Meredith was laughing at him when she resumed her human form. Not a single drop of blood marred her face now—there was only the bright red lipstick, perfectly applied. She waved airily at the body and commanded the remaining guards, "Get this out of here and find somebody to clean up the mess. I like this carpet." As they hastened to comply, she walked slowly, sensuously over to Travis. At first he feared another kiss—until she grabbed him by the hair and yanked his head back with astonishing strength. If he'd been human, the move would have broken his neck.

"Blood is very powerful, you know, but not all blood is created equal," she crooned. "You, my dear, are something quite special. I could become very, *very* fond of you." She kissed him lavishly then.

It might have been smarter to play along with the crazy bitch, but Travis just couldn't manage it. In fact, if his damn wolf hadn't gone missing, he'd probably try to bite her. Alone, the best he could do was try not to gag—

And choke her with his wrist shackles.

She was too busy forcing her attentions on him, and far too confident, to see it coming. In an eye blink, Travis had the chain wound around her neck like a garrote and was doing his best to strangle her.

A sudden blast of blue light slammed him against a marble pillar on the other side of the room. The impact rang in his ears and made him see stars. And the very last thing he saw was a silver wolf shaking its head and snarling at him.

SEVENTEEN

It was hard to believe she could run this fast. Neva's lupine body was stretched full out, belly close to the ground, her hind legs overreaching her front ones like a cheetah. She was glad her wolf was in charge, because she couldn't imagine thinking on the fly at this speed, swerving and dodging and leaping, making dozens of decisions per second. Under bush, over rock, through thickets, around roots. She had no idea where on earth she was headed, and perhaps her wolf didn't know, either. Escape was all that mattered, and while her pursuer was still hot on her trail, he'd been unable to close the gap between them. *So far.* She wished she was more experienced, but at least the bigger werewolf was as new to his animal state as she was—and she'd had the benefit of Travis's reluctant mentoring. As far as she could tell, Baker was on his own.

Why is he so pissed at me? She wasn't responsible for what Meredith did. For crying out loud, she'd even attempted suicide to avoid serving her sister, to prevent the harm she would be forced to cause to innocent people, and perhaps to take a weapon out of Meredith's hands. Didn't that count for something? *What does the goddamn universe want from me?*

She yipped in surprise as her wolf made a sudden swerve into what looked like an impenetrable wall of thornbushes. Head lowered, eyes squinted to mere slits to protect them, the creature simply crashed through the unforgiving brush. *Ow, dammit!*

Long spines raked through her thick pelt, cutting her deeply, but Neva's alter ego didn't slacken its pace in the slightest. In fact, it seemed to be trying for even *more* speed. That's when she felt it gathering itself. *What the hell are you—*

The ground disappeared below her as the wolf burst through the branches into open air. *You're going to kill us!* Neva held her breath as she sailed over a wide ravine she would *never, ever* have tried to jump in a million years. The wolf hit the edge of the opposite bank hard, scrabbling for purchase with its hind claws until it once again stood on solid ground. Before Neva could even muster a sigh of relief, the creature was racing away at breakneck speed again.

A panicked yelp sounded behind her, followed by a frustrated howl. Her wolf slowed at last and pranced—actually *pranced*—obviously pleased with itself. It came to a welcome stop by a spring that bubbled up through some twisted tree roots.

Good trick.

The creature sounded downright smug, and Neva was forced to agree. *Helluva good trick.*

Like wolf now?

Neva was taken aback by the question. In all her attempts to reject the creature she was becoming, even destroy it, she never once considered how *it* felt. Before she'd made her first Change, she remembered Travis trying to reassure her inner wolf, and telling her not to scare it. She'd thought he was nuts at the time. It didn't seem so crazy now. *Er, good wolf. Very good wolf. Nice going.*

A pleased sensation spread through her like good whiskey.

She took her time slaking her thirst at the spring as angry howls continued to echo through the forest. Finally they subsided, and she ambled back toward the ravine, sides still heaving and tongue lolling as she panted to cool herself. *Let's see if Baker's willing to listen to reason now.*

The first thing she noticed was that the ravine wasn't really a ravine at all. It was a sinkhole about thirty feet across and just as deep, a place where the roof of a cave had collapsed in the distant past. There was no meandering creek at the bottom of it, just a ton of rocky debris and a small, stagnant pool. And Baker. His chin rested on his paws as he lay on a slab of rock that looked to be the size of a Buick.

Hey, you all right?

He started and stared up at her. *What the fuck do you care?*

Look, I'm not my sister, okay? I was trying to tell you that when you went all Cujo on me. I don't work for her, I don't like her, and I'm trying to get away from her.

You're a werewolf just like she is!

Duh. So are you, smart guy. I didn't want to be a werewolf, but she only cares about what she wants. I got forced into it, and I'm betting you did, too.

The gray wolf looked down at his feet and sighed. *Yeah. We both did, me and Riley. He didn't get away. He's—he's still there, but I don't know if...*

His voice in her head trailed away, and Neva sighed, too. He didn't know if his friend was still alive. *So maybe we should get you out of that hole.*

I can't jump it, not straight up. I haven't got the distance to get up enough momentum.

You'll have to Change so you have hands to climb with.

I don't know how.

Man, did she ever understand that problem! Only Travis wasn't here to deliver instructions. Could she remember enough of what he'd said to be able to explain it to Baker? Sure, she could shift her form now, but being able to *do* something and being able to *describe* what you're doing were two very different things. She looked down at the big wolf that had threatened and chased her. He looked small and kind of forlorn now. Yet there was no guarantee that he wouldn't attack her the moment he was free. *Crap.* She couldn't just leave him. She didn't know where the hell Travis had gone, she didn't know the phone numbers of any superheroes, and she was the only coach available to help Baker.

Look, I'm not really good at it myself, but I'll try to help, okay?

Yeah? The gray wolf scrambled to his feet. That was when she saw that he was favoring one of his front legs.

Jesus, you're hurt.

It's a sprain. Maybe an ankle, at least I think that's what it is. A wolf leg doesn't quite match up with a human one, or even a horse leg—the joints are in the wrong places.

Her wolf's voice interjected in her mind: *All right places!*

It sounded indignant, and Neva rolled her eyes, not an easy feat in a lupine body. *Hush,* she said to her alter ego, then turned her attention back to Baker. *Look, if we can get you to shift, your leg'll probably heal up in the transition. I don't know how it works, but it does.* She was *so* looking forward to her own punctured hide getting fixed when she Changed. *Picture your human self in your mind...*

((((●

I'm sure getting the frickin' grand tour here. Travis had drifted in and out of consciousness while being dragged through the luxurious mansion once again, getting glimpses of its elegant rooms and lavish decor as he passed. He couldn't say that he liked *this* room much. The first thing he'd noticed, before he'd even opened his eyes, was the cloying stink. The air was thick with blood and death, the same scents that he had detected on his shackles, but amplified to nauseating levels. The windowless room was dark, and he sensed he was deep underground. His natural night vision adjusted to show that the space was enormous, almost ballroom-size, and perfectly round. Cold as a wine cellar, too—or a morgue. He wasn't usually bothered by the cold, what with his high body temp and all, but he shivered just the same. Of course, it didn't help that he was currently shirtless and hanging upside down from his shackles against a polished marble wall. Or that his head pounded with every heartbeat.

Hundreds of candles stood ready all around the perimeter of the room, and every one of them flamed to glorious life when Meredith came in hours later. *Some people just like to make an entrance.*

The white marble floor was vividly illuminated then—and what he saw there made his skin crawl. Signs and symbols were carefully drawn with black and gray powders, as well as strange words in languages no longer spoken. Many were drizzled with blood in complicated patterns. A fresh corpse with its chest torn open lay at the foot of a marble dais, upon which was the only furniture in the entire room: a throne-like chair.

As before, Meredith casually ordered the guards to remove the body as if it was simply trash. *Christ, where does she put them all?* It hit him like a punch to the heart then—the powder that formed all the creepy drawings on the floor was actually made of ashes, and the ashes weren't from anything innocent like wood. It accounted for both the god-awful smell and the oily feel of evil that clung to it.

As soon as the guards left, Meredith casually stepped out of her clothes, revealing a lithe figure that was breathtaking in its perfection. Her only ornament was a silvery chain with a black stone pendant on it that swung between her full, round breasts. She faced him, making sure to display herself as fully as possible as she twisted her long blonde hair over her head and bound it with a jeweled clasp. "I like to work sky clad," she announced with a sly smile.

Travis didn't give a damn what she liked. He had a throbbing headache, and his body felt like it had been worked over with a baseball bat. That could easily have happened while he was out, but it was more likely the aftereffects of being in close proximity to a powerful werewolf when she shifted form. *Werewolf.* That's what she was, a devouring monster beneath an appealing human exterior. He wouldn't grace the insane bitch with the word *Changeling.* He had taken lives himself, and he lived with the regret every day, but this woman killed casually, whimsically— and goddamn frequently.

With a word, she doused all the candles but one, a squat black one the size of a coffee can that stood in the midst of the mysterious artwork on the marble floor. The candle had three wicks, and the flames burned at least a foot tall, yet its light was all but lost in the vast, cavern-like expanse. Thick black shadows veiled much of the room even from Travis's Changeling sight. Meredith appeared unconcerned, and he assumed she had enough night vision for whatever task she planned. She knelt at one side of the room amid a variety of small clay pots and urns and struck a red spark from a pair of stones. Instead of fizzling out, the spark grew larger, rising from the marble floor until it hovered a couple of feet over her head. In its ominous crimson light, Meredith began to add her ghastly powder to the drawings, only pausing to make notes in a leather-bound book. Wholly focused on her work, she ignored Travis completely. Whatever words she uttered now were in a language he didn't recognize. Sometimes she sang, but the notes were discordant, in a strange minor key that raised the hair on the back of his neck.

He could swear that unnatural things writhed in the shadows.

Years ago, at a ceremonial sand painting in a Navajo community, Travis had watched the *Hataɫii,* the medicine man, create beautiful colored drawings on the floor of large hogan. The man had sung intricate blessings and chants for hours as he worked. His purpose was to heal, to restore balance and harmony. If there was a polar opposite to that ritual, Travis thought, it was happening in this room right now. His bones felt like ice, and this time it had nothing to do with the temperature.

Maybe this is karma come calling. Perhaps the universe was finally balancing the scales and Travis would pay for what he had done in his younger days. He couldn't take his own life—it was the first thing he'd thought to do after his wolf had killed the hunters, but of course, the damn wolf wouldn't allow it. Chances were good, however, that his life was soon to be taken from him. *Maybe that's the way it's supposed to be.* And for once, his wolf probably couldn't save him.

He still didn't know where the hell his alter ego had disappeared to. The bitch had probably worked some weird-ass hoodoo that separated him from his wolf. However it had happened, he'd never felt so naked in his life. Taking stock of what he had left to work with against Meredith and her foul magic, he was forced to admit things didn't look promising for him.

The only good thing in all of this was that Neva must have escaped. Aware of his relationship with her, Meredith would surely have taunted him with her by now if she had her. He hoped he'd taught Neva enough to manage her new life as a Changeling. He hoped, too, that she'd remember him. Maybe she'd remember him as a pain in the ass. Or maybe, he hoped most of all, she'd remember what she told him: "You can be a real jerk sometimes, but you're *decent*."

As epitaphs went, it wasn't bad.

((◖ ◖ ●

If ever there was anyone who didn't have an aptitude for shape-shifting, Baker figured it was him. Geneva had done her level best to coach him—although she claimed it was a case of the blind leading the blind—and still, it took most of the fucking afternoon before he finally sensed something different, something faint and elusive floating just at the edge of his perception. Mentally, he reached for it with everything he had.

And stood on two feet.

Stunned, he looked down at himself. Geneva had promised him it wouldn't hurt, but he hadn't expected that to be true, not after the hell he'd been through turning into a wolf in the first place. And he was downright amazed at how *fast* he had Changed—well, if you excluded the hours of mental exertion that preceded it.

He gave himself the once-over, flexing his fingers and then his toes. Whatever part of his leg he'd strained as an animal seemed to be just fine now. In fact, everything seemed fine—except he was buck-assed naked. Hastily glancing upward, he was relieved to see that the dark wolf, Geneva, was politely sitting with her back to him.

Turning his attention to the sheer sides of the sinkhole, Baker studied the limestone walls until he found a route he liked. He didn't have gloves and climbing shoes, but he didn't seem to notice the lack at all. Not only was he somehow tougher and stronger, his balance was heightened and he was surer of himself, confidently reaching for handholds that were mere pockmarks. Baker scaled the rock face in record time.

Still, when he hauled himself over the edge and got to his feet, the dark wolf had already been replaced by a pretty woman with thick dark hair that tumbled over her slim shoulders in waves. She stood just out of arm's reach and turned as he stood up, thankfully keeping her golden-brown eyes strictly on his face.

He could almost count the freckles on her nose and cheekbones and—

"Hey, you're *dressed*!" he protested. "How'd you pull that off?"

"With difficulty, believe me."

"Well, Jesus, tell me how to do it, will ya?"

She sighed and put a hand to her head. "Look, it took me all afternoon to teach you how to shift—I doubt I could explain how to keep your clothes. It's a lot more complicated than Changing your form. Maybe Travis could tell you once I find him. He's a much better teacher."

Geneva. *Neva*. One and the same. Baker felt like a complete idiot for not catching on sooner. "Um, he wouldn't be a big yellow wolf, would he?" He hoped he was wrong, even as he knew damn fucking well he wasn't. The golden wolf had called out a warning to *Neva*.

She brightened at once. "Yeah, that's him. Did you see him? Do you know where he is?"

"I'm really sorry. The bitch queen's got him."

EIGHTEEN

Neva sat with her back against a fallen log, staring at the campfire Baker had insisted on making. She would have been too cautious to risk it, but they were near a town and it would be less obvious to anyone looking for them than if they built it out in the middle of nowhere. And she had to admit, the flames were strangely comforting. It was probably part of the human DNA, needing to build fires to keep the monsters away. What did Changelings use to keep *their* monsters away? Did they have any, or were they just not afraid of anything?

She was definitely afraid. Her sister was a monster, and now the monster had Travis. Meredith also had Baker's friend Riley. Hell, Meredith had a whole bunch of people, each of whom must matter to *someone*. How on earth were two green Changelings going to go up against the bitch queen, as Baker had so aptly named her, and not be captured, killed, zombified, or worse, within the first three minutes?

All Neva knew was that she had to try. Her inner wolf was pining for Travis, and frankly—though it was mortifying to admit it—she was, too. Who'd have guessed? But even if she didn't care about him a bit, there was no way she could leave him in Meredith's merciless clutches, any more than she could maroon Baker in the sinkhole. It would be unconscionable. And if that was true, if that's what she really believed, then she'd had a responsibility all along. The damn universe did indeed have a plan for her, a totally insane get-yourself-killed-or-worse kind of plan. It wasn't enough to escape from her sociopathic twin, not enough to prevent herself from being used by Meredith to hurt people.

Neva had to stop her.

If this was destiny, then her destiny sucked. How the hell was she going to accomplish such an impossible task? Baker was determined to go back and free his friend, but he didn't have any ideas, either. In fact, they hadn't even found him any clothes yet, other than a torn-up plaid shirt in a ditch that he'd fashioned into what he laughingly called a *kilt*. It was more like a loincloth, really, but they were both more comfortable now that his dangly bits were covered up.

A glowing branch collapsed in the fire, sending up a shower of yellow sparks. It put Neva in mind of the static buildup that occurred during shape-shifting, and its telltale shower of blue sparks afterward. A new thought occurred to her. When she'd faced Meredith before, Neva had been wholly human. Now she was more than that, with a repertoire of lupine skills she hadn't begun to try out yet. She was Changeling.

Wolf can help?

Sheesh, was she ever going to get used to her alter ego listening in on her thoughts? It might be a handy way to communicate, but it was still disconcerting. And so was talking to herself, but hey, maybe it was past time to have an in-depth conversation. *Yes,* Neva said simply, tightening the focus of her mindspeak as Travis had taught her so that only the glossy dark creature that shared her existence could hear. *Yes, need wolf's help.*

Overall, Meredith was pleased with the results of her experiments. She'd begun with small and simple spells, of course, adding drops of blood to them from the pint obtained earlier from the big blond shape-shifter. And when she'd run out of that, she simply went straight to the source and lightly scored his chest with the curved steel blade of her boline, collecting the precious drops in a blue clay pot the size of a robin's egg. She used her fingers to wipe up the few drops that remained glistening on his skin—after all, it wouldn't do to waste them—and tasted them as soon as she turned her back to him.

There was no doubt about her body's reaction. This werewolf's blood was far more powerful than any human blood she'd sampled before. More powerful than *any* blood. She'd been working all night now, and she felt as fresh as if she'd just begun. If only she'd thought to try Andrei's blood while he was still alive, she could have known all this a long time ago. She might even have kept the dear old guy around. At the time, however, she wasn't as advanced magically as she was now, hadn't even begun to consider that there might be a more potent substance than human blood out there.

After all, none of her books had ever mentioned it.

It was certainly written in her own grimoires now. Who knew, perhaps she was writing a new chapter in magical history. Of course, no one would ever know, because she didn't plan to show it to anyone else. *The first rule of power is don't share it.* Meredith glanced over at the shape-shifter hanging upside down on the wall. Dozens of long, razor-thin cuts striped his chest with minute beads of blood welling up here and there. She giggled as she imagined writing a blog of magical tips. *Helpful hint—Always have a live source ready at hand when you're spell crafting.*

Tapping her lip with her finger, she considered him. Her new toy was big, strong, powerful, and a born werewolf. She'd bet he was even better than Andrei in bed—and not only did she deserve a little fun after working so hard, but the energy could also power some fabulous spells.

The only wrench in her plans was his poor attitude. *Of all the bad luck...*As it turned out, her latest prize belonged to that utterly frustrating 1 percent that seemed completely immune to her control. Magic couldn't even charm his name out of him. There was no help for it; he would simply have to be killed as soon as she was done with him. He was too dangerous otherwise. In fact, she should have that Riley slaughtered, too, and sooner rather than later.

She chided herself then. *Now darling, that's how you've always handled the situation.* Those who opposed her were simply killed. It was effective, it was convenient, and it was cheap, but it didn't get rid of the long-term problem. Plus it prevented her from fully utilizing that curious 1 percent. She should be experimenting to see if there was something valuable in *their* blood, too. What if she was missing something? *Besides,* she said to herself. *Think of the challenge it would be.*

Drawing herself up to her full height, she dusted the ash from her hands. A challenge always excited her, and she idly fondled the curls between her legs with one hand as she contemplated what she might do with this big, handsome specimen. She would break him. She *would.* Because if she could find a way to compel him, then there wouldn't be a werewolf or human left in the world whom she could not bend to her will.

Her laughter echoed throughout the great empty expanse of the marble-clad room, startling the subject of her plans into opening his eyes.

(((((●

Baker shook his head. "No, I'm telling you that Riley wasn't taken over and neither was I. I don't know how this mind-control thing works, but nothing happened to me *or* him. In fact, the dumb ass picked a fight with your sister."

"You're kidding me. That's suicide," said Neva.

"It almost was. She wanted him alive, though, at least for now, so her goons dragged him off after she beat the living shit out of him."

"And when she ran off with the rest of the pack, you didn't want to follow? No impulse, no urge, no compulsions, *nothing*?"

"I don't get why you find it so amazing—you left her, too. And nothing's dragged you back yet."

Nothing except her fear for Travis and her reluctant acceptance of an impossible task: to stop her twin. "Maybe I was able to get away because Meredith hadn't put a spell on me yet. She may have counted on her ability to control me without it." It made the most sense. Meredith had been bossing her around since they were babies sharing a playpen together. Taking her toys. Hitting and pinching her. Working up tears and successfully blaming Neva for things that got broken, wrecked, or went missing around the house. When they went to school, Meredith stole away her friends, spread rumors about her, tattled to the teachers about made-up crap. In general, Meredith had done her utmost to make Neva's life a misery. In high school, she'd told *everybody* that Neva had STDs. The fact that it was completely untrue didn't stop the teasing. Still, Neva had managed to have one new boy interested in her enough to ask her to the graduation dance—until Meredith convinced him to take her instead. She even had sex with him in the parking lot at the back of the high school, knowing that Neva would hear of it.

So of course *Meredith expected to continue controlling me,* she thought. *Why waste magical effort on a dog that was already trained?*

Or has magic been involved all along?

169

Neva frowned. She'd never thought to ask that question before, perhaps because it was only recently that she'd learned of Meredith's powers. Many little memories began coming together to form a frightening picture. Sure, Neva had been surprised to see her sister's command of magic, but if she really thought it through, hadn't the signs been there much earlier? Exactly how had Meredith fooled so many people into believing that she was the "good" child? Almost everyone—Mom, Dad, uncles, aunts, in fact *any* other adults—immediately accepted Meredith's version of events as the truth. Neva was almost never asked for her side at all. No one seemed to consider for a moment that she had an identical twin. Not even the police who showed up at the door when she was sixteen and charged her with driving a stolen car into a convenience-store window. Neva had been home all night, but nobody seemed to be able to hear her when she told them that. Even her lawyer didn't question a thing.

So just how long had Meredith been practicing magic? Since high school? Middle school? Hell, what about *kindergarten*?

Unaware of her train of thought, Baker poked the fire with a stick, causing a collapse of several glowing branches. "You know, maybe it works like hypnosis."

"What does?"

"The bitch queen's magic. I mean, some people can't be hypnotized, right?"

"So maybe some people can't be compelled by her magic?"

"Yeah, like that. Or maybe it's an animal thing, because we're werewolves now. They say that animals can't be hypnotized, but I think they *can*. I've seen a guy who could handle some pretty mean-spirited horses like they were pet dogs, but nobody else could do it. He said he started out practicing with small animals when he was young—"

Whatever else Baker said was lost in the roaring noise between her ears. *Omigod, the pets.* Every hapless creature that was ever adopted by the Ross family had vanished. Turtles, fish, parakeets, cats, dogs...all ran away or were "lost." As an adult, Neva figured the pets were probably dying and her parents were just covering it up, unwisely trying to spare their kids. But what if Meredith was involved with the disappearances? Was she practicing magic on them? Or something even worse?

Neva felt ill, but gave herself a mental smack in the head. *I'm asking all the wrong questions,* she told herself. *It no longer matters when it started or how. There's only one question to consider—can Meredith control me or not?*

"I think you might be right," she said to Baker. "Meredith put a helluva lot of effort into controlling everyone around me, but I don't remember any occasion where *I* did something against my own will or something out of character." It was an epiphany. She'd spent her growing-up years in a whirlwind of drama, far too busy struggling with the latest nastiness inflicted by Meredith to notice that *everyone was a puppet but her.* Perhaps that was the real reason Meredith hated her so much.

"Damn, but I'm starving," Baker said suddenly.

"We ate everything I had in my backpack," she said. Even some tins of sardines in mustard she'd chosen for protein and portability—and they'd tasted every bit as appealing as the labels promised. *Not.*

"Can't we get some real chow someplace?" Baker clutched his stomach like he was in pain. "And I need some clothes, too. I'm not cold, but I sure as hell can't go to many parties dressed like this."

Party. Dressed. Party dress. An outrageous thought occurred to Neva right then, and she wondered if she was gutsy enough to follow through on such a plan. It would only work if Baker had been right and Meredith couldn't magically control her, or use her position as Neva's sire to compel her. If Baker was wrong, the plan *still* might work if Neva could just stay under her sister's radar as long as possible. Meredith couldn't command her if she didn't know she was there.

"You know, I think I need a new outfit, too," murmured Neva. "An expensive one."

"What?"

"Never mind. Come on, we're going to town."

((((● ●

His concrete cell had all the comforts of a morgue locker, but Travis was relieved to be back in it. Even if he *had* been thrown onto the unforgiving floor like a bag of potatoes. He crawled up onto the cold metal bench and lay there with every cell in his body yelping at him at once, but it was *still* a relief. He'd lost track of how many hours he'd hung upside down in Meredith's dark, death-filled room while she worked happily away on her spells like a first grader absorbed in finger painting. It hadn't been fun, but he got through it by focusing all his thoughts on Neva—her dark, wavy hair that was so soft to the touch, her espresso-brown eyes, her freckles, and even her smart-ass mouth. She was going to be so pissed when he explained how his wolf had claimed her. That thought alone sent a ghost of a smile across his face. He drew strength from his feelings for her, even looked forward to her kicking his ass, and he felt confident he'd get through his present situation…

Until Meredith decided to summon up some company… and a pair of orange-eyed demons with shining iridescent scales stepped from the deep shadows to answer her call.

Elliptical pupils like those of a cat fastened on him immediately, but no cat ever had eyes the size of a frickin' coffee-cup lid. He never saw the creatures move. In one heartbeat, they tow-ered over the woman who had called them, and in the next beat they were hovering over *him*. Small but scythe-like talons began scraping off tiny fragments of skin from his chest and arms, like bloody snowflakes, which they licked up daintily with long, anteater-like tongues.

Meredith had been as delighted as a child with a new puppy. Still naked save for her necklace, gold hair tumbling from the clasp she'd bound it with, she'd squealed and laughed and clapped her hands as she watched him writhe under the effects of those hellish claws. Christ, it was like being worked over with miniature vegetable peelers. Travis gritted his teeth and deter-mined not to make one single sound—damned if he was going to add to the crazy bitch's enjoyment. If it could be called a good thing, the demons' mouths were very tiny in proportion to their size. There'd be nothing left of him in short order otherwise.

Of course, that just meant it was gonna take a whole lot lon-ger for them to kill him.

Without warning, the creatures vanished like greasy soap bubbles, leaving behind nothing but an oily mist that drifted back into the deep shadows. Meredith cursed, and Travis fig-ured they'd used up whatever magical pass she'd bestowed on them. Still cursing, she added notes to her book with vicious strokes of the pen before throwing it to one side and striding out of the room. The guards rushed in almost immediately then, which cheered Travis considerably. He appreciated their speed even when they'd punched him in the head and gut a few times. And he was still thankful for the guards' efficiency even though he was dragged from the room by his feet, facedown along the marble floor tiles.

Because several sets of enormous orange eyes were watching him from the blackness of the shadows.

NINETEEN

Neva had no idea how Travis managed to live with his light-fingered lifestyle. Did he hate it as much as she did? She hadn't thought so at first, but she saw him differently now. Between his fierce independence and the mile-wide streak of decency he tried to hide, he probably despised stealing as much or more than she did. He claimed it had become necessary from a sheer lack of ID, but couldn't he buy some fake ID? *Oh, crap, that's illegal, too.* Maybe a person could get used to thievery, but she didn't want to find out. If Changelings really lived as long as Travis said they did, she promised herself she'd figure out some other way of getting along, even if she had to sell macramé bracelets by the side of the goddamn road.

Of course, if her plan didn't work out, she wasn't going to live long enough to worry about little details like ethics.

Early evening in Jackson, Nebraska, meant that the bar was open for sure. A green-and-orange neon sign on the roof proclaimed it to be ELO. Not a very catchy name, she thought, until she got closer and read the simple painted letters over the door: *El Lobo Oscuro.* If there was such a thing as omens, this had to be one, although it was hard to tell if it was good or bad: *The Dark Wolf.*

Neva opted to walk down both sides of Main Street first, sauntering casually as if sightseeing. The town was quaint. The facades of the old buildings were brick, and the street itself was made of brick paving stones. There were few stores and fewer window displays, but at least she learned that everything was open late tonight. She watched everyone out of her peripheral vision, looking for just the right person. And by that she meant, sadly, *victim*. She had to have money, and she had to spend some of it right here in this little town. Therefore, it would be a very bad idea to snatch a credit card from anybody local.

Eventually she spotted a brand-new SUV with out-of-state plates, and followed a young couple into El Lobo Oscuro. Their clothing was casual but expensive—the woman's purse alone was easily worth five hundred dollars—making them exactly the kind of folks that Neva was looking for. She couldn't stand the thought of taking money from someone who would really miss it.

The pair sat up at the bar instead of getting a booth or a table—and there was an empty stool right next to the woman. Neva couldn't have asked for a better opening—maybe the Dark Wolf *was* a lucky place. "Hi, I'm Janet. Are you new here?" she asked.

In less than a minute, she knew all she needed to know. Jack and Linda Ballister, a tax attorney and a software programmer. Heading home from a three-day business seminar that had featured an open bar, they'd stopped at ELO simply to maintain their buzz.

Thirty minutes later, she escorted a very tipsy Linda into the cramped restroom and offered to hold her purse for her. As soon as the stall door closed, Neva began rooting through the large handbag for a wallet. Fumbling badly from nerves, she almost dropped it twice. Finally she found what she was looking for and selected a single credit card from a large repertoire of them, hoping its absence wouldn't be noticed. On second thought, she took the driver's license, too. *Just in case I get asked for ID.* The photo was bad enough that it could be almost anybody, and Linda had dark hair. *Besides, Linda definitely should not be driving.* Neva nearly snorted at the irony—here she was, a *thief,* passing judgment on what somebody else should or should not do.

She managed a smile when Linda emerged from the stall, and handed the purse back to her. They returned to the bar together, and Jack bought another round of imported beer. As before, Neva made small talk and only pretended to drink from the cold, green bottle. When she judged that enough time had gone by, she stood up and stretched. Had to get going, she said, had to get her errands done and go home. Linda hugged her before she left.

And didn't that just make her feel like *crap.*

Heat rose in Neva's face as she left El Lobo Oscuro. She knew that two telltale spots of color marked her cheekbones, signaling her embarrassment and guilt to the entire world. Stealing and lying were Meredith's specialty, not hers. She assuaged her conscience somewhat by reminding it of future lives she hoped to save by her actions now—and hoped her conscience didn't bother to calculate her pathetic chances.

Three doors down, she entered the farm supply store and bought the highest-fashion items she could find for Baker: loose-fitting work jeans, wool socks, a plaid flannel shirt, a black tee, and some dark construction boots. She rounded out the outfit with a denim jacket sporting a black corduroy collar, plus a black baseball cap that announced *Farmers Do It in the Dirt.* There wasn't much for chow in a place like this, so she threw a half-dozen chocolate bars and a fistful of beef jerky sticks onto the pile on the counter.

At the edge of town, where Main Street officially became US-20 again, Neva crossed a field and entered the small stand of trees where Baker was hiding. Her knees jellied the moment she was safely out of sight, causing her to sit abruptly on the ground.

"Are you okay?" he asked.

"I have no future as a thief, that's all. Here, get dressed." She thrust the bags at him, and he began going through her purchases and laughing.

"Jesus, I'm going to look just like my dad."

"You don't like what I picked out, you do the shopping next time."

His favorite item seemed to be the hat, which he promptly put on backward, skater style, and began yanking tags and stickers off the clothes. He held up the jeans and looked around. "What, do I have to go commando?" He grinned.

"Don't paint pictures like that in my head," said Neva. "I'm afraid the only underwear that Sandhills Farm Supply stocks is thermal long johns."

"Check. None is better. I like to be cool in the crotch anyways—"

Ugh. She stuck her fingers in her ears and turned her back to him. "La la la la la la…" When she figured he'd had enough time to dress, she glanced over her shoulder.

Baker didn't look half bad. She'd chosen the colors of the outfit well. The black tee and hat highlighted his dark hair. His deep-gray eyes borrowed some blue from the plaid shirt and denim jacket. In that outfit, he looked like a typical farmer's son: big, muscular, and unfailingly cheerful—unless you knew what to look for. She guessed that the humor he displayed so readily was only partly due to his nature. The rest was likely a way to cope with the horrors he'd witnessed.

"Well, am I gorgeous or what?" he asked as he bit off half a Butterfinger at once, narrowly leaving the wrapper. Jeez, he looked young, much younger than she was—or perhaps she was just feeling old these days. *Destiny'll do that to you.*

"Stunning. Let's go."

"Where?" he mumbled with his mouth full.

"We gotta get back to the bitch queen's palace."

"All right. How?"

"Right through the front door." She told him what she had in mind, and watched his eyes widen.

"It's crazy. Brilliant, simple, but totally crazy. Of course we haven't got a chance, but—*shit*, that's not a bad plan at all." He swallowed hard then, and cleared his throat. "So I gotta ask, you're not thinking of turning me in for a bounty or something, are you? Don't get me wrong, I'm sure I'm worth a fortune, being so good-looking, but…"

The joke fell flat as she fisted her hands on her hips and kept them there to keep from hitting him. "Listen, mister," she said. "We both have people we care about who are in Meredith's nasty hands. And there are a lot more people whose lives are being stolen by her every day."

"No shit?" Baker snorted and spat at her feet. "Riley and I went out for drinks, just to blow off a little steam. We'd been working like crazy on a project, lots of overtime, no days off, for almost a month. So we put away a lot of beer. And we'd been chatting up a couple cute girls all night, and they invited us to a party after the bars closed. Sounded like fun, you know?

"Only when we got outside, we were jumped by a half-dozen guys who threw punches like fucking anvils. Last thing I remember was being thrown onto the floor of a van. I woke up in your sister's complex—and not in the goddamn penthouse, either."

"I was a prisoner, too!"

"Oh yeah? I was kept with the newbies, the ones that hadn't turned yet, just one level up from the prisoners. I never saw you there, anywhere, not once. You lived in the great wide *above*. As in *above*ground, *above* servants, and definitely *above* any of us. You're blood to that crazy bitch, and you watched everything she did. So excuse me for being a bit cautious about what your real motives are. How do I know that you're not her partner?"

Neva erupted. "Meredith doesn't want a partner! Jesus, the last thing on earth she'd want is to have to share any of her power. And I sure as hell wouldn't *want* it if she did." She banged a fist on a tree, hard enough to bring down a shower of leaves and leave a slight depression in the bark. Hard enough to bloody her knuckles as well, but she welcomed the pain. She had no tears left for the things she had seen, but that didn't mean she didn't remember every last one of the people, or the wolves who had once been people, who had died horribly in front of her.

She had told Travis the truth—she saw Meredith's face in her dreams, her triumphant smile sharply edged in red lipstick and dripping with blood. But she hadn't told him about all the other faces that haunted her dreams, too. The faces of the dead.

Slowly, carefully, Neva recited her twin's efforts to impress her, to win her over—or corrupt her. Either would have been fine in her sister's dark books. She didn't know if Baker would believe her or not, and maybe it didn't even matter, but going over the horrendous checklist of homicides jogged loose a sudden insight...

"What Meredith really wants is an audience to show off to. And for some reason, she thinks I'm the ideal spectator. Maybe because we're alike in looks, maybe because I'm so different from her at heart. Whatever the reason, she needs me to *see* the sick and twisted things she does. She doesn't even want my approval. The more I'm shocked and horrified and sickened, the more she likes it."

"That is seriously fucked up," said Baker.

"Tell me about it. What it comes down to is that I've seen as much blood as you, maybe more," Neva said at last. "So I'm going there to do whatever I can do to stop her. I think we'd be more successful together, but either you trust me or we call it quits right here." She realized with a sharp pang that those had been Travis's exact words, but she managed to keep it from showing on her face.

Baker held her gaze for several moments, then nodded at last. "Okay, I'm in. You didn't have to get me out of that hole, and you didn't have to come back here with clothes and shit. I figure you could have just left me several times over. So you've got my trust until you break it. But"—he folded his arms over his chest—"if you sell me out, I'll fucking kill you."

"Good. Same here," she declared. "By the way, tough guy, you have chocolate all over your chin." She stalked toward the highway. She didn't need heightened senses to hear the crackling sounds of Baker hastily picking up his treats and stuffing them in his pockets.

Travis's internal clock said it *should* be about dawn. With no outside light, however, he wasn't 100 percent certain. How many days before he couldn't even hazard a guess? Best to assess his surroundings and check again for a way out. The steel bench that jutted from the wall was harder and colder than anything had a right to be, but still he had to force his aching body to get off of it. As he sat up, he gripped the edges with his hands for a while until his head stopped spinning and his eyes focused. His olfactory nerves perked up right away, however. There were new scents in addition to the thick, industrial-strength cleanser that permeated the atmosphere and every surface in it. He glanced over in the direction of the door, and didn't know which was more surprising—that there was food inside his cell, or that he hadn't heard it arrive. The metal tray on the floor held four items—a squat tin cup of coffee, a large bottle of water lying on its side, a cold beef roast, and a crusty loaf of bread.

He only hesitated a moment. Sure, Meredith could have poisoned it all, but if she wanted him dead, she'd already had ample opportunity. Besides, the bitch would probably want to *watch*. He sipped the coffee. It was warm rather than hot, but strong, and his head cleared a little. Rather than chug it down his dry throat, however, he set it aside and swigged down half the bottle of water first.

Better.

Travis took a bite from the roast. The savory meat was a surprisingly decent cut and very lean. Hefting it in one hand, he estimated it approvingly at about three pounds—somebody obviously knew how to feed Changelings—

No. No, they don't. They know how to feed frickin' werewolves. *Monsters. Killers.*

Travis suddenly felt like heaving the roast against the door. He wasn't anything like the murderous creatures that lived here. Or was he? He'd killed, but...*ah, hell*. What made him any better? He sighed deeply as the same old misery kicked him in the gut. His first impulse was to refuse the food, refuse to eat. Damned if he wanted to cooperate in any way, shape, or form. But common sense prevailed. He needed every last bit of energy he could get in order to survive and escape. Even if he didn't give a crap about his own life, he had to get back to Neva. Intentionally or not, she was his *mate* now, and he was quickly becoming aware of some significant changes in his being—as if something of her essence lived within him, surged through his soul and beat in his blood. Like natural wolves, Changelings mated for life. Whether she accepted him or not, he would live for her, die for her, and, if he had any choice about the matter, drag her off to Outer Mongolia.

Anything to keep her safely away from her deranged sister.

He took another bite.

TWENTY

In her glass-walled penthouse, Meredith lolled between red satin sheets, but sleep eluded her. Conjuring demons was difficult, demanding work, and keeping them in this dimension so long had left her utterly drained. She'd recorded what she'd done and how, as she always did—she hadn't gotten this far without taking the scientific method seriously—but the spell she'd created needed a number of refinements. The blood of that big blond werewolf had given her amazing personal endurance and high energy, not unlike a drug—but also like a drug, she'd crashed hard afterward and was now far too tired to fall asleep on her own. She would allow herself just a little while longer to think through her spells, make her plans for the next session—and then she simply had to get some sleep. It would probably take a couple of days' worth to restore her. She'd call Zarita to bring her lovely little bag of tricks upstairs. A shot, a pill, or both—her kindhearted doctor would find something that would work. Really, what would she do without her?

Meredith watched the sun rise over the ocean. It should have soothed her, but she only wondered how to harness its power. She simply *had* to find more power for her spells. The new werewolf's blood was interesting, but still not strong enough. She had finally breached the demon dimension, but she had yet to achieve her goals.

Blood contained life, but by itself it just wasn't strong enough. She would have to kill something, no, some*one*, to get the kind of energy needed, to take her spells to the next level. The only question was, who to choose? She supposed she could make use of that insolent werewolf, Riley. After all, she had a replacement for him now. Or she could send the pack to gather up a few more humans. If she cut the throats of several of them at once, it might give her what she needed.

Decisions, decisions. Her head hurt and she was so, so tired. She patted the shelf of the hand-carved walnut headboard until she found her phone, its gold casing reflecting the brightening light. The power button was set with a large square-cut diamond, and she pressed it now. Immediately the screen sprang to vibrant life, its crisp white light a beacon of hope.

"Zarita? I need you right away, darling. I've had another one of those terrible nights."

((((● ●

Hitchhiking had brought Baker and Neva all the way back to Oregon, but he didn't like having to head north for Portland instead of straight south to Meredith's lair in northern California. Neva had insisted that what she needed couldn't be found in any of the small towns they'd passed through, and definitely not on the way to her sister's isolated mansion. It was only the fact that Neva's idea was all the advantage they would have against the bitch queen that made Baker finally agree. Concern for Riley, though, was eating him up—was his friend even still alive? This was all taking too damn long. *Hang on, bud, hang on.*

They were in the Pearl District, an artsy place with high-end shopping. He'd gone into the first store with Neva, but felt he was risking whiplash from doing double takes at the price tags. He left within the first few minutes. From that point on, he let her do the shopping, and he went in search of chow. Baker had always been a big eater, but becoming a werewolf had definitely revved up his metabolism. Jesus, he was taking in more calories now than when he was a linebacker for the Bobcats in college. It wasn't a bit like Christmas dinner, though—his waistband never felt too tight for a moment.

Still, the waiting was killing him. He was antsy to get going, to head south and do whatever they could to free their friends. They probably didn't have a snowball's chance in hell, but he had to try, both of them did. The only thing that helped him keep his shit together was the fact that Neva didn't seem to be dawdling. It was only a couple of hours before she sought him out and handed him an armload of fancy shopping bags. The hair salon was next. She'd warned him it was going to take a very long time, and assigned him to get them a place to stay for the night.

He almost lost it then and there. Stay? He didn't want to fucking stay! Baker stomped away and tried to walk off his impatience and his frustration. His thoughts were as ferocious as his pace. *Riley could be dead already, and here I am fucking off in yuppie land. I should go on my own. I should have gone a long time ago. I should never have fucking left him there in the first place.*

Fortunately the Pearl District had no shortage of green spaces. At last he came upon an enormous stepped fountain in Jamison Square and sat on the edge overlooking it. Eventually, the sight and sound of running water helped him chill out. Neva's plan was a good one, if they could pull it off. And he knew damn well it would be better to storm the bitch queen's castle during the day—Meredith was definitely a night owl. It wouldn't hurt if he and Neva were fresh. They would need all their strength, both mental and physical, if they were to succeed in freeing their friends—

Water. Like.

Baker jumped to his feet, startling a couple of teen girls with a laptop a few yards away. "Sorry, sorry." He held up his hands in a calming gesture. "Just nearly fell asleep, that's all." They giggled and returned to their shared screen, talking a mile a minute. His acute hearing picked up the words *cute*, which pleased him, and *crazy*, which didn't.

He settled back down, wondering if the excuse he'd given the girls was true. Maybe he *had* been on the edge of sleep—why else would something so weird pop into his head?

Not strange.

And the girls had been right. He was now officially crazy. Wait—Neva had talked in his head with some kind of telepathy when they were both on four feet. It had taken some doing, but he'd managed to answer her. Was there another werewolf around here? *Hello? Um. Who am I talking to?*

Wolf. Baker wolf.

Holy shit, he was talking to himself. *Where the hell did you come from?*

Always here.

Baker felt the color drain from his face. He thought he was doing pretty damn good at coping with the whole werewolf gig. But he didn't expect the four-legged side of him to have a personality of its own. Wait, *wait*, if he was hearing voices, then maybe he was schizophrenic. Maybe that was a side effect of the whole shape-shifting thing. The transformation had scrambled his fucking neurons.

Not crazy. Wolf.

Sure, why not. Baker headed for the street then, figuring it was long past time to fulfill his assignment to get a room for the night—and he was feeling a definite urge to lie down. There didn't seem to be any hotels in the Pearl District, but that wasn't a problem. He hailed a cab, confident that its driver would know exactly where to go.

As the bright-yellow car headed north, Baker fingered the disposable cell phone in his pocket. After he'd checked in, he'd let Neva know which hotel he was in. And then he'd make use of the minibar.

(((● ●

Following the concierge's directions, Neva headed to the elevators. They were large and as sumptuously appointed as the lobby, with real walnut paneling and framed works by local artists. *I can hardly wait to see the room.* She quashed that thought immediately, still feeling the pang of guilt. Linda Ballister's credit-card bill was going to be a doozy. She'd make a note of the address on the driver's license. If she survived long enough, Neva determined to pay the money back someday.

Go help Travis now? Her wolf had been pestering her all day. She'd spelled out the plan and all the whys and wherefores of the situation, but the creature was as eager to help as a child—and just as good at being patient.

Tomorrow morning. Neva tried to send soothing thoughts to her alter ego, and imagined stroking its thick dark fur. *That's when we go help Travis. We have to eat and sleep so we're ready. We want to be very strong.*

Wolf is strong now.

Well, I'm not. If Meredith catches us, there'll be nobody to help Travis. We're all he's got.

It wasn't the answer her inner wolf was looking for, but it finally left her alone for a while. Between reassuring it and trying to help Baker with his new reality, Neva felt like she was babysitting. Holy crap, had Travis felt like that with her? How embarrassing was that?

She emerged into a wide and elegant hallway, with plush, patterned carpet that cushioned her aching feet. Victorian sconces glowed by every entry. There were fewer doors than she would have guessed, then realized it was because the rooms were big. The quality of the place was even reflected in the door lock—it only took one swipe of the key card to open it.

Baker was propped up on one of the two king-size beds, watching TV with a remote in one hand and a tiny liquor bottle in the other. The bottle had a large group of friends on the nightstand, all empty.

"Hey," she said. "I brought food." She extended the bags she'd been holding, and he turned his head—

She never saw him move. She didn't even have time to yell as a massive gray wolf bore her to the floor. Neva hit her head hard enough to see stars, but she was more concerned with the long, sharp teeth that were bared inches from her nose. Her own wolf tried to launch itself, but she struggled to hold it back. If she Changed now, there'd be a helluva fight. "Baker," she said firmly. "It's Neva."

He growled loud enough that she could feel the vibration clear through to her bones. *You goddamn bitch. What have you done with Riley?*

"I'm *Neva*! Neee-vaaah."

The growling stopped, and he looked confused. The big head leaned forward and—

He sniffed her. The rubbery black nose inhaled deeply as it passed back and forth over her face, along her throat, her ears. Jeez, it was like being vacuumed—only most Hoovers didn't have the potential to bite her face off.

Neva?

"Yes, yes, it's me." Relief flooded her system until she felt like a pile of limp spaghetti. "I'm Neva and you're Baker. I was going to ask what you think of the new 'do, but I think we've answered *that* question. Hey, can you get off me now?" She drew in a full breath as the big wolf backed awkwardly away.

She'd rather have remained lying down, but decided she'd look too much like prey. Neva rubbed the back of her head and got carefully to her feet, keeping a wary eye on her hairy roommate. His fury was spent, however, and now he just looked sheepish. In a few minutes, he shuffled over to the center of the room and resumed his human form.

"You're a lot smoother at that now," she said as she gathered the food bags.

Naked, Baker shoved a pillow in his lap as he plunked down on the nearest bed. "Lost my clothes again."

"That's okay. We have more."

"It talked to me, Neva. You didn't fucking tell me it was going to talk to me."

"What talked to you?"

"Baker wolf. The Baker wolf talked to me. Said it liked the water."

Okaaaay. She'd hoped the shape-shifting would take care of his inebriated state, but apparently no such luck. "You sure picked a great time to get shitfaced." She extended the bags again. "Here, get some food into you."

Neva ended up unwrapping the food and placing his hands around a pastrami panini the size of Rhode Island that she'd picked up at a deli. As he settled in happily around his first bite, she took her own meal over to a table by the window. Now that her roommate wasn't going to kill her, she took a moment to appreciate the decor. The table was far from the standard motel melamine-and-steel pedestal. For one thing, it was real wood, and for another, the elegant Queen Anne legs spoke of a possible antique or at least a very good reproduction. It matched the tastefully ornate headboards and other pieces of furniture in the expansive room. Only the big-screen TV contrasted with the feeling of opulence and luxury—until the press of a button lowered it out of sight into what she'd thought was an extra dresser. "Wow, this place could be on the cover of *Better Homes and Gardens,*" she breathed.

"I like the Jacuzzi in the bathroom." Baker's mouthful of food made him mumble, but he applied plenty of volume so she could hear him anyway. "The wolf said he likes water, so I gave him a bath."

"What are you talking about?"

"The Baker wolf!" he shouted, probably not realizing how loud he was. "It was in my head at the park. So I came here and gave it a bath. I thought I was crazy at first, but now we're good buds." He looked around. "Who took my fucking sandwich?"

"You ate it, bud. Here, I got an extra for you." She'd seen his appetite in action and guessed rightly that one would never be enough. She'd brought him three, but even a dozen might not put a dent in his hunger. She removed the panini from the paper and again wrapped his hands around it, then stepped back to watch him devour it. *Men.* It just didn't take much to keep them happy. The classic joke seemed a lot less funny when she thought of Travis, though. He was deeper, more complicated, somehow. She couldn't picture any mere sandwich distracting him from the task at hand—or from the weight of the world that he carried around. Oh, crap, she thought as she teared up suddenly. She missed him, and his damn wolf, too.

"We're gonna talk in the morning, okay?" she said to Baker, and put a finger to her lips.

"'Kay."

She left him to it and entered the bathroom, where there seemed to be more mirrors than walls—and was jolted as a striking woman with very long blonde hair looked back at her. Sure, she'd seen her image at the hair salon, but she'd been watching the transformation every minute of the hours it had taken. Now, not having looked at herself for a while, the impact was enormous. The hair extensions had been astronomically priced, but the results were plainly worth it. With makeup hiding her freckles, she looked exactly like her twin, Meredith.

No, wait, she *didn't*.

Frowning, Neva struck a pose, then another. Yeah, more like *that*. Pouted her lips just so, and practiced what she'd always called *The Look*—that confident, mocking expression that her twin seemed to have been born with. But it wasn't complete. She rummaged through her handbag and came up with one of several lipsticks she'd bought that day. The shade had to be just right, a combo of Fuck-Me Scarlet and Fresh-Blood Crimson. They weren't the real names, of course, but where Meredith was concerned, they ought to be. Neva took her time, carefully applying the color with a brush. And stood back.

This time it was right. Coupled with The Look, it was almost perfect. Meredith might as well be in the room with her. Neva practiced the smile then, the million-dollar diva smile with her freshly whitened teeth.

And shivered at her own reflection.

TWENTY-ONE

Three pounds of prime roast and a loaf of bread later, Travis had to admit he felt considerably better. His muscles and joints still ached, but the skin on his chest was regenerating nicely where unnatural claws had scraped appetizers from it. He peered out the tiny grated window in the steel door, as he had countless times since he'd awakened, but there still wasn't much to see—only that there were many doors just like his, all facing into a circular room with a concrete floor. When he'd been dragged here, he could swear he'd gone up a couple of stories—but was he still underground? He murmured a fervent thanks to the goddess for the ever-present fluorescent light, despite its greenish tinge and its irritating buzz. Anything was better than being left in the dark to wonder if those creepy orange-eyed creatures were wandering the shadows.

There were no guards in sight, but that wasn't too surprising. *Why should there be, when there's nothing for them to guard but locked doors?* He hadn't heard a single sound from outside his door, though. Surely he wasn't the only prisoner here? "Hey! Hey, can anybody hear me?" he finally hollered through the small grate. Grabbing the tin cup from the tray, he banged it against the door, like James Cagney in some old black-and-white movie. "Hey out there!"

Just as it seemed he was alone in the complex, he thought he heard a soft tapping. Travis strained to discern where it was coming from. To the right, two or maybe three doors away and—it stopped. No. *No, you don't.* "I can hear you," he called. "Tap twice for yes if you can make out what I'm saying."

There was a pause and then two soft taps.

He blew out a breath, a little surprised at how relieved he was. "Okay, that's more like it." What could he ask now? He considered the possibility that it was one of Meredith's minions messing with his head, but decided not. His sense of smell was still pretty good, even if he couldn't figure out where the hell his inner wolf was. Inside his cell, the smell of the high-powered cleanser masked everything except what was closest to him. Through the grated window, however, the cleanser was unable to mask the underlying odors of blood and filth and misery that emanated from one of the cells beyond. And it was *Changeling* blood.

Travis took a chance, immediately switching to mindspeak and narrowing his focus so the other prisoner would be the only one to hear him. *The chow's not bad here, but I hate the decor. How about you?*

Needs curtains. I'm Riley.

I'd rather not say.

I'm cool with that. Names are power. You never know who's listening.

You okay?

Healing slow. Had a run-in with the proprietor of this establishment.

Yeah, well, I'm looking for someone to help me complain to her personally about the accommodations.

Love to. Zarita thinks the bandages can come off soon.

Shit. The guy's condition had to be rough, because if there was one thing a fast-healing Changeling seldom needed, it was first aid. Even after the demons had sampled Travis's chest like a smoked-salmon buffet, the bleeding had stopped fairly quickly and the damage was becoming less noticeable by the hour. If Travis could just shape-shift, it would be healed immediately—but his wolf was still a no-show. *Who's Zarita?* He was concerned that Meredith had a partner in crime.

Dr. Zarita Arandas. I figure she must be damn good, because she's Meredith's "personal physician." Mostly, though, Zarita ends up looking after the pack. Not because we have a swell health plan or anything. Just 'cause we're usually the ones bleeding. So far I might be her most regular patient. Riley laughed a little, but it turned into a coughing spell. It took him a few moments to recover before he continued. *She brought you the food—guess you were still out of it.*

She'd given him the roast? The woman's credentials went up a few notches. *Is Zarita a Changeling, too?*

What's—oh, you mean werewolf? *No, but she was recruited by Meredith years ago. One of the early ones, apparently.*

The early ones. Christ, how long had this been going on? *Do you trust her?*

Mostly. She hates Meredith. 'Course, everyone does who still has a mind of their own. Most don't even seem to know who they are anymore. They think they've always been here.

What about you? You been here long?

Over a month. Been in the cell for a week. Maybe more.

Travis thought of something. *Can you Change? Can you call on your wolf to help you heal?*

Hell, I don't have to call it, it's right here. I haven't walked on two legs since Meredith handed me my ass. She blocks all shape-shifting—from what I've seen, no one can become human or wolf unless she allows it. Zarita says it's some kind of magic spell. Riley snorted. *Sounds like fairy-tale shit, but I didn't believe in werewolves either until this happened to me. So, magic? Sure. Unicorns are probably real, too.*

Travis frowned. According to Neva, Meredith was the sire of almost all the wolves in her pack. Among Changelings, nature had made provision for the very new or the very young, allowing their sire to be able to control them until they were in control of themselves. But that natural influence gradually waned. Within a few months, Meredith's wolves would normally be free of her constraints. Compelling someone to Change or not Change should be impossible for her—and yet she continued to control a large number of wolves. What had gone wrong?

He shook his head, realizing that nothing had gone wrong at all. Something had gone very, very right—for Meredith. He'd witnessed for himself that she practiced a ghastly type of blood magic, at a frighteningly powerful level. Neva had once said that her twin considered herself a pioneer in spell crafting and experimented a great deal. He'd seen that, too, and also that the woman was obsessive about documenting the results. *Of course the bitch had found a way to harness that initial natural control every sire had. In fact, she wasn't just continuing it but magnifying it. Judging by the fact that his own wolf was MIA, Meredith's unnatural control even extended to Changelings that she hadn't even sired. This just gets better and better.*

Sure does. Riley thought Travis was still talking to him. *Zarita will be here in the morning. Maybe you could ask* her *some questions.* The voice in Travis's head went silent as the shape-shifter drifted off to much-needed sleep. It was a troubled rest, however, as shouted words and snatches of strange one-sided conversations could be heard from Riley's cell over the next few hours. And the coughing fits. Travis was no doctor, but he was willing to bet the other Changeling had broken ribs.

For the next few hours, Travis focused on his memories of his grandfather. He sifted through them, hoping to find some tiny nugget of wisdom or information he could apply to his current situation, *anything* that would help him understand how Meredith was operating. And maybe from that he could figure out how to stop it.

All that came to mind, however, was a seven-sided chunk of clear quartz that his grandfather kept in his pocket at all times. It had no color, and the once-sharp points were a little worn with age. No matter what else Travis tried to remember, his mind's eye saw only the crystal lying in his grandfather's palm, looking like the plainest of glass. It didn't even cast rainbows or gleam with hidden inclusions, and as a small child, he hadn't been interested in it—until he was invited to hold it. *Make your thoughts quiet,* his grandfather had instructed. *See. Hear. Feel.*

He'd seen and heard nothing, but suddenly he felt something strange, as if a vibration was thrumming in his cupped hands. As the pleasant pulsation continued, steady and sure, up through his arms, into his chest, and somehow into his very being, he realized the crystal was causing it. *It amplifies energy,* his grandfather explained. *It takes that which already is and makes it greater. And it channels information from places outside yourself.*

Frustrated, Travis paced his cell. He wasn't his grandfather. He didn't have a damn crystal, and if he did, he wouldn't know the first thing about how to use it. Maybe if he'd stuck around, if he'd stayed with the pack, he would have learned some of his grandfather's skills. *If, if, if...*

Christ, he hated that word.

TWENTY-TWO

The rented SUV was a full-size gas hog, but it had four-wheel drive, and Neva knew they'd need it to get close to what Baker called "the bitch queen's fortress." She elected to do the driving—he was hungover, of course—and headed south on I-5. At Grant's Pass she turned southwest to access the Redwood Highway for the rest of the trip. Within the hour, they would be in Del Norte County, California, and zeroing in on Meredith's isolated mansion on the coast.

The sky was that vivid shade of blue that only occurred in the fall, with wisps of icy cirrus clouds airbrushed across the zenith. Everything seemed brighter, colors more intense, details more noticeable, from the calm ocean and the lush landscape to the green highway signs and even the flowering weeds that grew along the guardrails. Sunshine lent a golden cast to all of it... With a start, Neva realized she was appreciating a world that she could be leaving soon. She and Baker were going to attempt the impossible, and if Meredith caught them, their lives would basically be over. Perhaps they would survive physically for a time, but nothing would be left of them and anyone they cared about. Her twin would see to that.

A royal-blue highway sign embellished with orange poppies came into view: Welcome to California. *It's too soon*, Neva thought. Meredith's estate was close now, but it seemed wrong to have arrived so quickly. What if the hobbits had simply taken an off-road vehicle into Mordor? They'd have been there in no time flat—and most of the story would never have been written. *If you're going into battle, it should take a whole lot longer to get to the damn battlefield, shouldn't it?*

She needed more time to prepare. On the other hand, no amount of time would ever be enough, not for this. Baker called it a covert mission, but with Neva's luck, it would morph into a full-scale confrontation. *Better to just get it over with.*

"Wake up," she said. "We're in the Sunshine State."

Baker grunted and slid his sunglasses down his nose. "That's Florida. California is the Golden State."

"Sunshine," she persisted, more to keep him talking than anything.

"It won't be fucking sunshiny where we're going."

"Well, didn't you wake up cheerful."

"I'm not awake."

"You'd better get awake. We're nearly there."

He sat up and stuffed the sunglasses into the visor, furrowing his brows and only succeeding in looking cranky. *Amateur,* she thought. Baker's forehead lacked the expressiveness of Travis's— and the attitude. *There* was a frown that could speak volumes. *And it would look really good to me right about now.*

Baker's substandard frown lifted when the road took them through a vast forest of redwoods and Douglas firs. The living giants were breathtaking, and it seemed as if the SUV shrank down to the size of an insect as it rolled by them. The shafts of sunlight that fell through the towering branches was nothing short of glorious, and Neva couldn't help but think this was a good thing to see before—well, before anything *final* happened.

So much for positive thinking. But then, she had no illusions about what she was up against and what her chances were. She glanced at Baker. *You're sure you know your way around?*

I know where to look for Riley. I figure your Travis is in the same place.

It would have to do. They were insane, of course, she and Baker both. Once having escaped Meredith's house of horrors, how could anyone go back there? Yet her resolve hadn't weakened. If anything, it was reinforced.

She had to find Travis. Migrating birds felt the tug of the seasons. They flew hundreds, even thousands, of miles because it was a life imperative. And they knew exactly where they were going, even if they'd never been there. Just like what she was experiencing now—Neva felt the irresistible draw of an invisible cord, a pulsing, living connection that pulled her toward Travis. *Has to be some kind of a Changeling thing.* She almost believed she could find him without knowing where he was, and that was disturbing. How far did this weird new ability go? Did werewolves automatically sense each other?

If so, how long would it take Meredith to find *her*?

Enemy territory loomed before them—literally. With the redwoods towering two hundred feet and more, and Douglas fir and Sitka spruce nearly as large, Baker's six-foot-one frame felt abysmally small. The giant trees shared their territory with smaller species, sure, but it was all relative—many of the big-leaf maples and red alders he could see were more than a hundred feet high themselves. What it came down to was the bitch queen not only had an unbelievable amount of real estate, but most of it was old-growth forest. *I didn't think anyone could still own that—isn't it like a national treasure or something?* Maybe the property dated back to an earlier time and laws that were more lax about such things. Besides, as his dad was fond of saying, money talked. And Meredith de la Ronde seemed to have more money than God.

Whatever the land title said, they were going to have to walk in from here. It was just as well. Although they'd filled the tank before they left, the gas gauge was already hovering near empty. *Remind me never to buy one of these*, he thought in disgust. Even his dad's '79 pickup got *way* better mileage than this shiny new guzzler.

Neva and Baker hid the SUV, pulling it off the road and stacking branches and leaves on it. With luck, no one would see it. They'd compared notes about their respective escapes, and their consensus was that the guards usually stayed clear of the forest area. Strange to have such a natural playground for wolves but not let anyone use it. Maybe Meredith was concerned that the raw appeal of the wilderness might lure her wolves to desert her. The patrols seemed to be reserved for the walled perimeter of the mansion itself, with its vast manicured lawns, flagstone patios, and a pair of lake-like blue swimming pools.

Baker stripped off his clothes—noting he'd missed a price tag on the jeans—and stuffed them into a garbage bag. The package fit into a scraped-out hollow between the forks of one of the more normal-size trees he'd seen since this morning, some kind of oak. He scattered a thick layer of dead leaves and forest-floor debris over the black plastic to hide it and stepped back. The camouflage gave away no secrets. If only he could disguise *himself* that well…Naked, he stood for a moment, calming himself, then signaled his wolf.

The transformation was almost instantaneous. And painless, too—he never failed to be grateful that it wasn't like the first fucking time. He shook himself all over like a wet dog, as if settling the wolf hide into place. Senses were in high gear now: eyesight, hearing, and most of all, scent. The intense smells of the primeval forest called to something wild in him, and he nearly strangled trying to keep himself from howling.

Behind a clump of ferns tall enough to hide her completely from sight, Baker knew that Neva had shed her clothes as well. She was pretty, and he'd love to catch a glimpse—fair was fair, and she'd seen *him*, right? But he was having enough trouble keeping his shit together just from the effects of the scenery. Fortunately Neva was putting more clothes on, an outfit that her fucking royal richness, the bitch queen, would actually be caught dead wearing. Baker had no doubt that Neva could pull off this part of their plan—it was scary how closely she could resemble her sister when she put her mind to it. It wasn't just the dramatic change in her hair—it was the attitude, the condescending tone of voice, the body language that screamed, *Look at me, look at me, look at me.* Neva could mimic Meredith to a fucking T.

Still, when she stepped out from behind the ferns, he lost his breath. Her newly blonde hair had been loosed into long golden waves. A satiny white blouse showed off the roundness of her breasts, and a black stone pendant nestled between them. Her black leather leggings looked painted on, and continued into tall equestrian boots with tiny silver spurs. "Meredith favors stilettos," Neva explained. "But I can't walk in the damn things, and I'd *never* make it through the woods to the mansion. I've seen her wear boots like these once in a while, though, so I hope I can get away with them."

They look fine, said Baker. At least he thought that was what he said, but he was no longer looking at the boots. His eyes had already traveled back up to more interesting places—until he noticed she had something in her hands. *Hey, what the hell? I'm not wearing a fucking dog collar!*

"It's not just any collar." Neva took a step toward him with the wide, coal-black loop, and the scent of rich leather assailed his nostrils. "It's designer," she said, as if that explained everything. "Do you have any idea how expensive this was?"

I don't care if it's got diamonds the size of peanuts.

She rolled her eyes. "There are *no* diamonds. Didn't you notice that some of her wolves wear something like this?" She waved the collar at him. "It's some kind of badge of office. I figured maybe you'd be less likely to be stopped or questioned if we get separated."

Okay, so he'd seen a few collars on members of the pack, but hadn't known what they were for. He eyed the leather suspiciously. *What happens if I turn back to human while I have that on?*

"Nothing. It'll disappear into the twilight zone, just like your clothes do. Besides, look at it, Baker. In order to go around your big, fat wolf neck, it's nearly the size of a belt. You're not going to choke or anything."

In the end, he allowed her to buckle it on. Loosely. Appearing to be somebody important might be useful—and he couldn't afford to pass up the slightest advantage.

Don't like.

He nodded as he recognized his inner wolf's voice in his head. *You and me both, bud.* As he led the way for Neva, checking for the easiest route, he wondered at the bizarreness of talking to his alter ego. If his inner wolf was on the *outside* right now, then his human mind was on the *inside*. So did that mean he was hearing the wolf's voice in the wolf's mind or in his own? Puzzling over that existential dilemma, he failed to sense a threat until it was upon them.

A pair of white wolves erupted from a tall stand of rhododendron trees. Fortunately, Neva's alter ego was paying attention and she dove to one side, shifting form as she rolled—

And came up biting and snapping.

The scene was confused and surreal, a mad scramble of dark and light pelts, as Baker and Neva battled their attackers.

A flurry of magenta blossoms filled the air as if someone had viciously shaken a water globe, and tufts of fur began to join them. Neva had never fought as a wolf before, but she didn't have to figure out what to do. Instinct was in charge here. Her wolf spun and dodged, bit deeply, and leaped away. Her small size was an advantage, and she was fast. Baker was duking it out with the biggest wolf, but she couldn't spare him a look. She could only feint and strike, slash and retreat out of reach.

Her vision reddened, and gradually she backed her opponent up against a fallen redwood. Snake-fast, she ducked under its guard and caught it solidly by the throat, just under the jaw. Neva sprang straight up, which threw the larger wolf off balance, and brought it crashing to the ground with her on top. Her jaws were still clenched around the vital spot, her teeth already breaking the skin beneath the thick snowy ruff. Every impulse was screaming at her to deliver the final bite, to kill her enemy and—

No.

Her wolf strained to fulfill its instincts, and Neva could barely hold it back. *I said* no! *I'm not a murderer, and I'm not going to start just because I'm a werewolf.*

No kill? Her alter ego was clearly puzzled.

Travis said Changelings don't do that. No kill, just hold on, okay?

It complied. Relieved that she'd won the battle with her own wolf—at least for the moment—Neva turned her attention to the owner of the furry throat that was oh so vulnerable between her teeth. Scent informed her of several things right away. One, the white wolf was terrified, and two, it was older than she was. Three, it was female. And four—

You're okay? Baker's mental voice sounded breathless, which was strange. That's when she realized there was only panting and gasping behind her—the other combatants had broken off their struggle to watch what she was going to do next.

Fine. You?

My dancing partner's really worried about his pal.

I want to know what's going on. Why was I attacked? She was directing her mindspeak to the wolf beneath her, but it was Baker who answered first.

Well, duh! You look like the bitch queen herself.

And thanks a lot for blowing my cover. Neva made a silent mental note to smack him in the back of the head later, and to get him to practice focusing his thoughts more. *You don't get it. Nobody attacks Meredith; nobody would dare.* At least not anybody in their right mind. She redirected her attention to the creature whose life she held between her teeth. *Who the hell are you guys?*

The white wolf's eyes opened wide, and the helpless jaws worked as if to form words. *I—I—you're not Meredith!*

Please don't kill her. The new voice sounded young. And scared.

((((● ●

Travis had gone over every square inch of his cell from floor to ceiling, looking for any possible weakness he could exploit. There were none. He'd examined the door in particular, to no avail. If any of it had been designed for humans, he might have been able to use his Changeling strength against it. As it was, the best he could probably do was tear the grating off the window. He'd be free as a bird then—if only he could Change into a tiny sparrow instead of a wolf.

He was dozing fitfully on the hard steel bench when suddenly his blue eyes snapped open. There were human footsteps, small but purposeful ones, in one of the outer corridors. He had to strain to hear them until their owner came a little closer to the lockup area. Then he didn't need to try at all—the person began deliberately scuffing the soles of their shoes as they approached. *Obviously someone knows better than to surprise Changelings.*

He rose and peered through the grated window in the metal door. Zarita Arandas was a small woman, pretty, nicely curved—and alert. Headed toward Riley's cell with a red plastic tote, she sensed Travis watching her. She stopped still and glanced around carefully until her black eyes caught sight of him. "*¡Hola!* You must be Ms. Meredith's latest toy." She smiled and approached his door, where she could peer up at him. "She is very excited about working with you."

"Yeah, well, I'm not very excited about it," said Travis. "And I'm no one's toy."

"A toy does not have to be willing in order to be played with," she pointed out. "The cat does not need the mouse's permission."

Zero points for her ability to cheer people up. He decided to cut to the chase and switched over to mindspeak. *So what's your story? Riley says you've been here a long time. Why aren't you gone?*

Many emotions crossed her face at once, and the smile disappeared as if it had never existed. Looking into her deep, dark eyes, it became obvious that Zarita Arandas was a haunted woman. She shook her head at him. *Do not ask questions like that here.* "I have things to do," she said and walked away briskly. "I will be bringing food and water later. Maybe two hours, maybe three." Reaching for the keypad on Riley's cell door, Zarita paused for a nanosecond, her body angled just so.

Long enough for him to see the numbers she was punching in.

Travis listened, but there wasn't much conversation after the initial greetings. He discerned the *snick* of scissors and rustling noises—probably removing dressings—and the *tsk*ing sound Zarita made. "Your wounds are not healing nearly fast enough," she said to Riley. "Your wolf body will help you, but you need more food, more nutrition. I will see that you get it, but you must make an effort to eat it." She whispered then, so low that Travis almost didn't catch it. "*Por favor.* If you do not regain your strength soon, Ms. Meredith will have you killed. *Comprende?*" Aloud, she said exactly what she had said to Travis. "I will be back in two hours, maybe three."

Why the repeat? Travis frowned. Zarita had shown him Riley's combination and specified a time period. What, did she think he could somehow rescue the guy? *I can't even get out of my own damn cell.*

If she heard him at all, she didn't answer, but a growing noise in the outer corridor made him look up. He peered out of the grating and recognized the men approaching. They were the same guards who had unknowingly "rescued" him from Meredith's underground lair earlier. Big, beefy guys, all of them, they'd make great bouncers for heavy metal concerts, or perhaps enforcers for biker gangs. Travis knew he could take them on one at a time and win, whether they were armed or not. Whether they were in human form or not. He could tackle three or four at a time and probably come out on top, even if his inner wolf didn't show up to help him. But there were ten of them, and they weren't stupid. One thing he'd noticed early was that Meredith didn't employ idiots. Conclusion: they were coming to get him, and there wasn't a damn thing he could do about it.

Of course, nobody said he had to go quietly. But then the honor guard would double up on their efforts, and he could end up knocked out, drugged, hobbled with heavier shackles—or all three. He could play along, but they wouldn't trust him if he was suddenly cooperative, either. No, he needed to pretend he was in dire shape—maybe even act a little frightened. Christ, that wouldn't be too hard if they were taking him back to Meredith's underground playroom. *Only a moron would go back there willingly. They oughtta believe it if I drag my heels a bit.* And while he was dragging those heels, he'd be watching for anything, anywhere, that might help him escape.

TWENTY-THREE

I started it. I was going to kill you.

Neva's jaws were beginning to ache, but she maintained her grip while shifting her position enough to get a better look at her vanquished foe's partner. The other white wolf was every bit as tall as Baker's gray form—but not as heavy. Not yet. It would fill out later, when the human who belonged to the animal persona was full grown. Crap. *How old are you?*

I'll be seventeen in—

You're a fucking kid? Baker sounded incredulous.

I'm not a kid! And I can kick your fucking ass!

Nathan! the fallen wolf interjected. *Don't hurt him, please. He thought you were Meredith. We both did. I'm sorry I wasn't fast enough to stop him.*

Double crap. As if being a werewolf and a thief weren't bad enough, now she'd been reduced to attacking mothers who were protecting their children. Neva wanted to just let go and slink away, but she needed a few more answers before she released her prisoner. *Who are you, and what are you doing out here?*

Sonje Berendsen. I've been head chef since we were brought here a couple years ago. Nathan helps me in the kitchen. But he's bigger now, really strong, and somebody noticed him. This week, they tell me, he's going to be assigned to guard Meredith's work-room. Downstairs! I had to get him out of there. Those guards— they don't come back, you know.

I've heard that. Neva had never been to the lower levels of the mansion, but according to the staff whispers, anybody who worked down there didn't last very long. As for why, there was no shortage of grim and ghastly speculations. Knowing her twin, the rumors were probably all true. She opened her jaws and drew back. *I'm sorry. You can get up now.*

Nathan suddenly wedged himself between Neva and the wolf she had bested, growling until his mother reprimanded him again. Sonje rose then, limping a little, and leaned against her son. That's when Neva looked around and realized they were all wounded. Baker had a long slash across his flank, and one ear looked positively *chewed*. Nathan had several gashes around the back of his neck and a savage bite mark down one front leg. Neva was bleeding as well, from claws that had raked her belly and muzzle. She resisted sighing, but goddammit, the whole purpose of her disguise was so they wouldn't have to fight their way *into* the mansion. Instead, all four of them looked like they'd just battled their way out of it. *How did you get away?* she asked suddenly.

Eddie told me about it. He'd been bartending on the third-floor balcony during a party, and he noticed that it opens out over a roof. He thought perhaps a person could jump down onto it, then follow the roof sideways, to the left, until you could jump down to the next, and the next. There are three.

Nathan piped up then. *We were the first ones to try it, and it works. But on the last roof, it's still a long way to the ground. I jumped into the pool instead.*

I wish I had thought of doing that, Sonje said, holding up her lame paw.

Neva was relieved that she hadn't been responsible for one injury, at least. *If you Change back to human, most of your wounds should be healed. Do you know how?*

Both white wolves nodded, and Sonje added, *Yes, and we hope it will work if we get far enough away from the control of that evil woman. But you—why are you dressed like her? You even look like her.* She narrowed her eyes. *Are you the sister?*

Neva figured that was exactly what she had been all her life: "the sister." Unknown, generic, and completely irrelevant next to her twin. She wasn't family in any sense of the word as far as Meredith was concerned, just a handy scapegoat.

Luckily, Baker fielded Sonje's question. *We escaped, too. Now we're trying to get back in and rescue our friends.*

Ik wens u nog veel sterkte, Sonje replied solemnly. *That is Dutch. I wish you much strength. Much courage. You will need it. But as for me and my son, we are going now before we are missed.*

Neva watched the pair until they disappeared among the giant trees. Baker was still suspicious, and he decided to follow them at a distance until he was certain they weren't going to return to the mansion and raise the alarm. It gave her a chance to shift form and assess the damage.

She was relieved that she was able to retrieve her five-digit clothing and accessories from whatever cosmic closet they'd gone to. And she was *ecstatic* that they were not only undamaged but still clean! Her face hadn't been so lucky, however. Peering into a mirrored compact from the handbag, the deep claw marks across her muzzle had translated to red scratches across her nose and cheek. Healed but not invisible yet. She found a place to sit down and apply some makeup, trying to hide the thin red lines as best as she could. A little time, perhaps a few hours or so, and the marks would disappear. Hopefully they'd be gone by the time she was in the mansion. If not, then she hoped Meredith's minions would be too afraid to stare at her face. Because Neva couldn't wait around until her complexion was perfect.

Sonje was right to take her son and get the hell out of here. For Neva, however, Sonje's timing couldn't be worse. Her twin tended to take escapes personally. If word of the head chef's disappearance reached her, she was likely to take out her anger on whoever was available.

And Travis was likely to top her list.

((((● ●

Travis was surprised that the elevator went up instead of down. He probably should be surprised that the elevator went anywhere, what with all ten of his guards crammed in with him. He figured it amounted to about a ton and a half of solidly packed werewolf, but the mechanism operated as smoothly as if they'd all been canaries.

The first floor went by, and not only could he not move, but all the advantages of a transparent elevator were moot—he couldn't see a damn thing for all the bruisers around him. So he made it up. *Lingerie, housewares, handcuffs, mace...*Hell, anything to keep his mind off the diminishing oxygen. Same with the second floor. *Leather goods, rocket fuel, guns and ammunition.*

The elevator came to a stop on the third floor, and he was hustled out as if he was the president being evacuated by bodyguards. Only if a bullet came for him, none of them were going to throw themselves in front of it.

((((● ●

Hiding just inside the tree line, Neva looked over the broad expanse of ground-hugging ivy that encircled the stone walls and grounds of the mansion like a rippling green moat, a buffer between carefully landscaped order and towering primeval forest. Intruders or escapees walking across it would be spotted immediately. The main entrance could be seen from here, boasting tall white iron gates covered with elegant scrollwork. She estimated she'd have to walk about a hundred yards, without a sliver of cover, in order to reach it.

The big gray wolf at Neva's side hesitated, and Baker's voice popped into her head for the first time in an hour. *Can't we be more subtle? You know, go through the side gate where the deliveries come in?*

"Not a chance. Meredith wouldn't be caught dead using the servants' entrance." *Unfortunately.* Neva wasn't keen on walking in the front door, either, but either her disguise would work or it wouldn't. And it could all depend on how well she could sell it. *Be bold. Be bold.*

In her mind she held fast to the last time she'd seen Travis—when they'd made love in the forest bower. She would never forget the expression on his face (who knew that he even frowned during sex?). Nor would she forget the phantom image of the golden wolf that she had seen in his eyes at one point. Her own inner wolf was a hair's breadth from the surface now, like a racehorse at the gate, as determined as she was to get to Travis. Maybe more so. Neva also planned to do her utmost to stop Meredith once and for all. For her wolf, however, saving Travis was the *only* thing that mattered.

"Try to look a little more subservient," she said to Baker. And she stepped forward, leaving the relative safety of the rugged forest for the unprotected danger of the delicate ivy.

High above everything, a pair of dark eyes snapped open like a predator's. Red satin sheets rippled serenely across Meredith's naked skin, stirred by the soft sea breeze from an open window. Her body was as flawless as an alabaster statue and just as unmoving—her physical being was still deeply asleep. Her mind had been, too, until someone ventured into the charmed ivy surrounding the walls of the estate and triggered her sudden awareness.

Geneva is here.

A soft sighing laugh escaped Meredith's red lips. Just as she'd predicted, the little bitch would be trying to return to her precious mate. Of course, he was no longer where Geneva would expect him to be. And Meredith would have such fun with both of them.

But not now, not now...*Effort versus reward.*

She knew from the sun in the sky how much time had passed since she'd given herself to sleep. Knew it wasn't enough—after all, she wanted to be at her very best. Slowly, her dark eyes closed again. She would sleep until the night came again.

And then she would play.

(((● ●

Travis didn't know what he'd been expecting, but this definitely wasn't it. No dungeon, no torture chamber, not even punching practice for the guards. Instead, he'd been dragged into an expansive bedroom with plush carpets and elegant draperies. Glass walls overlooked the estate and the forest beyond. He hadn't been able to enjoy the view for more than a moment, however, before being tossed on a bed the size of a small country and tied down.

He stared at the ceiling, where an antique map of the constellations had been painted, and tried to make sense of the situation. At least he wasn't in Meredith's room, thank the goddess. But a guard had called this "the guest room," in a tone that implied it had all the hospitality of the Bates Motel.

The shackles and chains were gone, replaced by a red silken cord that didn't look like it was tough enough to restrain a butterfly, never mind a full-grown Changeling. Yet despite its delicate appearance, it might as well have been steel cable from the Golden Gate Bridge. Try as he might, Travis couldn't budge it in the slightest. Magic was obviously in play here. The strange scarlet cord was all one piece, looping back and forth under the bed so it could tie his feet and hands to carved wooden bedposts as thick as power poles.

One of the guards had tucked a pillow behind his head, not to be kind, but to be funny. "There," he'd said. "You're to be made comfortable while you're waiting."

"Yeah? Waiting for what?"

They'd all laughed then and left the room without answering his question. Bastards.

Magic or no magic, Travis set to work trying to loosen each one of his hands and feet in turn. Christ, if he could reach the cord with his human teeth, he'd *chew* the damn thing. But there was no stretch in the strange material, no give at all. The act of shape-shifting alone might have torn the cord to pieces...but some strange spell still divided him from his wolf. He hadn't grown up hating magic, but he was sure hating it now. The way that Meredith used it, it was more like cheating. Stacking the deck in her favor. If there was any way of getting the crazed woman's magic off the table, Travis would welcome a fair fight.

He'd heard once that evil had to be resisted, even if you couldn't win. At the time he'd thought that was a pretty dumb saying, one guaranteed to get you killed. Right now, however, he was in the mood to resist plenty. Travis reassessed the situation. He couldn't do a damn thing physically. His wolf was out of the picture. The cavalry wasn't coming. All he had was whatever was in his head. Exhausted, he closed his eyes and thought of his grandfather. In his hands magic had been used to heal, to teach, to enhance and uplift. *Make your thoughts quiet*, said his grandfather. *See. Hear. Feel.* Travis saw the big quartz crystal again, plain as a chunk of glass and about as fascinating. Brows furrowing, he tried again to think of what his grandfather had said about it. *Amplifies...it amplifies something or other...*

A Latino woman in a white lab coat came in, her black hair braided back into a long tail that hung to her hips.

What the hell. He gave his best Goldfinger impersonation. "So, we meet again, Dr. Zarita."

"Zarita *Arandas*," she corrected, apparently not noticing his lame attempt at humor. She rummaged in a red plastic tote and began assembling a syringe, rubber tubing, a number of empty rubber-stoppered vials, and more. "And what about your name, sir?"

"Trouble."

"Ah, yes. Ms. Meredith said you were not very cooperative." She wrapped the tubing around his upper arm and began tapping the vein inside his elbow. "I hope you will not give *me* any trouble today." She was surprisingly gentle as she skillfully inserted a double-ended needle.

"I don't seem to be in a position to give anyone much of a problem today."

He watched as she filled vial after vial, and finally hooked up a tube to a vacuum-sealed bag. His blood dribbled into it as slowly and fitfully as fresh brew from a coffeemaker. "Hey, I need that stuff. Exactly how much do you plan on taking?"

"A little over a liter. Ms. Meredith has found it to be an excellent restorative."

"I find it pretty damn restorative myself—what the hell is she doing, drinking it?"

"Of course. It will be chilled and waiting for her when she awakens."

He stopped asking questions at that point. *Of course* someone who had mastered such dark magic would drink blood by the carton. Christ.

"Be sure to eat everything you are given, so you can replace what I've taken today and what I will be taking tomorrow," the doctor said as she gathered her equipment. She paused before she left the room. "I'm sorry to tell you that it will likely be a daily procedure, Mr. Trouble."

Every frickin' day? He felt drained—literally—and dizzy. Weren't you supposed to get goddamn cookies or something if you gave blood? He slid into a dreamless sleep.

TWENTY-FOUR

As Neva walked, she loosened her hips and lengthened her step, seeking that fluid runway gait that was so characteristic of her twin. Meredith never, ever failed to make an entrance, even when she was simply crossing a room. She was always on. And she was always in charge. There was an air of absolute authority that clung to her, as palpable and intoxicating as her Clive Christian perfume. Neva approached the gate at full stride and didn't slow down a bit. Nor did she say anything—Meredith certainly wouldn't bother to speak to whoever was behind the security camera. At most, she'd give a very slight but regal wave of her hand, and that's what Neva did. *This is going to look really stupid if I walk face-first into the—*

The gate parted before her immediately, with plenty of time to spare. Neva had to struggle to keep the surprise from appearing on her face. Instead she wore the patented Meredith mask—the look-at-me-I'm-beautiful blended seamlessly with the look-away-I'm-powerful. To anyone else, it would have been impossible to mimic such a one-of-a-kind expression, but Neva had witnessed it all of her life. She might not have the temperament for it, but nature *had* given her the same facial features as her twin. Neva now turned The Look on everyone, two-legged or four-legged, and they all responded the same way—with lowered eyes and utter deference. With her Changeling senses, she could smell the acrid tang of fear radiating from each and every one of them. No one dared speak to her; they just hurried to get out of the way. So this was what it was like to be Meredith? She probably loved it, but Neva was sickened.

Right now, though, she had no choice but to keep up the scary-bitch act. Baker played his role perfectly, walking at her left side and slightly behind her like a heeled dog. They'd decided to leave his bloody wounds as they were—it created the illusion that Meredith had either beaten or bitten him. He'd managed to appear afraid of her, too, even as he glared threateningly at everyone else. Maybe it was because he was experiencing as much déjà vu as she was. The first and last time she'd passed through the front gates, she'd been wholly human.

The front door was opened as rapidly as the gate had been, and she passed through without slackening her purposeful pace in the slightest. This could all come to an abrupt halt if Meredith happened to be anywhere on the ground floor, but unless her sister was going somewhere, Neva thought it unlikely. There was a grand foyer and an opulent reception area the size of a small department store on the first floor—but the rest was devoted to vast kitchens and staff accommodations. Like a cruise ship, the best rooms were all upstairs, and that's where guests were entertained.

Which meant that any kind of prison would be in the opposite direction.

Neva bypassed the main glass elevator and headed confidently down the high-arched hallway. Three people and two wolves fled from the area at her approach.

Baker was clearly puzzled. *We aren't taking the stairs, are we? 'Cause I'm sure your sister wouldn't do that.*

You're right, but she also doesn't take the main elevator very often. Neva rounded the corner and ducked behind a thriving group of tall potted palms, and voilà—another elevator. She'd been in it many times over the three or four weeks she'd been held here. It was large and bright, more like a room than an elevator, with mirrored walls set in such a way that she and Meredith had been reflected into infinity. And still Neva had felt claustrophobic, as if her twin sucked all the air and the energy out of the confined space.

Ow! Baker hadn't gotten clear before she punched the down button, and he left a handful of hair from the tip of his tail in the door. *You could have waited a fucking second.*

She shook her head. She *had* to stay in character. *Meredith wouldn't wait.* Her twin wouldn't spare a thought for anybody or anything. Her underlings had to fend for themselves—and if they weren't fast enough to get out of the way of a door, a car, or an oncoming train, that was simply too bad. So if someone happened to see her pause even a fraction of a second to allow Baker's tail to get clear of the elevator, it would be shocking enough to be memorable. Neva didn't need the staff to start comparing notes on Ms. Meredith's behavior.

Not until she found Travis and got the hell out of this place.

Baker slapped the stop button with his paw when they were just two floors down. *I think this is where it is. Us newbies were kept one floor belowground. But anyone who got out of line was taken down to the next level for a while. Solitary confinement. Riley went there twice.*

What about the rest of the floors? She had no idea how deep the mansion actually went. It was like Bruce Wayne's house, dwarfed by the Batcave beneath it. Because *holy crap*, there were at least three more levels below this one. Maybe even more, because there were two keyholes directly below the row of buttons. She hoped fervently they didn't have to search them all.

The big gray wolf shook his head. *All I know is that anyone who went to the bottom floors didn't come back. Ever.*

Thanks for that perky little thought. I feel much better.
Sorry.

The sumptuous elevator opened onto what looked more like a subway station than a floor in a luxury home. Floor, ceiling, and walls were lined in glaring-white tile that looked both antiseptic and cold under the fluorescent lights. Neva's gaze fastened at once on two small red spots that marred the otherwise snowy tile grout. The color told her the stains were fresh—and although she didn't know the source of the blood, she was chilled to the marrow just the same. Meredith had dragged her to many courtyard, and even *poolside*, demonstrations of power. Plus she'd killed casually in whatever room she happened to be in at the time. But her twin had never brought her to any of the floors belowground. *Why?*

Corridors stretched away in two directions, lined with white metal doors. *Cells.* Each door was plain, boasting only a keypad above the handle and a metal grating on a six-inch window that was five feet above the floor.

Mimicking her sister's runway gait on the tiled floor made a horrendous noise that echoed and reechoed throughout the entire story. She'd much rather have tiptoed, but it was too much out of character. Her twin never, ever tiptoed anywhere—and making noise that called attention to herself would simply be a bonus. Neva was just thankful she'd chosen the riding boots over the stilettos.

There didn't seem to be anyone occupying the cells on this end. Baker was casting his nose back and forth like a bloodhound, occasionally standing on his hind legs and peering into cell windows. They detected nothing until they rounded a corner and entered an entirely different wing. Baker was just ahead of her when he suddenly broke into a gallop.

Riley! Hey man, are you okay?

Stop broadcasting! Dammit, I'm going to make you a tinfoil hat and glue it to your—

Neva stopped abruptly, drawing air along her palate, trying to sift a sudden mix of scents. *Travis!* She could smell Travis, that unmistakable all-male blend of earthen elements—mountain trails and high lakes, summer days and sex-filled nights. He was here!

She knew it was better to stay in character, at least until she got a better look at the situation. Couldn't she just walk very briskly? But there was no holding back her inner wolf. It was determined to get to Travis no matter what she had to say about it. Neva managed to hold back from shifting to her animal form by her fingernails, but she couldn't stop herself from racing down the bleak, white corridor at top speed. Her heart pounded in her ears; her boots pounded on the tile until she couldn't hear anything else.

Which was probably why Neva collided with a small Latino woman wearing a white lab coat.

The impact of the collision sent the women careening against opposite walls of the corridor, even cracking a couple of the stark-white tiles before they both landed in heaps on the cold floor. Neva recovered first, getting to her knees and shaking her head to clear it. It felt like she'd hit a granite pillar, not another human being. Correction, she'd hit another *werewolf.* No wonder she'd gotten her bell rung. She held onto the wall as she got to her feet, and had to take a couple of breaths before she could spare a glance at whom she had run into.

Recognition made her heart sink to the very soles of her expensive boots. Meredith's doctor, Zarita, lay unmoving, and Neva could see that her lip was split and bleeding badly. A red plastic tote had burst open, and she scooped up some of the gauze pads, tearing open packages until she had a thick bundle to press against the injury. "Are you okay?" she asked, leaning over and gently shaking the woman's shoulder. "Are you hurt anywhere else?"

Zarita's dark eyes flew open and then widened considerably. The worst of all possible words spilled from her bleeding lips. "You are not Ms. Meredith!"

Crap. Neva had forgotten to stay in character—obviously she should have kicked the woman when she was down or something. Looking to save the situation, she adopted Meredith's trademark smile. "Of course I am, Zarita, darling. You poor thing, you've hit your head. Now you know I simply can't do without you, so please tell me you're all right."

Slowly, Zarita took over holding the gauze pad to her lip, staring at Neva's face the entire time. Gradually she sat up and leaned against the wall, but suspicion still flickered in her eyes. "Are *you* all right, Ms. Meredith? I checked on you not long ago and you were sound asleep. You asked not to be disturbed until nightfall."

Play along, play along. "I remember dreaming that I was looking for something." Neva put a hand to her head. "But I just found myself walking and walking along all these hallways, and I didn't know where I was going. I don't even know what I was looking for. It was very strange."

"It is indeed very strange, miss. You never come to this floor. Ever."

Great time to find that out. Well, it might be out of character to show concern for anyone else, but it was totally like Meredith to be worried to the point of hypochondria about herself. Neva turned it on full. "Oh, Zarita, dear, I'm not sleepwalking, am I? I'm so glad I met you before anyone else saw me like this. Please take me back to my suite now."

To her surprise, Zarita shook her head. "You are very good. But you are not Ms. Meredith."

Neva promptly folded her arms and mimicked one of Travis's custom frowns. "You bet I'm good. I'm her bodyguard, lady. She pays me to act as her double."

"I have seen that movie. Twice. You are the sister."

Neva was getting damn tired of this "the sister" crap, but now was not the time to complain about it. *Baker!* She focused her thoughts for him only, not wanting to give away his presence to Zarita.

I'm trying to get into Riley's cell. He's in bad shape, but he's alive.

Zarita looked startled. Baker had once again completely failed at shielding his mindspeak. That wasn't surprising, but the woman's next question was. "You are trying to help Riley?" More surprising was the sudden hope that lit the doctor's face.

"Yeah, we are. And Travis, too. Why?"

"I can help you. Riley will die if he doesn't get out of here soon, and—and I do not want that to happen." Zarita set her lips—gingerly—into a small, thin line, as if to prevent any more details from spilling out.

"And Travis?"

"I do not know his name. There was a big blond man in a cell near Riley who calls himself Trouble. Blue eyes, frown *here*." Zarita pointed to a spot between her brows.

Neva almost laughed until she reran the words through her brain. "Wait, *was* here? But I can smell him…" Her senses told her the truth then: the scent was a leftover, and it had already faded slightly in the small amount of time she'd been here. "Where is he now?"

"I was too late. He was taken upstairs before I came back here." Zarita hung her head. "I was going to help him escape if he would take Riley with him."

Upstairs was not good. Downstairs was undoubtedly a death sentence, but upstairs was her twin and that could be worse.

"*Where* upstairs?" She knelt and gripped the small woman by the shoulders. "Please tell me where!"

"Your Travis has been placed in a guest room on the third floor. Meredith has been sleeping for many hours in her penthouse, and she will be ravenous when she wakes. She finds his blood appealing."

Horror gripped Neva by the throat and squeezed hard. She stepped back until she could feel the cold wall behind her. "Is—is she a vampire?" If there was such a thing, she was certain that her crazed sister would aspire to become one.

"Not in the physical sense of the word. But blood has many, many uses in dark magic. Your man's blood is particularly rare and powerful, and she will make use of it as long as she can, for anything she can think of. Perhaps it is a small comfort, but I don't think she will kill him very soon. I just do not know when—or if—he will be returned to his cell."

"You're sure giving me a lot of information. Why?" Neva narrowed her eyes at the woman. "You're her personal physician, and I'll bet she pays you plenty. Why should I trust anything you say?"

Zarita stood with a curious dignity. "Meredith does not pay me in money. She knows where my children are, and she allows them to live. To keep them safe, I would have served her my entire life."

Which was worse, Neva wondered—being kidnapped yourself, or having your family held hostage? If the doctor's story was true, she wouldn't want to be in her shoes. "But?"

"But lately...her madness has been growing in leaps and bounds. She has always been selfish and cruel, but careful and calculating. Something has changed. She kills on impulse, even when she does not want to, even when it ruins her own plans. She loses control and destroys the very things she likes, and weeps over them afterward. Most of all, she does great damage to her own pack, the pack she is trying to build. Many were slaughtered simply because Meredith was angry that *you* had escaped."

Neva felt the color leave her face. *People died because of me.*

"See? You feel pain because of this. You are nothing like your twin. Nothing. I was afraid at first when I saw your golden hair, the way you are dressed, that you were trying to be like her. I was afraid that I could not trust *you.*"

Jesus. "Look, when I left this place…well, I tried to make sure that Meredith couldn't use me to hurt anyone. Travis saved me. And I need to go find him now. Please help Baker and Riley get out of here, and for heaven's sake, get yourself out, too. Go to your children and hide them."

"They are grown, and they will not hide. They do not believe in werewolves and magic. But I will help Riley and your friend."

Zarita could be lying and her offer might be nothing but a trap, but Neva's instincts and those of her wolf detected nothing amiss. She was just going to have to take a chance and trust her. *Baker, I found you some help! I'm going after Travis.*

Impulsively, she hugged the small woman, then ran back the way she had come, all the way to the private elevator. She didn't care how out of character it looked or sounded. On this floor, at least, it no longer mattered. If Travis was on the third floor, then that was where she had to go, and fast.

TWENTY-FIVE

The soft stroke of a hand across his forehead roused Travis at last. Had the doctor come back? "Don't take any more out," he said muzzily. "It makes me too tired." He must have been out for a long time…there was a glow on the horizon, but the rest of the sky was dark and the room with it. The feminine shadow by the side of his bed, however, was familiar. He knew that scent, that shape, that—

"Neva?" he whispered, then came fully awake. "Neva, what the hell are you doing here? I told you not to come here. I told you to stay away!"

"I couldn't leave you here," she said, leaning close. "Besides, the wolf wouldn't let me."

His night vision made use of the ambient light to study her, mentally checking off her features. Her soft dark hair was in its usual careless ponytail, the scattering of freckles across her nose and cheekbones in all the right places. Most of all, her golden-brown eyes were warm and kind. Did he dare believe it was really her?

Before he could decide, she knelt and began untying the cords. "Are you okay? Can you walk?" she asked.

"For Christ's sake, Meredith will kill you!" he protested. Shit, shit, *shit*! He cursed his wolf, cursed it for taking over and claiming Neva without the approval of either one of them. The terrible consequence was plain—Neva couldn't help herself from coming here, might even think it was her own idea at first. Her wolf would drive her here to be with its mate. In his head, he shouted at his lupine self: *You put her in danger!* And cursed it again when there was still no frickin' response.

"I doubt it. She doesn't want me dead," said Neva. "Besides, Meredith's not even here. She flew off to go shopping for a couple days. Now get up, we have to hurry. The guards are drunk off their asses, but somebody might still be awake."

He sat up and rubbed his wrists. Every inch of skin the cord had touched was now throbbing with pain, as if it had been burned with acid. He grabbed a silken red loop of the stuff and stared at it, as trying to discern its secrets. "I should have been able to break this."

She simply took it from him and began gathering it into a neat coil, gradually pulling it from under the bed where it had been crisscrossed in order to reach all four bedposts. "Fenrir's Cord," she said simply, winding the end around the bundle and hanging the whole thing on her arm like an oversize bracelet. "In Norse mythology, Fenrir was a giant wolf whose destiny was to kill Odin. The gods—"

"The gods bound him with a silken cord," finished Travis. "It was enchanted so he couldn't break it."

"Everyone thinks that's a myth. But I'm finding out that nothing is just a story, not where Meredith is concerned. Either she found the real cord or she made one like it. So I'm taking this with us in case we need it." Neva tugged at his sleeve and tried to pull him toward the door. "Get a move on, will you? We have to get going."

He was all for leaving, but he wasn't going to be fooled again. He seized Neva's hand and yanked her hard against him. She felt like Neva. Smelled like her. Thumped him with her fists and glared at him just like Neva.

"Hey, we don't have time for this crap right now!"

She sure sounded like Neva, but Meredith would know how her sister smelled, how she acted, how she talked. In fact, Meredith would have an entire lifetime of knowing almost everything about her twin. There was one thing she wasn't likely to be aware of, however. He cupped her head with his big hands and tipped it up so he could press his mouth to hers. He took his time with the kiss, deepening it, needing to be certain beyond all doubt.

And there it was—or rather, there it *wasn't*.

She doesn't taste like Neva! That unique hint of apple wine and warm spice was completely missing. And oh, by the way, his body's natural reaction to Neva was missing, too. He should be trying to hold himself in check, yet his physical self couldn't be less interested if he'd been kissing a cold bronze statue in the park. The thing in his arms was neither woman nor statue—it was a monster, and its name was *Meredith*.

His first instinct was to throw her away from him like a rattlesnake and spit as if he'd been poisoned. Instead he drew out the kiss as if she was made of honey, slid his arms around her and pressed those round breasts tight against his chest, even grabbed her ass. Whatever it took to convince the crazy bitch that her disguise had completely fooled him, because it was his one and only chance to get the hell out of here.

Christ, he hoped he didn't throw up...

((((●

Neva made use of the mirrored walls of the elevator, straightening her clothes and adjusting her hair, until the car stopped at the third floor. She strode out confidently, startling a young housekeeper into dropping a small stack of towels. "You," she said, pointing at the girl, who was trying to refold them with shaking hands. "I want to inspect the guest rooms on this floor. I'm thinking of redecorating. Open them up for me."

The girl half walked, half ran ahead of her. Neva knew from experience that all nine rooms were kept locked—including the one at the far end in which she'd spent her captivity. She had no idea which one held Travis, though. But she was certain it would arouse suspicion if *Meredith* was to wander the hallways, trying doorknob after doorknob.

The girl drew her keys from her apron pocket, dropping them twice before opening the room closest to them and reaching in to switch on the lights.

Biting her tongue to keep from saying *thank you*, Neva entered the room as regally as if she was a queen inspecting her troops. Recessed lighting revealed the room to be pale grayish white, with all the hues of the ocean gathered in the carpets and the bedding—but this was no cottage. The colorful paintings of seashells were O'Keeffe, and undoubtedly authentic. "I think I'll move those," she pretended to muse, tapping her red lips with the tip of her finger. *Crap. I haven't got time to go through eight more rooms. How can I cut to the chase?*

She had no idea if more than one room was in use at present, but she took a chance. "Take me to the bedroom that's occupied. I think I might switch these paintings with something in there."

The girl led the way without hesitation. Neva was relieved to see that they were passing several rooms along the broad hallway—now she was getting somewhere! Best of all, she passed a large reception room that opened out to a terrace. Was it the one that Sonje and Nathan had used?

At the second-to-last door, the girl was about to put the key in the lock when the knob began to turn in her hand. "Oh, it's not locked," she said in surprise.

"I'll take it from here," Neva said quickly. "I need some time to study the decor, and I require absolute silence in which to concentrate. Take your towels and leave this floor."

"Right away, Ms. de la Ronde." The relief in the housekeeper's voice was undeniable, and she wasted no time leaving.

As the light footsteps died away, Neva took a breath and opened the elegant door. Reaching for the light switch proved unnecessary. The light from the hallway behind her spilled into the room and illuminated Travis Williamson—

And the brunette in his arms he was currently lip-locked with.

Travis's eyes were closed, not in bliss, but in an effort to distance himself from the creature he was kissing. The sudden change in light made him crack open a lid, however—and then both eyes shot wide. *Meredith!* Her long blonde hair tumbled to her waist, and her red, red lips were open in a perfect O as she stared at him from the open door. He froze, unable to make sense of the rabbit hole he'd just fallen down.

"Travis, what the hell are you doing?" she demanded, and it was Neva's voice.

In his arms, the creature/woman/monster/whatever sprang behind him and tugged hard at his arm. "She's found us! Run!" She had Neva's voice, too—but not her taste.

For Christ's sake, did he have to go around kissing *everyone* to figure out who was who?

Travis cursed the absence of his alter ego, knowing that his wolf would recognize the real Neva no matter what, because it knew her wolf. And maybe neither one of these women was Neva. But there was something about the blonde at the door, some elusive quality that called to him in spite of the fact that she looked like their worst enemy. Suddenly his shocked brain kicked into gear. *Travis! She called me Travis!* He hadn't revealed his name to anyone in this house, *especially* Meredith. Immediately he leaped for the door—

And was yanked almost off his feet by something around his neck. He clawed at it, his fingertips identifying the silken thread as Fenrir's Cord. High-pitched laughter behind him chilled him to the bone, and he glanced back to see exactly what he had seen in the forest bower—Neva's face bearing Meredith's mocking expression.

"Oh, my goodness!" She giggled, and it reminded him of her delight over the demons she'd conjured. "I simply can't keep up the charade any longer. You should see your faces! Too, too funny." She was holding the other end of the scarlet cord in her hands, but only loosely—it was moving on its own like a live thing. As Travis choked, the rest of the cord undulated around him like a python, squeezing until he was brought crashing to the floor.

"No!" shouted the real Neva. She ran toward him, but she was knocked back by some invisible force just as his vision started to gray at the edges.

"Oh, *yes*, my dear, darling little sister. And don't bother trying that again, I'll just finish strangling him and save us both a lot of trouble later."

"Let him go, Meredith. It's me you want, isn't it? Aren't I at the center of some grand plan of yours? You don't need him."

"*Au contraire, ma soeur chérie*, I need him very much, because he means something to you. It's just like when you had a doll you liked and I came and took it away from you. I didn't want it, you know. I didn't ever want your silly things. I just got such a kick out of seeing how upset it made you."

"I already knew that. You like getting a reaction out of me. That's what you always want, isn't it?"

Meredith walked in a circle around him, but Travis only knew that by the sound. He couldn't see her. His vision had tunneled down to the size of a nickel, as if he was looking in the wrong end of a telescope. Christ, he was going to pass out, and there wasn't a damn thing he could do about it. Most of all, there was nothing he could do to help Neva.

At that moment, however, Meredith snapped her fingers, and two things happened. One, the cord loosened from around his neck, and two, as he sucked in welcome air, he began to Change. Connecting with his wolf at last should have been a good thing, except it was nothing like the shape-shifting he was accustomed to. His body contorted violently as if resisting the transformation, as if he'd never done it before in his life. And it was painfully, agonizingly slow, taking long minutes to accomplish what was normally instantaneous. *Goddammit, what the hell is happening?*

"Stop it," Neva yelled.

Her twin clapped her hands. "See? Some things never change. I still love getting a rise out of you."

"You sick, twisted bitch! All you do is use people to amuse yourself. Let him go."

Gasping, Travis hunched on the floor as his spine rearranged itself, his fingernails tearing up chunks of the expensive carpet and underlay—until his fingers shortened into toes. *Don't piss her off, Neva,* he warned, focusing his thoughts narrowly in spite of the searing pain that was exploding throughout his system. *She's not stable.*

Jeez, ya think? I told you that a long time ago. Are you okay?

Sure, fine. Gimme a few minutes and I'll come up with a heroic plan to save us.

In other words, I'm on my own.

Unaware of the silent conversation, Meredith only laughed at her twin. "You've seen how things work around here, Geneva.

I'm in charge, and that means I do whatever I like. *Of course* I use people. I tell my pack when to walk on two legs and when to walk on four. And I've decided that I'd like your boyfriend better in a fur coat.

"Mind you," she pretended to muse, "I could decide he looks better without balls, too. You know, I'd never have believed it if I hadn't gone to the woods myself—imagine my baby sister mated *for life* to a werewolf she hardly knows."

"Cut the crap, Meredith. First of all, being born ten minutes ahead of me doesn't make you older, and it sure as hell doesn't make you any wiser."

"No? Then why do I know things about this man that you don't? You've never been impulsive in your life. Always playing by the rules. Never taking a risk. Never really living at all, so what do *you* know about anything? Oh, and you're *so* squeamish about spilling blood and taking lives." Meredith shook her finger at her. "You've judged me very, very harshly because I dare to do these things. So imagine how hurt I felt when I discovered you'd suddenly mated with a murderer!"

Travis's Change was slowly nearing completion, but a brand-new pain knifed his heart. Christ, he'd known the bitch would use his accidental confession against him. *Neva, don't listen. Please, please don't listen.* He couldn't tell if he was talking mind to mind or just praying like hell. It felt about the same.

"Uh-huh, sure, sis." Neva folded her arms and regarded her twin. "Like I'm going to take your word for it."

"You don't have to take my word, darling Geneva. Ask *him* about it sometime. Ask how he slaughtered seven help-less humans, young and old. Tore them into little tiny bloody pieces." She knelt and put an unwelcome arm around his neck, but he couldn't control his body yet, couldn't stop her. "My, my, just look at these big teeth," Meredith said as she struck a provocative pose, stroking his giant fangs with a manicured finger.

Keep it up, Travis thought to himself, furious and frustrated that the Change was taking so goddamn long. *Stay right there until I'm fully wolf, and I'll enjoy chewing you into tiny pieces.*

"These are the very ivories that bit and slashed without an ounce of mercy—" She cut her fingertip on the razor edge of one of his giant carnassials, the meat-shearing teeth that all wolves possessed. "Oopsie." She giggled. A normal human being would pop their finger in their mouth and suck on it, or run for a Band-Aid. Or both. Instead, the bitch had it poised over Travis's tongue and was milking drops of her vile blood into his mouth. He fought to get away, even to just close his jaws—hell, he didn't care if he bit his own tongue off in the process—*anything* to get away from that foul substance. But his body still wasn't listening to him. He couldn't be more paralyzed if he was frozen in a block of ice.

For some crazy-ass reason, the memory of his grandfather popped into his head. *Make your thoughts quiet,* he had instructed. *See. Hear. Feel.*

I'm not exactly able to do anything else right now. Travis forced himself to relax, to let go, to reach out with his senses, and just *feel.* He certainly felt something dark and evil—that had to be Meredith. He felt something oily and almost venomous on his tongue—her blood, for sure. But then there was something else, something that pulsed like a live thing, vibrating as powerfully as his grandfather's crystal had vibrated in his hands all those years ago...

Suddenly something large and heavy struck Meredith in the side of the face, jarring her from her loathsome task and smearing her ever-perfect lipstick. She shrieked as a second object hit her squarely in the head. Neva was standing over by the bookshelves, hefting a third volume in her hand. "That's the trouble with spells, dear sister," she said. "They're very, very specific. You've put up a shield against me, but apparently not against these." Neva fired off the book, and this time her twin ducked.

Meredith rose up in a fury, forgetting Travis completely and turning her back to him. "You're protecting this *killer*?" she shouted, putting up her hands, palms out, to ward off any more projectiles. "How fair is it that you love him, and you don't love me?"

Neva threw another book, but cursed as it bounced off an invisible shield without even striking her twin's hands. "First of all, I never said I loved the guy, and second of all, you've done nothing but make my life a living hell since I was born. You called me, remember? I came here in good faith, Meredith, hoping you were serious about reconnecting and making a new start, but you lied. Like you *always* lie. I can't love a liar *or* a killer, and you're both."

The devastating words fell on Travis's heart like sledgehammer blows. *You did this*, he said to his wolf. *I told you we would never have a mate.*

His alter ego, maddeningly practical as always, simply addressed the situation at hand. *Wolf here. Cord gone.*

Travis looked down. Distracted, Meredith had let go of her end of the cord—*and it had simply fallen off during his transformation.* With the Change complete and his body finally under his control, he used each of his paws in turn to push the jumble of scarlet coils behind him and under the bed. The bedcovers fell back in place as if they had never moved. Next, Travis subtly gathered himself as he trained his attention on the back of Meredith's neck, where the dark ponytail swung from side to side as she spoke.

"There's no such word as *can't* around here, Geneva. I *can* make you love me. Just like all my wolves love me. You're going to stay right here with me, and either be my adoring little sister or my obedient little sidekick," Meredith hissed, and fisted her hands, her voice gaining volume until it bounced from the walls all around them. "You're going to worship the ground I walk on right up until it's time to visit my spell-crafting room. And then you'll *thank me* for allowing your blood to be part of—"

Travis sprang.

TWENTY-SIX

The great golden wolf knocked Meredith down with such force that her face slammed against the floor, stunning her. Neva gasped as his enormous jaws snapped shut at the back of her twin's neck. There was no blood and no bite, however, and the big animal didn't linger. Within a nanosecond of his teeth ringing together, his powerful hind feet pushed off of Meredith's body, driving the air from her lungs as he launched himself for the door. Travis's voice filled Neva's mind with a single word:

Run!

Startled, Neva spun and shifted to wolfen form, then raced beside Travis down the long hallway. *I know a way out.* That is, as long as Sonje had been telling her the truth, or this would be a damn short trip…In her mind she could hear her twin screaming for her pack to *stop them.* Meredith's voice increased in volume and power, a stabbing, twisting knife in the head, and Neva felt sorry for the wolves who could not resist such a painful compulsion.

As the terrible voice ceased, she couldn't help but be glad that Meredith wasn't going to lower herself to chase them herself. Of course, it also meant she had total confidence that they couldn't escape.

Neva veered to the right, straight into the grand reception room where Meredith had once held a fake party in her honor— and instead, had changed her life forever. This time, however, she wasn't hanging around for her deranged twin to grab her. Running full-out, she crossed the expansive floor in a handful of bounds and lowered her head to ram the glass doors leading to the patio. Travis was there a heartbeat ahead of her and broke the glass for both of them. It exploded into a shower of beads that clung to their fur, but they didn't slow down. *This way,* Neva said as she ran to the edge of the stone balcony—

And leaped over the side.

Sonje had been right about the roof that lay directly below. Of course, *now* Neva remembered that the white wolf had said to run along to the *left,* not straight down. Because no other roof jutted out beneath this particular area.

Neva scrabbled with her claws to gain purchase on the sloping surface. Travis dropped down beside her and likewise struggled to keep from sliding. She could see the other two roofs, about a hundred feet away, which would act almost as stair steps if they could make their way over there. If she fell off this spot, however, it was a sheer drop of forty feet or so to a flagstone patio—and she didn't want to find out if werewolves bounced.

Lie down flat! Travis dropped to his belly. *Now!*

She followed suit and was relieved that the skidding and sliding stopped immediately.

Get your head down—we need to be invisible.

Neva dropped her chin between her paws and even flattened her ears. She made sure that her tail was stretched out along the shingles as well before she followed Travis's gaze.

Crap. Dozens of wolves seemed to pouring in from the outer walls, other buildings, courtyards, and gardens, all converging on the mansion. Meredith had obviously called for all hands on deck. But that wasn't necessarily bad. Neva shared her thoughts with Travis. *She thinks we're still in the building.*

It won't take long for a search party that big to figure out we're not. *Are we heading for those rooftops over there?*

Yup. And we do a one-and-a-half gainer into the pool from the last one.

Not very quiet, but at least we won't break our necks. Okay, be ready to move. As soon as those wolves are close to the house, we're leaving.

Do you think we can avoid being seen?

Not a chance in hell. But we're going anyway.

They watched, not daring to move until the last stragglers disappeared from their line of sight. Neva was first to get to her feet—if it could be called that. She elected to slink along with her belly almost touching the shingles. She didn't look back to see if Travis was following suit. Knowing him, he was probably trotting along as if it was a ground-level sidewalk. She jumped down to the next roof and then the next, hoping that it wasn't making a huge amount of noise indoors. She crept along to the side of the roof that overhung one of the sparkling blue pools. Travis pulled up beside her as she contemplated the drop. Water or not, it was still a long way down from here.

Do it this way, he said, placing his front feet far beyond his nose. *Just like a human, point your arms—your front legs—out ahead of your face. Tuck your head.*

It doesn't look deep enough for a dive.

Trust me, there's lots of water. And this way, we'll keep the splash down—this is the wrong time to do a cannonball. Without any further warning, Travis launched himself.

The splash was minimal, just as he promised. It seemed to take awhile for him to come back up, but then she spotted him swimming along the bottom, staying under the water—and out of sight—as long as possible. Neva took a deep breath, then another. Truthfully, she was afraid to make the leap herself, but it was all relative. Jumping into a goddamn active volcano would be less scary than being recaptured by her psychotic twin.

Forgetting to tuck her head, Neva hit the surface awkwardly, sending chlorinated water jetting into her sinuses as she arrowed straight to the bottom. At the last moment, she managed to pull up before she smacked into the bright-blue tiles, and floundered her way along. Swimming underwater in a lupine body was nothing like swimming as a human—and she wasn't particularly good at *that*, either. She flailed in an approximation of a sideways dog paddle until she reached the big golden wolf and came up coughing.

Quiet! He'd been waiting for her in the shaded shallows, where tiled steps led up and out to the patio. Every part of him was submerged but for his nose and eyes. Somehow he'd folded his ears to keep them below the waterline, too.

She thought she'd strangle as she attempted to suppress her sputters and coughs, and settled for exposing her nose and snorting out as much water as possible.

Where do we go from here? He glanced toward the house, watchful for any sign they'd been discovered.

She hadn't asked Sonje that particular question, but it wasn't hard to decide on a plan. Neva knew the layout of the grounds—and she remembered exactly where she'd managed to get over the wall herself. *On the west side, behind the greenhouse. We can get there in short runs so we have cover—from the pool house to the stand of cedars, along the rose hedge and west of the garage.*

Kind of like a covert military operation.

She snorted some more. *Maybe they'll make a movie out of it. On three…*

They mounted the steps until they were on dry land—or rather, dry tile—but they didn't take the time to shake the water from their pelts. Nor did they move like wolves. Instead, they crept, panther-like, from point to point, as fast as they dared, keeping close to the foliage or in it. Everything went smoothly until they wriggled between the junipers and the brick wall of the enormous multicar garage. A howl sounded long and loud from the mansion steps and was taken up by a multitude of voices around it. Neva could hear the excited yips and barks of the pack as it spread swiftly over the grounds. *They're hunting us.* Should they lie low or run for it? They were well hidden where they were, but—

Travis had already thought it through. *They're just going to pick up our scent if we stay here. We have to make a run for it now.*

They loped along the side of the garage under the protection of the prickly junipers, then bolted across the short open space to the greenhouse area. Neat nursery rows of tall, ornamental trees and thick rosebushes surrounded the big glass building, providing replacements for gardens and beds all over the estate—and welcome cover for the two fugitives.

Neva led Travis around the back, where a pallet of mulch had once helped her climb up and over the high stone wall that surrounded the grounds. Except the pallet wasn't there anymore. *Crap!*

We don't need it.

What? Are you kidding? That wall has to be a dozen feet tall, maybe more. And the top is about two feet across.

Did you climb over it on two legs or four?

Two, of course.

Exactly. Now that you're a Changeling, you can jump this, easy. You just need a running start. Come on.

Neva wasn't sure about that at all. He'd said the swimming would be easy, too, and she was still leaking water from her sinuses, but she followed him anyway. A long row of red-flowered rhododendron shrubs ran perpendicular to the wall, and Travis crept all the way back to the very last bush. *That's about a hundred feet of runway. More than enough to give you momentum if you run as hard as you can.* He checked to see if anyone was looking in their direction. *We're clear if we go now.*

But I—

Just do what I do. You'll be fine. He launched himself like a sprinter, and for a moment she was mesmerized by the sheer power of the big wolf. Muscles bunched beneath the golden pelt, and legs gathered and released in long flying strides, his tail a banner behind him. Neva caught her breath as he was suddenly airborne, up and up, front legs tucked high. As he passed the top of the wall, he kicked off it powerfully with his hind legs and disappeared from sight.

Over there!

The words were loud in her mind, but it wasn't Travis. Neva turned to see a group of wolves heading straight for her, ears flattened and teeth bared. *Jesus.* She ran for her life, straight for the wall. Certain she was following Travis's example to the letter, she launched herself upward—only to discover that she'd leaped a couple of strides too soon. Her chest hit the top edge of the wall hard, knocking the breath from her. Still, she clung with her front feet while her hind claws scrabbled for purchase on the vertical stone. She could hear the pack approaching, but wolfen paws had no fingers, and she couldn't get enough of a grip to pull herself up and over. *Help!* Just as she thought she was going to tumble backward, a familiar tawny figure appeared on the edge of the wall and ran to her.

Neva didn't know what she was expecting. Maybe that Travis would shift to human form and grab her with his big strong hands. Instead, he simply closed his massive jaws tightly on the thick ruff and the tender underlying skin between her neck and her shoulders, and pulled. *Ow, dammit! No, wait, don't—*

But he did. With unbelievable strength, the golden wolf heaved her straight up and *over* the wall, then jumped down after her onto the field of ivy. Any other time she would have cussed him out, complained about the treatment or the new scrapes and bruises she'd just picked up. Or maybe she'd just plain slug him. This time, however, adrenaline overrode everything as Neva picked herself up and ran with everything she had. Together, she and Travis raced flat-out for the forest beyond.

Just as the first of their enemies gained the top of the wall.

(((● ●

Shaken and furious, Meredith stalked to her private elevator and headed down to the lower floors. She needed to soothe herself with the caress of magic, but not something strenuous. No demons today. She couldn't stop rubbing the back of her neck, still feeling the hot breath of the big blond werewolf on the vulnerable skin, even as the deafening ring of his long sharp teeth still echoed in her ears. The first time she'd met the golden wolf, he had shown her no fear. And promised her no mercy. She'd been excited then, aroused and titillated by the threat, and amused at the novelty of it.

This time, the entertainment factor was distinctly lacking. The swiftness of the attack was the worst. Why, the creature could have severed her head from her body before she could react, before she could shape-shift and shock him away from her. Her own fault, definitely, *oh yes*. She'd been so caught up in the confrontation with Geneva that she'd forgotten all about Travis. And especially forgotten the fact that she'd called his wolf to come out. In fact, the little bitch had probably been trying to distract her on purpose, hoping her lover would succeed in killing her big sister for her.

Instead, the golden wolf had mocked her—*her!*—by knocking her down and walking over her, as if she was *nothing*. Her beautiful face had been marred by the impact, her nose bleeding and one eye puffed nearly shut. His hind claws had marked her back, gouging deep as they sprang off her body.

Her rage flared again at both the insult and the injury, and her silver wolf struggled to break free. But there was no one nearby to vent her feelings on, no one to tear asunder, no one's entrails to yank out. *Now, now, be patient a little longer,* she told the creature that lived within her. *We're going to take care of ourselves first, darling, and then I'll turn you loose. You can start with that awful Riley wolf, and then we'll go hunting.* Slowly, reluctantly, her alter ego settled, placated somewhat by her promises.

She had to pause a moment before her fisted hands could unclench enough to turn the key in the lock of her most loved sanctuary. Candles flared as she entered, but this was not her vast marble spell-crafting room. No, this was a much more intimate setting, a combination of study, spa, and elegant kitchen. Like a cook relaxing by trying out new recipes, the combining of ingredients for potions would help to ease the stress from her shoulders. And she needed to whip up something to take the bruising and swelling from her face. If she couldn't restore it to its natural perfection quickly, she might have to put together a temporary glamour spell. Oh, and a hot soak would do her nerves such a world of good.

She'd tried to call Zarita, of course, but the doctor wasn't answering. No doubt she was out there, driving the van, helping the rest of the pack search for the fugitives. Meredith wished she'd thought to call her first, before issuing the general command to recapture her little sister and her lover…but as a master of magic, Meredith could take care of herself if she must. As she gathered the elements for some of the spells, an unopened bottle of Black Pearl cognac caught her eye.

Dear old Andrei had once said that quality brandies—and this was among the very best—were designed to be savored in tiny amounts, but where was the fun in that? Her face hurt, she had a pounding headache, and her favorite toys had left the building. Meredith wanted to feel better *now*. She filled the crystal snifter past the halfway point and sipped steadily while she leaned over the elegant bronze bathtub and turned on the golden faucets. As it filled, she threw double handfuls of crushed juniper berries and geranium leaves into the water, and then carefully added three vials of blood from Geneva's blond werewolf, Travis. The other three vials she emptied into her glass and watched as the crimson liquid spread ghostly tendrils throughout her dark drink like a tiny apparition.

She was going to feel much, *much* better very soon.

And really, didn't she already have everything under control? Geneva and Travis would be recaptured any minute now—*you can run, but you can't hide*—and then Meredith would unlock the mysteries of the blond werewolf's blood, even as she used Geneva's to power her most beautiful spell yet, her masterpiece. In fact, once she had her little sister back in her hands, Meredith would make certain Geneva *begged* to help with the project. The image cheered her immensely, and she giggled. She drank deeply from the crystal glass, almost draining it, then shrugged out of her clothes.

((((● ●

Hours later, Travis and Neva were still running. Natural wolves were built for it, able to keep up a ground-eating pace that would carry them thirty to fifty miles in a single day. Experienced Changelings could travel even farther and faster. Even a newbie like Neva could run like a greyhound, but here, the rough terrain and steep slopes made any kind of speed difficult. The only upside was that it was similarly hard on their pursuers.

And their pursuers were still with them.

It had become painfully obvious to Neva that the very best they could hope for was to maintain their slender lead, and she was starting to flag. Travis wouldn't allow them stop for rest or for water, but even he couldn't run forever. His voice sounded tired in her mind.

Christ, I really thought we'd lose them by now.

They'll never stop. She'd reached the point of exhaustion where even mindspeak took a lot of effort. *Never. If Meredith set them on us, they'll chase us until their feet bleed and their hearts give out. We're gonna need the Marines or a damn miracle in order to get away.*

What about magic?

Neva snorted. *Where the hell are we going to get some of that? They don't exactly sell it in corner stores like fireworks.*

I've been wondering if this damn necklace is good for anything.

What are you talking about? What necklace?

He ran closer to her so they were muzzle to muzzle, then curled back his lip for a moment. Gripped between his teeth was a black egg-like stone and a coil of silver chain. In the intense light of the setting sun, the dark gem glittered and flashed with brilliant colors.

Neva stumbled in sheer surprise. *You're kidding. You stole her pendant? Why? And why the hell didn't you tell me that before?*

I figured it was some kind of magical tool—Meredith probably owns a million-dollar necklace for every outfit in her closet, but did you ever see her not wearing this rock?

That was an easy question. *No. She's forever playing with it, rubbing it, holding it. I thought at first that she just liked to fiddle* with it, like a worry stone or something. But, yeah, it makes sense that there's more to it.

Look, my grandfather said crystals can amplify, intensify things. I've been thinking—maybe that's how your sister managed to maintain control of her wolves. What if she magnified the normal abilities of a sire?

Yeah, but it didn't work on everyone. It doesn't work on you and me.

No, but it works on most *of her wolves. So what would happen if we used it?*

Us? Are you crazy? We have to destroy it, not mess around with it. Or what if it works like a homing beacon and she can track us with it?

With this many wolves after us, no one has to work very hard to track us. They all know exactly where we are. But as for being dangerous, I can feel this thing vibrating like a damn dentist's drill, and it hasn't done anything more than irritate the hell out of me. I think you should put it on, see what you can make it do.

Why me? If you're so eager to try it out, you put it on.

Because magical objects are usually tuned to their owner somehow. This belongs to Meredith. And nobody on the planet is genetically closer to her than you are.

So is that why you were kissing her? You couldn't tell the difference? Neva was surprised how much anger surged through her at the memory, and her pace increased accordingly.

No! For Christ's sake, I was trying to fool her into thinking she'd fooled me with her disguise, so I could escape. He cursed himself then. *It sounds frickin' stupid, even to me.*

Let's just say it's on the list of things we're going to talk about later.

He sighed. *Won't that be fun. But if we don't do something soon, there won't be a later. Think about it—your DNA has got to be virtually identical. And I'm betting it's close enough to fool the magic.*

Was the man insane? *We're not carbon copies. And you don't "fool" magic. Especially hers. The stuff she plays with is lethal.*

Okay, but our other choices are to keep running until we die or be recaptured by Meredith's goon squad.

We got away before. In a damn dump truck, no less! We'll find a vehicle, we'll hitch a ride—heck, can't we steal a plane?

Travis was shaking his head. *Five wolves, Neva. We were being tracked by five wolves. And we had some really close calls before we shook ourselves free. How many wolves do you think are after us now?*

Her heart sank. They had at least ten times the problem, all as tireless on their trail as Arnold Schwarzenegger in the *Terminator* movies.

Crap.

TWENTY-SEVEN

Baker held out his hands to steady Riley as the wounded wolf rose and stood on four shaky legs. *He should be in intensive care, not walking around.* Zarita had given Riley a big shot of morphine, so he was feeling no pain, plus some kind of stimulant to help make up for strength he didn't have. Baker had protested at first, thinking the combination sounded fucking dangerous, but she assured him that the simultaneous use of the drugs had been well tested. *On humans.* He supposed he'd have to be satisfied with that—and really, what choice did they have? His friend had always been a big guy, and he was an even bigger wolf. Carrying him was out of the question, and if they left him here, he'd die.

Zarita knew the complex inside and out, and damned if she didn't take them directly to an honest-to-god tunnel. Built from an enormous culvert, big enough for even Baker to stand up in, it looked like it went on forever. "Shit, this is like a movie!" he said as she closed the door behind them and swung an iron security bar across it.

"It's for the guards to use to take the bodies out," she said quietly, dampening his enthusiasm considerably.

Glad I'm taking my own damn body out of here. Riley's voice sounded good in his head. It was still an odd way to communicate, but after practicing it with Neva a few times, Baker had to admit it was practical.

They walked in silence most of the way, a row of bright lights along the ceiling keeping the claustrophobia down. In fact, it reminded him of the passenger boarding bridge to a plane—only the fucking jet was parked on the other side of the terminal. "Where's it come out?" he asked.

"It goes under the wall and comes out in the forest." She still carried the red plastic box with her, hugging it in front of her as if to comfort herself.

"Are you okay?"

"I have been with Ms. Meredith a long time. It's frightening to think of what may happen when she finds me gone."

"Your kids?"

She nodded. "Others, too. She will take out her anger on anyone left behind."

"She'd do that just because Travis and Neva left," he said, hoping that the couple really had managed to escape. "In fact, I think Neva's more important to her than any of us. That might distract her from going after your family just yet."

"I cannot get my children to believe me. They are grown, and think they know everything about this world. They will not move or hide, or even take precautions."

"Yeah, but you've been gone for a while, right?"

"Years. I've written letters, but Meredith has had them mailed from other places, so my family has never known where I am."

If her story was true, it sucked. "Maybe Riley and I could convince them. After all, look at the condition he's in—that should scare anybody. I could Change into a wolf right in their living room. They'd have to believe then. Hell, *you* could Change into a wolf and show them."

"Unfortunately, I can't. She never turned me. I don't know why."

Zarita lapsed into silence, and Baker was glad for the respite. He didn't know what to say to that last little revelation. The bitch queen seemed to want to convert the whole fucking world to werewolfism, so why would she draw the line at turning Zarita? He gave up thinking about it and focused on Riley. The big wolf's gait was stiff and halting, and from time to time he'd lean against his friend's leg for support, but he kept moving. *Can you Change back to a human, bud? Neva said it helps with healing.*

Meredith controls everyone around the mansion—none of them can shift their form without her royal high-and-mighty's permission.

Maybe it'll wear off with distance. Kind of like mindspeak, you know? The farther away you are, the harder it is to hear anything.

A door came into sight. "There shouldn't be any guards, but I will go out first and make sure," said Zarita.

Baker wasn't about to trust her that far, no matter how good she'd been to Riley. "We all go out together. If somebody's there, just tell them we're taking this injured werewolf out for exercise and fresh air."

"Okay."

The absence of argument made him feel like shit, but he still wasn't taking chances.

They emerged into a rocky ravine, with rough-hewn steps leading down the side of it. Baker's sense of scale, however, was thrown off by the ginormous trees. They towered overhead like skyscrapers, making it hard to tell the depth of the ravine. Finally he cupped his hands around his eyes to block out the forest and studied the terrain below. The remains of a fire could be seen smoldering in a stone basin maybe twenty feet down, but the thick stench it gave off was like no campfire he'd ever encountered. There was an oily sweetness to it, mixed with the scent of badly charred meat. The stink seemed to crawl into the pit of his stomach, nauseating him. "Fuck, is that what I think it is?" he asked.

"This is where they burn the dead. That's why I was fairly certain no guards would be here. No one will come near here for days until it's time to collect the ashes for Meredith."

The bitch keeps the ashes? Riley sounded appalled.

"What the hell does she want with them?" demanded Baker.

"Dark magic requires such ingredients. Blood, bone, hair, ashes. And lives, *especially* lives. Several guards have disappeared lately. The staff believes that she's killed them to enhance her spells."

"And then she cremates them and uses their ashes for even *more* spells. Nice. A murderer who recycles. Let's get the fuck out of here."

Her face was grim. "I don't like this place, either. If we follow the ravine south, it's only a few miles to Redwood National Park. If Riley is able to Change by then, maybe someone there will give us a ride."

Don't worry, Baker said to Riley. *I'm fucking stealing a car for us if I have to.* He wanted to put as many miles between him and Meredith's creep show as he could before nightfall.

((((● ●

In order to try and use the dark pendant, Neva figured she needed her human form. According to Travis, however, they needed a *defensible* spot. That sounded ominous. She couldn't imagine trying to fight so many wolves. They would be dragged back to Meredith for certain.

This way.

He led her down yet another steep slope, and she could feel her strength ebbing as she strained to keep from sliding. It wasn't long before the big tawny wolf was almost twenty feet in front of her—and her Changeling senses could hear her twin's hordes not far behind her. Previously such sounds had spurred a burst of adrenaline, but not this time.

Christ, it's about time! Neva, come this way.

In her mind she was hurrying, but her pace remained the same. Finally she caught up to Travis and looked over his shoulder. There was a groomed path, and he nosed her hard toward it. *Come on, it'll be easier for you.*

It'll be easier for what's chasing us, too.

There's no choice. We have to get to a spot where you have time to Change and work with the stone. It'll be a race, but this'll help you.

She loped beside him, her nose to his hip. It was comforting somehow, and he adjusted his pace accordingly. She couldn't help but wonder if he'd read the sign beyond the path, however: Damnation Creek Trail.

The terrain was a welcome relief at first. The giant redwoods began to thin out and get smaller. Giant groves of huckleberry trees and rhododendrons gave way to spruce-covered hillsides. The trail would be a challenging one for a human, but on four legs, it wasn't bad at all. They crossed a small wooden bridge with a strange triangular frame. She assumed the water below it was Damnation Creek itself. Farther on, a similar bridge recrossed the creek. Then the trail narrowed and began to climb once more. Her muscles felt like wet ropes.

Neva looked back and saw a handful of their pursuers crossing the first bridge. Ahead of her, Travis galloped up to the trail's summit.

Shit. Shit! Goddammit—who builds a fucking trail that doesn't go anywhere?

She climbed up alongside him and looked down at a small rocky cove. There were steps carved into the rock face leading down to it—but the tide was in and the stairs led only to water. *Well, at least they can't get behind us.*

I'm so sorry, Neva. I thought this would connect with one of the coastal trails.

S'okay, I needed a break anyway. Give me the stone, and stand back so I can Change.

He deposited the pendant on the rocky ground. But he didn't stand back. Instead, he took up a position on the narrow path in front of her, facing the trail they'd just ascended. His voice in her head was quiet and sure. *Take your time, Neva. I swear they won't get to you as long as I'm alive.*

No words seemed appropriate. She sent him a burst of emotion instead, hoping it would come across as the virtual hug she intended and not a jumble of tangled thoughts and feelings.

Now she had to persuade her animal persona to let her return to her human form. All of its instincts were poised to protect her with tooth and claw. The best she could do was promise her wolf that it could come out and fight if any of the enemy got past Travis. Reluctantly, it stopped arguing with her—

And she stood on two feet. She wobbled for a moment, a little dizzied from the height, and less stable on the rocky terrain without four legs. Neva had never really thought how much the human form relied on constant balance. She picked up the black opal and nearly dropped it again as it seemed to pulse in her hand. Did that mean it recognized her, or was that an example of the vibes Travis had spoken of? She looped the heavy white-gold chain around her neck—wet from wolf drool, of course—and held the black stone with its hidden fires firmly in her fist.

That was when she felt the magic.

Cold fingers of power wriggled over her skin like tiny slugs. Neva wanted to throw the pendant away from her, toss it into the ocean behind her, but instead she held it tighter and clutched it against her chest. Her twin wouldn't fear the stone and neither would she. Much.

Wolves were approaching, gathering at the base of the rise. Travis snarled at them and warned them off, head lowered, muscled shoulders hunched, showing all of his formidable teeth. She stopped looking. She had to let him take care of that, had to trust him to hold them off. Her job was to make this last Hail Mary effort, to take control of a magic that wasn't hers.

But that's Meredith's way. Neva thought of her twin, how she sought to control everything and everyone around her. How she took power away from others, wrested it from the elements, chained it and forced it to serve her. Looking back over the ocean, Neva suddenly began to breathe in and out in rhythm with the waves. Silently calling. Inviting. A great peace settled over her as she lifted her gaze to the tree-covered hillsides before her. Calling. Inviting. She settled the stone between her breasts and raised her arms slowly, slowly. Calling, inviting. An immense energy followed the movement of her hands, as if she were drawing it up from the water, the earth, the plants, and finally, as her hands reached above her, energy poured down from the air above, filling her.

The stone was hot now, maybe hot enough to burn through her shirt, but she ignored the discomfort. She didn't dare touch it right now. Instead she kept her hands above her head and looked out over the wolves gathered at the bottom of the path. They stood perfectly still, gazing up at her. Waiting. They needed something, yearned for something—what was it?

Travis's voice was a whisper in her mind. *I think they're waiting for your orders.*

So many of them, she murmured. *So many lives stolen.* It wasn't orders they needed at all. Determined, she concentrated on the skill she'd learned only recently—mindspeak. And did the very opposite of what Travis had tried so hard to teach her. She *broadcast.* Only it was more than words that she sent to the dozens of wolves below. The energy, the living power that she'd collected from nature itself, channeled through every cell of her being like a strong wind, and delivered her message for her. *You're free. Every one of you. You're free to live your own lives, never to be compelled again, never to be subject to any will but your own. Meredith has no power over you and neither does anyone else.* After a moment she added, *Never harm a human being. Never turn anyone against their will.*

The wolves looked puzzled. Some sat and scratched at their ears, others shook themselves. But none of them were snarling, growling, or threatening in any way.

Exhausted, Neva slowly brought her arms down. She sat beside Travis and leaned against him. *That's all I got.*

I think it's enough. Whatever the hell you did, I think it's working, he said, and licked her face. *Nice touch with the Changeling rules, by the way.*

I figured if we're going to turn that many werewolves loose on the world, we'd better give them some guidelines.

A few of the wolves lay down where they were, as if they were tired. Others wandered away—but not together. It took well over an hour, but eventually all of the wolves dispersed and disappeared from sight.

Travis nuzzled her. *I wonder where they'll go?*

Home, I think. Wherever that is for them.

Wherever that is, I know where it's not.

She nodded. *Me too.*

(((● ●

Meredith awoke in the bathtub, the water cold, the bottle of cognac two-thirds empty, and her thoughts muzzy. She could simply work a small spell and reheat the water, of course, but that seemed like too much trouble. Besides, she was getting hungry. *Have to keep up my strength.* Her inner wolf growled. *And yours, too, darling.*

She stepped out and patted herself dry with soft French linen towels, then checked her face in the mirror. The swelling was gone from around her eye, but a slight bruise lingered. The golden werewolf was going to pay for that—perhaps she would remove one of *his* eyes. Into what spell could she incorporate a werewolf eye, especially one from a natural-born shape-shifter? Meredith contemplated that as she did her hair and applied her makeup, calculating what magical effects she might glean. She didn't feel like dressing—really, clothes were so restrictive—and selected a black satin wrap instead. The hue didn't favor her complexion, but black was the color of power, which favored her personality. She paired the wrap with woven stilettos in the same shade.

Relaxed and confident, she poured herself another drink and left the room, wobbling only once on her trademark heels. The elevator door opened at once, as if anxious to get out of her way. As the car rose, she surveyed countless images of herself in its mirrored walls and smiled with pure satisfaction. Until it occurred to her that something didn't look quite *right*. She examined her makeup, took a long sip of the cognac, and pulled at the collar of the satin wrap to reveal more cleavage. The drink had brought color to her cheeks, and the mirror, ever her friend, declared that she looked not just good but positively *resplendent*.

Yet something teased at the corners of her mind, something she should know…

The elevator opened at ground level. Meredith planned to check with her pack on their progress and then order a meal to be sent to her room. She was hungry, and her alter ego was positively *starving*. A brace of quail perhaps, or a fragrant rack of lamb? *Both, I think, and—*

The house was dark. The elevator doors closed behind her, taking all the light with them. There was no sound. No scents of food being prepared. No army of attendants appearing to cater to her whims. Confused, Meredith wandered through the vast rooms, the businesslike *click* of her stilettos the only sound. Where in heaven's name was her pack? She reached out with her mind and called. And called again for someone, *anyone*, anywhere. Anxiety rose, fluttering in her chest like a panicked bird, and she called aloud.

She threw aside the glass and ran then, her heels beating a tense staccato that echoed off the walls. As she approached the great front doors, the turmoil of her emotions sent them crashing open ahead of her with such force that they bounced against the walls of the house, cracking layers of stucco and brick. The noise resonated in her ears, but it was the only noise, the only sound, and it faded into nothingness. The expansive grounds were as empty as the house, dark and foreboding under a new moon.

Meredith reached for her pendant—and collided with harsh reality as abruptly as if she had run straight into a wall.

The exquisite black opal was gone.

In the elevator her liquor-soaked brain hadn't been able to discern what was wrong. It had no problem comprehending the implications of the missing gemstone, however. The immense monetary value was meaningless. The opal's real worth was in its ability to collect and channel power, enhancing her control over her pack, magnifying and extending her influence as their sire indefinitely.

And now?

She had to find it. Had to. Her heart and her heels pounded out a rhythm of terror and rage as she retraced her steps. Every light in every room she entered flared into chaotic life as if a surge had passed through the lines. She chanted every locating spell she knew of, crawled on the floors looking under furniture. Returned to the elevator and kicked off her stilettos as she bashed the buttons with the heel of her hand. And as the car began its descent, she bashed the mirrors, one after another, with the spiked heels of her shoes.

The search of her sanctuary turned up nothing. She hadn't set aside the pendant before getting into the tub. Hadn't left it on the counter. Hadn't even soaked it in a crystal bowl to replenish it. Furious, Meredith ransacked the entire room, turning out drawers and cupboards, breaking jars and vials until she was emotionally and physically exhausted.

As she leaned against the wall, sides heaving and stomach churning, she thought of her penthouse bedroom. That was where that brutish yellow wolf had knocked her down. Perhaps the chain of the pendant had broken? Perhaps the clasp had loosed itself? Of course it had. It *had* to have come apart in the struggle...

But it hadn't. Hours later, the penthouse resembled the sanctuary, furniture upended, windows broken, and entire sections torn from the carpet. Sober at last, Meredith looked even worse than the room, the former rosiness of her skin replaced with a ghastly pallor. Her hair was dull and tangled, and mascara pooled beneath her lower lids. She stood at a ruined window, clenching and unclenching her fists until her palms bled from her now-ragged nails. Her satin wrap was half on, half off, but she was heedless of the cold ocean breeze on her naked skin. The only thing she was aware of was the realization that *her wolves were gone.* Her carefully created, painstakingly accumulated army of wolves was never coming back. She was completely and utterly alone.

A wailing sound bubbled up from somewhere deep within. By the time it emerged from her throat, it was a long, lingering howl of purest anguish...

And terrible retribution.

TWENTY-EIGHT

Travis curled himself around Neva, placing himself between her and the night. He'd found them a shallow cave-like space beneath an overhanging tree on the hillside. She was too tired to make another Change, and he decided he could keep her much warmer if he remained a great furry wolf. She needed to rest, and as far as he was concerned, she could sleep for days if she needed to. He was in awe of what she'd achieved. She believed the power of the black stone was responsible for what had happened, but thanks to his grandfather's teachings, he knew better. *It could only amplify something that was already there.* Neva had been the one to call together the natural energies around her and use them to deliver an amazing act of compassion. Instead of taking control of the wolves for herself, she'd freed them completely, now and always. It was a masterstroke, a brilliant move against Meredith. The bitch would have to start all over from scratch if she wanted to keep her little empire together. Except that Neva probably hadn't given a single thought to any of that. She hadn't planned it. To her, releasing Meredith's army was simply the right thing to do.

Travis was so proud of her, he could burst.

He watched over her until the sun rose and flooded the cave with light. Neva rolled over and rubbed her eyes, and he couldn't help but nuzzle her. *Go back to sleep. You don't have to get up yet.*

"But I have to *pee*," she protested, struggling to climb over him.

Travis wisely got out of the way, and took the opportunity to shift back to his human form. When Neva returned, the sun was behind her, shadowing her features and highlighting the long blonde hair she'd adopted in order to pass for her twin. He frowned. "You're going to change that back to your natural color, right?"

"I dunno. Blondes are supposed to have more fun." She laughed as she sat beside him, and tried to push back the furrows in his brow with her fingers. "But after the last couple days, I've had enough fun to last me a long time. Maybe I'll dye my hair red. Or hey, what about purple? I saw someone in Portland with the most beautiful violet—"

He groaned.

"Was that you or your inner wolf?"

"Both, I think."

"So what do we do now?"

"We get the hell out of here. Meredith may not have an army, but she's dangerous all by herself, and now we've *really* pissed her off." He paused, as if measuring whether or not to say anything more. Finally he did. "It was too easy, you know. Way too easy."

"What? What the hell was *easy* about these last few days?"

"Think it through, Neva. If Meredith had come after us herself, we'd never have escaped."

"So why didn't she?"

"Overconfidence," he said. "She underestimated you. She expected you to—"

"She expected me to just roll over and let her have her way. Let her win. Just like always." Neva rested her forehead on Travis's shoulder. "You're right."

"Here's something else I'm right about—she won't make that mistake twice."

"Jeez, are you *trying* to cheer me up?"

"Come on. We'll walk back until we cross another trail that'll take us someplace civilized. I know we passed a fork not that far back."

Neva pulled a cell phone from her pocket. "Nope, that one would take us north, toward Meredith." She showed him a map of the Damnation Creek Trail she'd pulled up onscreen. "Ta-da!"

He squinted at the small image. "So if we pass the point where we stumbled onto it, it looks like it heads southeast."

"And the trailhead is right on Highway 101," said Neva, tracing the tiny line with her pinkie. "We could hitchhike south from there." She snapped the phone shut, folded her arms across her chest, and looked him straight in the eye. "If we're still together, that is."

Travis's heart plummeted to his shoes. "I know you have some questions, but this isn't a good time."

"There *is* no good time. We've been on the run ever since you found me. So I'm asking my questions right now, at least the important ones. You told me that the Changeling code forbids the killing of humans. You said it was the highest law in your world, and I believed you."

"It *is* the highest law."

"I wasn't about to take Meredith's word for anything, so I want to hear it from you. She said you killed people. Is that true?"

He'd dreaded this moment. How many times had he rehearsed different things he could say to her? Reasons. Excuses. Explanations. *Anything* so she wouldn't look at him with disgust, loathing, or worst of all, fear. In the end, there was nothing but the truth—and she deserved nothing less. He felt like the bleeding remnants of his soul were laid bare as he managed to choke out a single word. "Yes."

"But you didn't kill Meredith. You caught her by surprise. All it would have taken was a single bite, and you didn't kill her."

"What? No—Christ, she's your sister. You don't want her dead, you told me so yourself."

She nodded. "Exactly. So I figure you're not necessarily a murderer by nature. Maybe you should try telling me what really happened to you."

The story didn't burst out of him, not like when he'd returned to the bower, determined to make a confession. Instead it came out quietly and slowly, sometimes haltingly. Through it all, Neva listened—and when he looked down, she was holding his hand.

"That's why you're alone, isn't it?" she asked at last.

"I'm related to most of the pack. If I'd gone back, they would have had to decide what to do with me—kill me or banish me. I was young, and I told myself it would be better to save them the trouble of having to make that kind of decision. I think I was actually just too ashamed to face them. I've often thought since that I should have gone back, should have tried to explain what happened. But they'd still have to make that decision, even after all these years. It's the law." For some reason, he suddenly remembered the cardboard sign he'd seen a homeless man holding outside a Denny's, back when Travis had first decided to get Neva out of the hospital. "You can't go back and fix the past."

"No. But you can make the present and the future a whole lot better."

He blinked at the simple wisdom. "Yeah, I guess that's right."

"So what am I going to do about my sister?"

"Simple. Stay away from her."

"But she's still out there, and maybe she doesn't have an army at the moment, but it won't take her long to recruit more *volunteers*." Neva made quotation marks with her fingers in the air around that last word. "She's going to steal more people's lives. I have to do something."

"Stay *far* away."

"But—"

"Look, Meredith is beyond anything that you and I can handle by ourselves. She's got a personal brand of dark magic going on that makes serial killers look like jaywalkers." He repressed a shiver as he remembered the scaly demons with the enormous orange eyes. "I don't want you exposed to that—she wants you for something, and whatever it is, it's not good."

"But I can't just ignore the fact that she's a murderer. She's hurting people, killing them. If she were an ordinary human being, we could just call the police. But she's not—and she's getting more powerful all the time."

"That's why you can't be the one to deal with her. If your twin has *you*, it'll further her plans somehow. I need to talk to someone who works with magic, see if I can get some help to beat her at her own game."

"Where the hell are you going to find someone like that?"

He spoke so quietly that only her Changeling senses allowed her to hear him. "I have to go back to my old pack."

"*What?* You just finished telling me that they'd have to kill you or banish you."

"I have to take that chance. Besides, banishment is just going to be more of the same. It's already what I've lived with most of my life."

"Yeah, well, what if they decide to kill you instead?"

"Meredith is a danger to everyone—human, Changeling, *everyone*. She has to be stopped, and it's in the pack's best interest to help."

"And the *killing you* part?"

"Well, maybe I'll be lucky and they'll hold off until we stop Meredith."

"I don't like this plan at all. If you go back to your pack, I'm coming with you."

"Listen, you don't—"

They both jumped when Neva's cell rang. She picked it up gingerly to look at the call display—then quickly flipped it open. "Baker!"

Travis's inner wolf reacted at once. He wrestled it down as he asked, "Who the hell is Baker?" No way would his alter ego tolerate a rival.

Neva simply waved her hand and shushed him. "I'm so glad you're okay. Really? That's wonderful. Hey, where are you? Good, we're heading south. I'll call you when I stop someplace, maybe tonight."

The phone hadn't snapped shut before Travis was growling. He couldn't help it. "Who. The hell. Is Baker?"

"For pity's sake, he's just a friend. He helped me get to Meredith's to rescue you. He got his friend Riley out of the prison, too, and Zarita escaped with them, and then he found Sonje and Nathan again. They're all down in Tucson."

Travis's wolf settled down as he digested all that. He was glad that Riley had gotten out. Poor bastard deserved something decent to happen to him. "I suppose you want to see them?"

"Of course I do." She sat astride his lap and put her arms around his neck. "But first, I'd rather see *you*. Naked. Now."

Neva nearly choked trying not to laugh. For the first time since she'd met him, Travis's characteristic frown disappeared. In fact, his brows nearly reached his hairline in pure and pleased surprise. How long they stayed like that, she couldn't say—she was suddenly being squeezed too tightly against his broad chest to see what his face was doing. His mouth was busy, however, kissing the top of her head, then roaming over her forehead, her eyes. His muscled arms released her, and he cupped her face so he could brush his lips over hers, teasing the corners with the tip of his tongue.

A shudder of arousal played down her spine, and she concentrated on capturing that elusive tongue and sucking it gently into her mouth. In and out. In and out. And in case he missed the suggestion, she rocked her pelvis in his lap. The answering bulge in his jeans was just right for rubbing against.

Travis released her face and sought one of her ears, breathing softly into it until he caught the lobe firmly between his teeth. Seizing her hips with both hands, he slid her rapidly back and forth over the front of his jeans. The sound of his breathing harshened. Wet with excitement, she gripped handfuls of his shirt and rode the rising wave of pleasure—

Until he stopped dead. She tried frantically to rub herself against him, but he merely picked her up by the waist and stood her on her feet. It was Neva's turn to frown, half disappointed and half frustrated. "What the hell is—"

"Take off your jeans," he ordered. "Just the jeans. For now."

She eyed him as she complied. He'd stripped naked and sat down again. His cock was high and hard and welcoming, but again her expectations were diverted.

"Stay standing." He kept his knees together and directed her until she stood straddling them. Slowly, his big hands rubbed circles around her hips and the sides of her legs, massaging gently up and down, dispelling all the tension from her muscles but building it unbearably in the untouched vee of her legs. Finally he slid a hand behind her and gripped her ass firmly. Neva moaned as her core clenched hard. Travis's other hand began caressing her inner thighs, moving higher by degrees until a single drop of moisture ran down the inside of her leg. He caught it on the end of his finger and licked it off, his blue eyes on hers the entire time.

Two more drops trickled down. She was going to start screaming if he didn't touch her soon. As if he'd heard her thoughts—oh, crap, was she broadcasting again?—his strong fingers softly massaged her curls, then parted them. A long, low moan broke from her lips, and she had to grip his shoulders to stay on her feet as his fingers circled her clit and then slid slickly into her.

She lost it then. There was nothing she could do to stop her hips from pumping hard against his hand. She wanted, needed, *had to have* more—he gave her two fingers, then three, all the while keeping his thumb on her rounded clit. *Faster, faster...now, now, now!* Neva could swear that fireworks went off behind her eyelids as she finally reached the top of the elusive roller coaster and rocketed down the other side. Thankfully, Travis gathered her to him, holding on tightly as she shattered into a million pieces. Neva had barely stopped shuddering when he placed her arms around his neck and settled her throbbing core within striking distance of his rampant cock.

"Take me in," he whispered to her. "Take all of me."

A single bump from his rearing arousal nearly sent her over the edge again. She wanted it, wanted him inside her, but her orgasm had left her so *damn* hypersensitive...Slowly, gingerly, she eased over his smooth penis—velvet over stone—and pressed gently against it, shivering hard as every nerve ending in her body reacted to the unique sensation. She was soaking wet and more than ready for him, but still vibrating. She caught sight of him then, jaw clenched, the cords in his neck standing out, and a scattering of beads of sweat on his face and chest, from the strain of holding himself back—she was probably torturing him just as he'd teased her. Neva pulled off her shirt, pressed her breasts to his bare skin, locked her hands together behind his neck, and thrust her pelvis just so...

It was Travis's turn to lose control. He was on his feet in an instant, rocking deep into her as she wrapped her legs around him. The perfect friction nearly caused her to climax again—and suddenly Neva became exquisitely aware of their surroundings. It was more than the warmth of the sun on their bodies and the soft caress of the ocean breeze. There was a push of unseen power in the air, and a vast reservoir of energy pooled in the ground below their feet. Something huge and primal gathered in them and around them, building quickly. Her body rapidly climbed toward a new and more powerful peak, and she gripped Travis hard, milking him with her sex, binding them together until he shouted out his release at the same time she did. In the same instant, the wild energies around them came together with all the force of a thunderclap, washing over them both until they collapsed in a heap.

When Neva opened her eyes, she was lying on top of Travis. His heavily muscled arms were still around her, protecting her, sheltering her—which made her feel a little better about being naked at the end of a hiking trail. She couldn't tell what time it was or how long she'd slept, but the sun was high, and she fervently hoped no outdoor enthusiasts had made the trip across Damnation Creek this morning and taken photos of her naked ass.

"Hey, gorgeous." Travis's eyes flickered open, and he smiled up at her as she struggled to free herself from his embrace. His frown was hardly even visible at the moment.

"What the hell just happened to us? Is that normal sex for werewolves?" She gathered up her clothes and checked the time on her cell. Two hours! They'd been asleep for two hours!

"Changelings," he corrected. "And no, I'd say that kind of earth-shattering sex is pretty damn unique. I think it's related to whatever you did yesterday when you used the stone—it's like the elements got involved somehow. Maybe nature approves of us getting together?"

"Is it going to be *unique* every time? What about when we had sex for the first time, in that evergreen shelter? It was totally *amazing* sex, by the way, but I saw your wolf in your face. It only happened that first time, though. I never got to ask you what it meant because we got separated right after that. Did you see my wolf, too?"

"Yeah. Yeah, I did..." He paused in the middle of pulling on his jeans and looked flustered. "I wasn't going to tell you about it until later."

"Really? Later when?"

"Later when you knew everything about me and didn't hate me for it."

"You mean like now? Okay, so spit it out. Are we bonded or something?"

"Yes. Like glue. Changelings recognize their true mates, and my wolf recognized you long before I did. And by the time I realized what was going on, it was too late. The animal persona bonds through sex, and the wolves—yours and mine—witness the bonding. That's what you saw. I guess you could say it's like a marriage, only I didn't get the chance to ask you."

"*Would* you have asked me?"

"I would now. Because now I have reason to believe you'd say yes." He eyed her appraisingly. "You would, right?"

"Hmm. You can be a real jerk sometimes, but you're decent. So probably."

"That's a good thing, because you're stuck with me, Neva. Changelings mate for life. And we live a helluva long time."

She mulled that over as she finished dressing. "So let me get this straight. We're tied together? You're going to follow me wherever I go?"

"And I'll know where you are, too. The wolf will always know exactly where you are."

"Is that so?" Walking a little ways ahead of him, she shifted to her lupine form, looked back over her shoulder at him, and wagged her ebony tail. *Let's test that theory, shall we?*

She raced away, a sleek, dark shadow against the forest floor. A moment later, a great, golden wolf followed her.

THE END

ACKNOWLEDGMENTS

This book was largely written in the middle of a move from an island in Alaska to southeastern Washington State. It was supposed to be simple—it wasn't. It was supposed to be quick—it wasn't that either. And it was supposed to be painless—not even close. We traveled with two pickup trucks containing the only belongings that were meaningful or essential enough to keep, plus our two opinionated pugs, and my laptop.

I credit my husband, Ron Silvester, with keeping me sane, and well-supplied with coffee and reassuring hugs. Ron and my daughter, Samantha Craig, once again tag-teamed as beta readers, and I could not have done this without them. Thanks to Stephany Evans of FinePrint Literary Management, who wore two hats on this project: one as my fearless agent and the other as an excellent beta reader.

Thanks to my editor, Eleni Caminis, and the team from Montlake Romance. They've been wonderful to work with, and I've been grateful for their enthusiasm. (P.S. On this project, I've been *extra* grateful for the talented copyeditors! I may yet learn how to use a comma.)

Finally, although it may sound odd, I simply *have* to express my appreciation to this book's main characters, Travis and Neva. Some characters are hard to work with—they fail to tell you what they're doing, keep their history and their motivations a secret, hide out when you need them to perform in a scene, or give you the silent treatment. Travis and Neva started talking to me one day in the Seattle airport between flights, and *never stopped*. In spite of the deadline pressures and the chaos of moving, I can honestly say I loved writing their story, and I'm looking forward to their adventures in book two.

ABOUT THE AUTHOR

Photo by Ron Silvester, 2011

Dani Harper is a former newspaper editor whose passion for all things supernatural led her to a second career writing paranormal fiction. A longtime resident of the Canadian north and southeastern Alaska, Dani recently ventured south with her husband to rural Washington to be closer to their grown children. She is also the author of *Changeling Moon*, *Changeling Dream*, and *Changeling Dawn*.